## Praise for Birds of Paradise

"I work with troubled, often homeless teens and really appreciate the way Kathy Handley depicts the honor and individuality of people on the fringes. Her characters are everyday people, under enormous pressures, drawn with extraordinary power. Kathy Handley depicts Southern California with a giddy mix of warmth and wisdom. Her keen eye for detail- a blue dress, tattoo or antique car- brings this setting to vivid, irrepressible life. It's impossible not to root for Handley' lost and searching souls."

~Perri Wexler, author of
*Left of Unsaid*

"Kathy Handley is an expert in matters of the heart, plain and simple. Her great gift is to show you the moments that matter and do it memorably. No matter how far away the setting, you always feel that Kathy's stories are happening in your own back yard and that her characters might just wander over to say hello."

~Sherri Ryan, friend

"Kathryn Handley paints a rich story about relationships lost and found and the search for self that affects us all. Rendered in fine detail, Birds of Paradise is a novel of redemption and belonging that won't easily be forgotten."

~Nancy Antonietti, Grub Member, author of forthcoming novel,
*Peace Knocking.*

Heart-warming and rich in detail, Kathy Handley's *Birds of Paradise* takes us on a journey into the lives of people for whom we genuinely care.

~Virginia Young, author of
*Out of the Blue and The Birthday Gift*

"With their insides bleeding out bad memories, the runaways in Birds of Paradise are not only fleeing their pasts but also seeking their elusive threads of future happiness. Their griefs will break your heart, and their triumphs will restore it."

~Kevin Donahue, poet

## More Praise for Birds of Paradise

"Kathryn Hope Handley's *Birds of Paradise* is a story that centers on
The Squat - the makeshift community home where a group of young
runaways huddles under the trusted guidance of father figure Onge,
in the loft of the LA garage of a '30s movie queen who is as elegant
with faded glamour as the 1939 Mercedes Cabriolet gathering dust
beneath The Squat.

"The cast of the story ranges from young to old; rich to penniless
aristocracy; middleclass to poor; male and female. Yet such is Ms
Handley's powers of imagination, that always we see the world -
whether it be the too-fast-moving lightshow that is LA, or the
holograms of America that are the towns the characters hale from -
through believable, individual souls. And individual senses, too, via
the author's beautiful naturalistic language.

"Ms Handley has been a judge for National League of American Pen
Women, Soul Making Contest - a contest of excellence in prose
poetry. And well she is suited to the task, as this her own first novel
often waxes prose-poetic in the telling. Too, it is *American* in the
sense that, while unmistakably Art, *Birds* doesn't get bogged down
in self-conscious "literariness": Ms Handley's ability to tell a plain
story keeps us turning the pages. In *Birds*, things *happen.*"

~Woodrow S Charles Willow, Boston writer, artist

# Birds of
# Paradise
## a novel

Kathy Handley

*Dear Ken—*
*Best of luck with your*
*inspirational book to*
*come.*
*Love,*
*Kathy*

Riverhaven Books
Massachusetts
www.RiverhavenBooks.com

**Also by Kathy Handley**

a world of love and envy
short stories, flash fiction, and poetry

Published in the United States by Riverhaven Books,
Whitman, Massachusetts
Printed in the United States of America
By Country Press Lakeville, MA

Photography: Amanda Borozinski
~ **Boro Creative Visions** ~
www.borophotos.com
Book Design: Stephanie Blackman
~ **Riverhaven Books, Inc.** ~
www.riverhavenbooks.com

*Excerpts from this novel have been published in
*a world of love and envy: short fiction, flash fiction, and poetry* by Kathy Handley under the title, "I Know My City," as well as back stories of Green and Stripe, titled, "Green," and "Up Baby."

Published 2011 by Riverhaven Books
Designed by Stephanie Lynn Blackman
Cover Photo, Amanda Borozinski - Boro Creative Visions

ISBN:978-1-4507-6177-2

Printed in the United States of America

A portion of the proceeds from this book will go to organizations that sponsor activities for special needs children and their parents and friends.

For my Eddie,
Elizabeth and Carolyn,
Eric, Grace, and Le'o

## Prologue:
## Joe-Mack, Winter

Joe-Mack stomped on the pedal of the faded aqua Pontiac, a giveaway car, the older of their two jalopies, the one he had meant to junk before winter's arrival. The engine coughed as he urged the vehicle up the icy hill. He braked and the car slid. It died at the crest. He twisted the wheel as it slowed to a stop, attempting to move out of the main traffic lane. Ramming the stick into neutral, he shoved it back to park and scraped the raw-red skin of his fingers on the rough underside of the rusted steering wheel. Instinctively, his tongue ran across the cut, making it sting; it felt worse rather than better. Joe-Mack, glad for deep breaths of frigid air, and the cold that gave him a reason to hyperventilate, exhaled great puffs of white fog in front of his face. The edge of sanity loomed before him and the possibility of freezing to death, to boot, served him right, and Gloria right. *Ultimate revenge.* You're acting stupid now, he thought. Calm down. There's no choice here. You have to do this.

The backseat had one dented cardboard box jammed with a toothbrush, seven or eight books, jeans, one navy blazer, and whatever else. After all, what would he need? Not a damn thing. The toothbrush was a joke. He used to be a nut cake about brushing his teeth after meals. Even during his school years he'd carried one in his pocket, heading into the crappy john after lunch, scrubbing furiously, and he kept one in each glove compartment: his car, her car, his truck. But now, who would care? Not him. Not Gloria. In the seat beside him, Gloria's Polar Spring bottles, half-emptied, frozen, sat next to Jen's silver butterfly hair clip and an old pair of yellow nubby slippers little Amy had shucked off a long time ago. He half thought about taking them back to her. After all, winter in Michigan meant those ten-below days; she'd need them running around on the hardwood floors. No, that would defeat his purpose. *No going back. Not for a while at least.*

After a couple of minutes of letting 'Ol Bess rest, he gave a quick sign of the cross and yelled, "Come on, Baby! Bessie, you can do it." The car started after the second try. "Yes, girl!" His mood was down, but just the thought of this old piece of junk starting in the middle of a crap-winter, he found he was chuckling. *Didn't that beat all? He was despondent, and here he was laughing at his old jalopy.* They used to trade off, but this time he left the good car for Gloria and the kids. Then he continued his drive to nowhere, playing mind games: left, left, left, now right, right, right, now drive through, get coffee, and follow the winding roads that circled the lakes. He'd been fixating on his plight for hours when he reached boredom and realized his location was only five miles from Wixom.

Parking in the visitor area, he sat, numb to freezing his rear, and then trudged through powdery snow, leaving deep boot prints on the path, to the apartment house entryway. Before buzzing number ten, he perused the names on the doorbells. He nearly passed Francis DuBois. He grinned at the thought of this fancy name for his buddy, who was unique. *One to a box*, Gloria had said. *A lunatic with major heart.* The crazy loon had chased skirts since junior high. He was the one who treated the whole crowd to 12-incher hot dogs — sometimes with his last cent. He adored Gloria — wouldn't take sides, but all this didn't matter. Francis had a Master's in charm. He noticed little things about chicks and complimented them up the ying-yang. "Nice pen," he'd say. "Sexy eyebrows, cool socks," anything to get them to grin and, next thing, he'd have his arm around one of them, squeezing her waist and reaching up to cop a feel. He had a way of making them feel special. They'd giggle, even at themselves.

Now, when Frenchy failed to buzz him in, Joe-Mack knew he was sleeping trucker's hours. He stepped out, packed up three snowballs and heaved them at the windows. When he heard the third crack the glass, he jumped. Frenchy opened the window, hung his head out. "What the hell? Who's that?"

"Me," Joe-Mack said. "Let me in."

Rubbing the snow and mud from his boots on the mat, Joe-Mack entered the foyer. A mixture of smells emanated from the hallway, the strongest stench of something burnt, perhaps onion soup or blackened toast, with an overlay of cleaning liquid. He missed the warm kid smells at home.

Frenchy opened his door. Standing there in his boxers, he smoothed down his wild hair that later would be slicked into a ducktail.

"What in holy hell you doing? Everything okay?"

"No. You should cut that hair, bud."

"You kidding me now, brother-man. Get in here. I need a java."

Joe-Mack went to the couch and slumped down, watching as Frenchy made the coffee in the kitchen, hauled on a pair of chinos that he located on the chair and then served the drinks. He reminded his friend that he hadn't made a visit to his apartment since Frenchy had his gall bladder out. "So, what's up? Trouble city?"

"You remember last month when you were over to the house. You made a big deal about Gloria's legs in her short skirt?"

"Yeah. It was kind of showy for her."

"She's cheating," Joe-Mack said, his voice weakening, his eyes searching the threads on the rug. "Son of a bitch, she's cheating. Been going on a while."

"I had doubts about that time, but hey, who am I to say? You know my track record with the opposite sex. Glo running with them snotty bitches from work– definitely not copasetic."

"Yeah, look what it got her into," Joe-Mack said, walking over to the window, running his fingers across the hole from the snowball. "Jesus, sorry about this. Can't do shit right."

"No bothers." Frenchy threw on a grungy sweatshirt and shuffled through a pile in his junk drawer. He found the electrical tape and criss-crossed two pieces over the hole. "I'll jingle Smithy. He got next to nothing to manage in this joint. I'll throw fifty on him. Be fixed in a jiff."

"Here, let me," Joe-Mack said, digging out his wallet.

"Forget it. No biggie, besides you look like shit. Hungry?"

"No. But I know you: you've got a hollow leg."

On the way back from Denny's, Joe-Mack said, "You know Glo's a good mother."

"You got that right," Frenchy answered. "You miss the little ones already?"

"I do. I'll get back after a bit. Check on them."

"Right-o. Hey, you want to crash here?" When he got no answer, he said, "Yep, take the couch. I'll be heading out at nine bells tonight. Alarm set on eight. Don't do nothing irrational, hear?"


The temperature the next day rose, causing the ice to melt along the gutters and the icicles to break from tree branches, cracking the quiet night. Frenchy coaxed Joe-Mack from the couch with a cup of steaming coffee, threw a cellophane-wrapped Venice Beach sweatshirt at him and hustled the guy into his truck after heaving the cardboard box into the cab. He said, "This ain't forever. Give the woman time to clear the air. No worries, have a little faith for Christ's sake."

Joe-Mack rode along, numbed by the landscape, the fat branches of the trees weighted down with snow, hanging precariously over some of the roads. Ice mixed with sand created a slushy mess they carved through with the slurpy sounds in their ears. Joe-Mack's voice was raspy, as though he had talked to himself all night. He was still in his wrinkled shirt with Frenchy's sweatshirt, a hair too short, over it. His heart was cold fractured ice. He finally asked Frenchy about leaving his car in Wixom. The guy said, "So what. Let them tow the sucker. Ain't worth the impound fee."

## Chapter 1
## Eleven Years Later On the Road: Joe-Mack and Freddie

The team in Phoenix had been quick with the load, a trail of arms lifting and heaving the boxes from the conveyer belt. Most of them could do it blindfolded, yakking about their night's prowess and big money to be made in other fields while grousing about damned politics and white-collar jerks who didn't get the picture. One fella had brought his son to fill in for a worker who had left town for a funeral. Joe-Mack, tickled, watched the young stud whose football jersey clung to his chest with damp perspiration, grunting with the first and the last of the load. But he made it through. Lummox the Huge said, "Okay, virgin boy! You done been christened into the land of the weak and the strong." His father mocked the sign of the cross over his son's head and said, "Let's go. Get you a nap before your first class."

Frenchy, his bud, said, "Whoo, whoo child, tell that high-school honey of yours, you the man, now."

All set, Joe-Mack settled into his cab with his thermos of coffee full up. Cresting a hill outside of the city, he saw the black mountain silhouette in the distance. It had amazing pink light rising from it, quivering in the mist, signaling the start of a new day. He liked beginning his trips early during the fresh morning before the corruption of a shitload of traffic and nasty news blaring from the radio. Four in the morning and rolling. Also, he could count on his trucking buddies out here on the road. They might be pulling all-nighters but they were professionals. Joe-Mack had seen each one of them driving dog-tired, drunk, pissed off, all of it and often; the road angel protected their fronts and their backs. It was the way it should be for these warriors of the road. He'd heard talk about the road angel, different versions of her. The one time he saw her was when he broke from riding with his bud, Frenchy, and went out on his own, the anger in his gut pushing him on through three nights in a row—eating speed all the way. Big money flew in, jamming every corner of his sleeper. Come to think of it, it was in this very edge of the map, just leaving Arizona, when, all of a sudden up in the pale cherry sky of dawn, he saw the outline of her figure. At first, he thought she was a cloud, a mist of smoke from a far off cabin or the light from a cluster of billboards in the next town – a dream. As he got closer, her arms lifted and she sang to him, a song rendered in a thin high voice like golden reeds whining in the wind, a sound of love. It pulled at him. Just before she vanished, he saw Gloria's face. It freaked him out but good; he thought she must have died. He stopped on the side of the road, barely up on its shoulder, took up his cell, and dialed the old number. She answered, groggy-sounding, and he listened carefully. She said, "Hello," three times and he thought he heard her lightly whisper, "Joey?" He punched the off button and was left wondering if she was alone or all wrapped up in the arms of another man.

Joe-Mack had a keen eye for detail. He checked the intensity of the rising sun, dust blowing or fine rain misting, a snake skittering across the road during these pristine mornings just as he had when he was a kid delivering papers. Back then, he sometimes felt that he was the first to notice the change in the seasons in Michigan; he thrashed through luscious fallen leaves, crunched first prints in snow mounds up sidewalks unless beaten to them by birds' feet or dogs, felt the summer sun over his shoulder as he rode the red bike along the route, and saw the first budding crocuses and daffodils in his mother's yard. He picked a few for her jelly jar in the kitchen. First dumping the pencils out of the jar, and then filling it with water, he arranged the tiny flowers like cousins at a picnic, dressed in sundresses and shorts. The things in nature became the beauty he could trust. Loving it all, pictures ran across his mind as he drove, the images he saw and the ones he dreamed: the wicked lightning; crashing waves over rocks and road alike; sheeting rain, a wall in the sky; a purple sunset; a field of cornflowers, bluer than sapphires; a quirky bunch of birds of paradise leaping tall from dry dirt—life's awkward mix signaled there was a man upstairs. Perhaps he was an artist.

Once a week when Joe-Mack rolled his rig through Las Vegas on short hops, he saw folks thumbing to and away from there, bright-eyed on their way and blurry-eyed broke heading back to LA. He usually didn't pick up hitchers, but there was something pathetic and lonely about this skinny kid dressed in black who bent over his bag like he thought a pack of coyotes would jigger up and carry it off. As Joe-Mack rolled past him, he saw the look of sheer panic on the boy's face, like a moose let loose in a desert and out of water. The rig rumbled as he swerved and braked. All the while, in his mirror, Joe-Mack kept an eye on the youngster, who wobbled in his dirt-cheap and likely new boots toward the door of the cab.

Up on his toes, the boy hesitated outside before he climbed up, and then, when he figured out where the handle was, he opened it, his face wary, yet seemingly grateful.

"Get in," Joe-Mack said.

Slinging his backpack up on his shoulder, his body curved with the weight of it. He used both hands to pull himself up.

"Thanks," he said, in a puny voice, his eyes darting from the trucker to the floor of the cab.

"What's your name? Where you headed?" Joe Mack asked.

"Freddie. I'm going to LA. Hollywood, to be exact."

"You can call me Joe-Mack."

Freddie, while sitting stiffly on the edge of the seat, sneaked looks at Joe-Mack. Joe-Mack knew the kid was checking him out—his wiry body with arms out-muscling the rest of him from hefting freight. Now forty, he had gained a little character on his face, a plus from the road hammer—so he'd been told by the ladies he met.

Shoving a hand forward, he said, "Since nobody ever taught you, it is polite to look a man in the eye even if he is a stranger." After giving him a respectably strong handshake, he wiped his palm on his Levis.

Rod-thin, the kid had tied a black sweatshirt around his hips, and wore two layers of tees under his shirt. A double strand of safety pins serving as a necklace bounced along his

Adam's apple. One pin as large as a diaper pin corkscrewed through an ear that looked freshly pierced. The kid's hands were trembling as though he was buzzed; he kept running his fingers across his eyelids and shifting his shoulders as though the weight of the pack was still bugging him. His eyes were gentle-brown, eyes perhaps the color of his mother's, which might have had that same innocence before her life got hard and she maybe became part of the reason this youngster was hitting the road.

"Belt up, kiddo. I'm not looking for trouble, but you can never read the guy on the other side of the white."

Freddie made a mess of untangling the seat belt. Joe-Mack reached over and clicked it for him. The Circus Circus bag between Freddie's legs was overflowing: a bunch of CDs, a camera, a corner of glossy blue fabric, and a Coke. *There you have it, Joe-*Mack thought, *a runaway survival kit. What a fellow totes along to start a new life. Had he even thought to bring along a jackknife?*

With a great deal of effort, Freddie jostled the pack up onto his lap and, with much digging, he located and opened a miserably beat-up map. A yellow marker line streamed from Vegas to Los Angeles with a hand-drawn star in rainbow colors set smack on Hollywood.

Age didn't matter much, Joe-Mack figured--not when a guy is leaving his home, familiarity. His guts twist up inside of him, yet he knows he has to go. Make the big exit. With him, it had been a leap without forethought, a reaction to enormous upheaval. His strangling anger propelled him from his home base in Michigan to this crazy road life. It had been eleven years since he left Gloria with her shook-up look, a mixture of guilt and terror, and the disbelief that he wouldn't forgive her. He hadn't seen her lying liquid smile, splendid body, or his little girls in all that time, but he heard their voices in the background that once in a blue moon when he called their mother. The old subconscious doing its duty—in dreams and daydreams and in a sunrise, distant, yet grabbing him to the point where he wanted to scream—the start of a new day without them. And when he slept, he'd pop up drenched; sure as hell, he could smell Gloria's wild-banana curls, as she called them, splayed out on his shoulder, her freckled breasts bare and slick against his ribs.

Mesmerized by the constant whirr of the tires, the whisk of the fresh air plowing in the windows as the sixty-footer cranked along in the middle lane, Joe-Mack and his passenger settled in, each glancing out his window intermittently. They sped by the oddball Joshua trees that stood in clumps, or alone on a rise, their branches with rounded knobs like children's knees. On occasion in the dusk, in a tired trucker's eyes, they seemed to walk across the hills. Now the desert floor was prickled with multicolored sand, as deep purple as a night sky and as white as moonstone. The landscape and scrub-brush was spiked with prickly cacti, blooming scarlet chuparosa and blue desert lavender. Vast patches of white and orange poppies tumbled along the side of the road in the midst of sand and bits of trash. *After all those endless bleak-gray winters, this,* Joe-Mack thought, *is a sight my girls should see.*

"You got a wife?" Freddie asked, out of nowhere.

"Used to. End of story."

Freddie hung his arm out the window like a child on a Sunday ride, as the wind whiffled his carefully gelled hair. He'd made the break, so where was his elation? If his money lasted him a week or so, he'd scope out the place and scam a few wallets. He knew how to distract people with a coughing fit or trip, some bumbling move that allowed him to throw them off guard. Picking pockets was easy for a boy who moved along in life slight in stature and dismally invisible.

Last night's final conversation with his mother was pitifully short. Freddie was packing and repacking when his mother rushed into his room, her jowls flushed, her floppy breasts jiggling. She failed to notice the piles on his bed but went right into her story. While watching the shopping channel, the ultra-lovely girl with whiter-than-white teeth had spoken to his mom when she put in the lingerie order. She said, "Rose, nice to hear from you. What did you purchase today?"

Freddie's mother was breathing hard as she spoke, the words flying from her mouth, "I heard my name on TV. It was so damn exciting. Nearly keeled right over." Then she ran back in to see what was up next.

"Great, Mom," he said to her back. *She lives with TV life. More than with her husband. The prick.*

Joe-Mack interrupted his thoughts. "Let's grab a bite and gas her up."

Freddie didn't want to spend any money yet, but he jumped out and followed Joe-Mack to a table at the stop. Most booths were full of men who sat alone, staring straight ahead except when they hollered across the tables to each other. They were young, bearded, old, ugly and two of them had women with them.

When Joe-Mack ordered the breakfast special, Freddie said, "Just water."

"No, no. Let me get it. Make that two specials, one for Freddie here."

"Yessiree," the waitress said, cocking a half-smile at the trucker. "That's two coffees then?"

"You bet," Joe-Mack answered, opening up the newspaper that sat on the table.

It was a lot of food for Freddie's nervous stomach to handle, but he went at it.

"Better chow while you can, young man."

"Sure, thanks."

Joe-Mack set the newspaper pages in order, folded them up before eating. After he sugared his coffee, stirred it, he said, "You ever have a paper route, Freddie?"

"No. I only had a bike for one day. It went missing."

"How so?"

Freddie avoided looking directly at Joe-Mack but told about the time his drunken father brought home a pink girl's bike from a bar where some guy was selling it for three bucks. That night Freddie rolled it down the street to a dumpster, heaving it up and over.

"I heard a raging crash. Gone-zo. Told my mother it was stolen. She gave me macaroni and two Hershey bars."

"It's not such a bad mode of transportation. You know kids outgrow their bikes, forget those routes anyway, but they darn well remember those early morning skies. Spectacular – every day a fresh painting up there. Then, later in life, if you have to get up and out early, you been there before."

Tracing a finger along the sunlight's bright path on the table, Freddie waited for Joe-Mack to speak again. Finally, he went eye to eye with Freddie and, with a softness in his expression, he said, "You know, Freddie, you're going to be out there on your own. Best you open your eyes. Start noticing the sky, feel the weather shifting and then narrow down to your surroundings.

"Like with a camera lens?"

"Yes, but use the brains you were born with. Check out how you feel. Is your gut telling you anything? Be aware!"

"Okay."

"Aw hell, I'm sounding like a father here, but be careful. Listen, if things get out of hand, here's my cell number," he said as he wrote it on a corner of the paper, tearing it off and handing it to Freddie.

"Right. I got money. A camera."

"Let's hike it then. Make up some time."

Hustling back to the rig, Freddie glanced down at his black nails. One had already chipped. Crap, he had left the polish at home. He wondered if Joe-Mack would have thought better of him if he had washed up better.

It had been a long day for Freddie already, what with a nearly sleepless night the night before bolting, and then rising at five to get out before his parents woke up, and then the ride with Joe-Mack that seemed like forever on his tired ass. But he liked being around this man and the idea of riding high above the cars. After dozing he awoke, drooling, still safe inside the cab. Nothing about this man was like his father, the casino rat, who dressed in greasy-gambler black. There was something easy looking about this trucker, his plaid shirt worn soft, open at the neck. If this guy had a family, Freddie concluded he would have been a warm, kind, young father who let his fresh-faced wife have a go at the slots while he held his toddler on one knee and bounced a baby on his shoulder, its soft head nestling into his neck.

As they approached Los Angeles, clusters of buildings came into view. The sky above the tallest ones was layered with dirty-yellow haze.

"Smog. What's up with that?" Freddie asked.

"Excess. Too many cars, people, not enough wind to carry the pollution off."

"We close now?"

"Twenty minutes unless there's a bottleneck."

Joe-Mack asked Freddie how much he knew about California. When the boy answered, "Not much," he told him that it was remarkable, especially off the beaten track.

"You can stand in Venice gazing out at the endless horizon and see the shape of an island, Catalina. From far away it looks like a lump of brown clay. You'd like the place. It could be anywhere: Capri of Italy, a Greek island off the coast, but it's a small world where tiny sailboats and big-time yachts surround the front side docking near an old 20's casino building. It's round. It would remind you of a carnival ride as you pull up. Everyone sees it. On the backside wild pigs scuttle through the brush."

"No kidding."

"Let's imagine we run into each other. Could be I'd stake you to a ride on the Big White Boat. It's a kick to watch the dolphins circling the boat. It appears they recognize it. It's cool. Something kids your age might enjoy. But look, what do *you* expect to see in California?"

"Hollywood, maybe Venice, Malibu—like that."

"You have to watch yourself in Hollywood. At night especially. But then the coastline, Malibu, Venice, Manhattan Beach, they're different. You can dig your heels in the sand, look over your shoulder. You'll see steep canyons. Topanga, where the Hippies smoked dope in the sixties, mountain ridges, sometimes snow on Baldy on a clean day. You'll even get used to the brown hills of Malibu."

"Yeah?"

"Just one thing. In your travels, try to be decent. It never hurts," Joe-Mack said reaching over to deliver a substantial slap on Freddie's back.

"I just want to walk the streets I heard about. Be myself."

"Okay, but get a practical thought in your head, will you?"

Joe-Mack asked him if he had money. Would he get a job? Freddie heard the words, but they blew past him, as the truck veered off the freeway at the Sunset Exit, and his body swung towards the door. He was treacherously close to the destination he had dreamed of for years, and yet he was battered with flip-flop thoughts of major excitement and terror. Clutching his backpack, he held his breath for a couple of seconds. The far-off view of the skyline and the rolling traffic offered him no clues as to what lay in wait.

The smog rested over the downtown buildings, a heavy, bruised, yellow blanket that had bullied aside the baby blue of a clear day. The kind of day a Southern Californian might brag about to his relatives stuck in the Midwest or back East. Even on this gray day, white fluffy clouds in the far-off distance skimmed across the sky. Tomorrow would be brighter.

Freddie had revealed precious little about his home life. Intent on getting to know more about the boy, Joe-Mack said, "So, your dad bought you a bike you hated, huh? What's he like?"

Freddie hesitated but then got into it. He told of the hopeful moment his father surprised him with presents, a ball and bat. He hadn't noticed the tilt of his father's walk, but he heard him slam against the bureau knocking off the pile of CDs when his father wandered into the bedroom saying, "I bought you something. Here." He plopped a shiny aluminum bat and real leather hardball with red stitching circling it on the bed. "Tomorrow we'll give this a go."

After mooning about baseball games all the next day at school, during the pledge, the times table drills, lunchroom, afternoon recess, he finally heard the last bell ringing, loud and obtrusive. Startled from his thoughts, he jumped up, leaving his homework papers crushed in his desk along with the goofy glasses he never wore, and rushed home. In his room, he hefted the bat. It was majorly heavy but he swung it around a couple of times. After knocking down the pressed-wood shelf, he sat on his bed surrounded by the fallen shelf, metal screws, and the crap that he had stored on it, a box of Cheetos, comics, Power Ranger bendable figures. He got a charge out of sliding his fingers up and down the cold, smooth aluminum. He could almost hear the roar of the fans as he hit the homer. Rolling the ball around in his right hand and then left hand, the leather had a good feel against his palm, a fresh smell; he sniffed it, then tossed it hand to hand.

Later that afternoon Freddie sat on the front step squeezing the bat between his legs. He held the ball in his hand, but when that hand got sweaty and tired he switched hands and finally placed it carefully on the bottom step. It was past his suppertime so he left his new things and went in to eat some sticky macaroni, flipping a glob of it upside down on the fork and timing how long it would hang there as he zoomed the fork over his head imagining it to be a Blackhawk. When he went back outside, he dug his tennies in the white stone pebbles, kicking flecks of stone and gray dust into the air. He scooped up handfuls of the stones and dropped them like petals on the cement steps, their sound pinging. He created curvy roads and pyramids and tiny volcanoes, punching in their tips. "Varoom. Kaboom. Swush," he roared, pretending there were massive explosions. Finally he bared his teeth, picked up the bat and smashed each one. *Yes! Power Ranger strikes again.* He used his hands to sweep all the stones back onto the yard where they surrounded the slate flagstone path. The path he'd seen all kinds of weirdoes walk up to enter his home, enter his living room that was a dumb chapel.

Just after eight he lumbered inside, his body tired and chilly from sitting on the steps all that time, his legs heavy. Inside he plunked down on the piano bench and banged on the bass keys. The sounds of his mother's shopping channel drifted from her bedroom. An hour later his father stormed in, clothing askew. He said, "Let's go. Turn on the outside lights, Rose?"

The floodlights along the overhang of the house and the White Chapel sign lit up the front yard but left patches of dark where Freddie knew he'd never see a moving ball, much less catch it, but he stood out a ways in the pretend field anyway. His father tossed the ball up with his left hand, then quickly grabbing the bat with both hands, he rammed it, expecting his son to catch it. After four attempts, the last in which the ball nearly came up missing, he yelled to Freddie, "Get over here."

Hunkering behind him, his father squeezed his hands hard over Freddie's on the bat. He smelled putrid, the stench enough to make Freddie vomit, but he didn't. Freddie's hands sizzled, vibrated when the bat connected with the ball, as though he held a shotgun. The ball zoomed past Rose to the side of the building next to the Joshua tree. His mom, wearing a paisley caftan and marabou slippers, was not much of a pitcher or outfielder. When his father took the ball to pitch, his face went mean; he knuckled it while moving back very far. Freddie trembled at the distance. He forgot that he was supposed to eye the ball. It sailed past him the first time. Rose missed it but scrambled to pick it up and threw it like a bowling ball back to her husband.

"Dirtball!" his father yelled.

"Give him another chance," she said.

Although the second pitch was above Freddie's forehead, he swung wildly at it anyway. His father's face was pinching. He rubbed his nose as though it was running.
"Jesus, Freddie, that was a ball. You blind?"

His father swung his arm around like he was winding up and threw what must have been the fastest ball he'd ever flung down the line. Freddie saw it coming but didn't have time to duck. He was hit smack on the side of his arm.

Dropping the bat he ran around in circles, clutching his elbow, crying from the pain. His mother took him inside, iced the arm, and his father threw the ball and bat in the kitchen trash and left—*for his hangout, the Crock,* Freddie thought. It was the first time of many times he wondered about his parents—why they were married. They so didn't belong together and having a child hadn't made things better.

Although they sat just outside of Los Angeles overlooking a city that was named after angels, Joe-Mack could see that Freddie was in his head, back in Las Vegas, back in his body when he was a little kid. The young man sat rubbing the arm that was hit, tears cupping in his bottom lids, tears that he quickly wiped away with his sleeve. He sniffed loudly, hanging his head.

"Buck up," Joe-Mack said, "you're not the only one with sad memories. Eat the pie. Frenchy says it puts hair on your chest."

"Who's Frenchy?"

"One in a million!"


Joe-Mack and Freddie slugged up the steps; the smells at the Over Easy wafted out the door into the late morning, where fog lingered. The weather was not what Freddie expected. as he entered the city of his dreams, yet he had made it to Hollywood. The combination of burnt toast, refried beans, sizzling bacon and customer stink lent a strong odor, distinct, to the place, the sort that deepens with time and memory. He wasn't quite sure what he had expected here in this old 40's-style diner but this certainly wasn't it. His mother never cooked bacon; he used to grab a couple of pieces of it stuffing his whole mouth from the buffet breakfasts back home. He could taste it now, its pure salt and grease, feel it crunching between his teeth. He was full from his breakfast at the Stop, but the bacon smell pulled at him. Unlike Las Vegas there were no bells ringing to welcome him, the indoor noise so common in casinos, no immediate familiar dealers' blank faces, the gals who sometimes threw him a wink, no come-on hookers grabbing coffee, rubbing their ruby-red toenails, aching arches – just a bunch of folks hardly noticing him and Joe-Mack. The people in the diner were all about themselves, in their own heads, he presumed.

The floor was worn soft and squishy in places, but swept clean of crumbs and napkins, gum wrappers, the crap that people drop when they don't care.

Joe-Mack glanced around, spoke to the kid behind the counter. "This place been around a while, I'd say."

"Yeah, I guess," the counter-boy answered. "The lady there live up the hill. She's old now," he said, pointing to a woman in a timeworn, grease-spattered painting hung high and to the right of the fry stove.

"Interesting," Joe-Mack said as he stared at the subject matter in the picture. There were four men in tuxedos, each with their arms supporting a section of the lolling movie star who dangled an ebony cigarette holder from her cherry lips. The actor or dancer, whatever he was, who held her hips was captured in profile, his Roman nose strong and straight. He appeared to be leaning his head against the taller fellow next to him. His smile was curious.

The woman's legs were shapely as was typical of the actresses of that time – no bulging muscles or out-sized calves – merely trim ankles and smooth knees revealed through the slit in the bias-cut dress.

"Coffee, all around here," Joe-Mack said as he and Freddie eased onto the cracked leather stool cushions.

"Thanks," Freddie said.

"Okie dokie."

"Sunny day."

"Usual L.A. weather. You got a plan, kid?"

"Sort of…"

Both of them leaned forward, elbows on the counter. Conversation between Freddie and Joe-Mack was sparse. After they drank their coffees, as Joe-Mack pushed himself up slowly, hesitantly, Freddie said, "Can you stay a little longer?"

"Not today I can't. I'm pushing it as is."

"Oh, then…"

The camaraderie that had developed during the ride and breakfast when the trucker and Freddie shared a bit about their childhoods seemed to have passed. Joe-Mack was looking like he was anxious to get back to his schedule.

Freddie folded his arms, looked behind him out the window, pretending not to notice when Joe-Mack scooped the check. He watched him turn it over where both of them could read a name on the back, *Gonzalez,* signed in loopy letters under a printed, "Thank You."

Once again, like he had at the Stop, the trucker pulled out a wad, peeled a hundred from it.

"Any change?" Gonzalez asked.

"You bet," Joe-Mack said. The hundred was still in between his fingers and then, he didn't even eyeball it, but without a care he slid it into Freddie's hand, dug out a twenty from his shirt pocket and popped it on the counter. Freddie crunched the large bill into a crisp ball and jammed it into his pants pocket. The bill was warm from Joe-Mack's touch.

"Keep you afloat," he said, standing, tucking in his shirt, adjusting his belt. "Now, do you want to keep the money or get a lecture?"

"I'll take the cash, man. Thanks," Freddie said, looking red in the face over his quick-handed greed.

"No biggie."

Although the man didn't grin at his own generosity, Freddie thought he might be pleased with himself. After all he was helping him out, even though he was a loser-geek. "Hey, I can pay you back. When you swing back this way."

Joe-Mack chuckled. "Good idea, kiddo. You have my cell."

"Sure, I got it."

"Listen, give a call. I might be a million miles away, but no hurt in trying."

"Just so you know, I seen big-buck daddies throw their stashes at the tables, never minding they got kids. Nobody ever give me a C-note before."

"No sweat, kid. Go on. Stay. Finish your coffee."

"Peace out, man."

Joe-Mack smiled at Freddie's attempt to be in the know. They parted ways. At the door he turned back to see the boy still following him with his eyes.

## Chapter 2
## The Home front: Starlet and Gloria

There was something different about the air the day Gloria and Jen ventured off to the lake. Heavy, it hadn't settled yet. Last night's fierce lightning had split a tree down at the cottage. Raw golden wood gleamed in the sunshine. Sap bubbled up, beginning its slow journey over the curve of the ripped bark. A large chunk of the oak's trunk landed on the battered rowboat; it bellied over with the force of the strike yet remained intact. It could have been crushed, but it wasn't. The boat had spent some sixty summers leaning against that tree that was close enough to the water's edge to have its branches dipping into the lake. When the water froze over, it captured trailing bare branches in the bluish ice.

The night before, as the thunder boomed and the winds roiled outside, Jen brushed her hair with a boar's bristle brush, counting the strokes, and, at the same time, her heart fluttered when she realized that she was dangerously close to leaving home. But then, if her mother were willing to kick Ralph out, she might postpone her secret plan to flee. It was hard to believe that her scumbag-boyfriend had been around for six months and actually living in their house for the last thirty days. He wormed his way in and was working up to something, and it wasn't good news. Jen knew that for sure.

As Jen and Gloria sat at the sturdy pine table drinking tea, they watched the roses in the garden quivering where a few bent to touch the earth during the storm. Gloria's baby rose bush, with surprisingly huge thorns and the one mauve rose, was nearly buried in mud. It seemed out of place tucked in the row of larger bushes with stark white blossoms that had burst out like cabbages but were on their way to wilting brown. Gloria dashed outside, with the storm whipping her blouse up, to cover the tiny bush with a plastic bucket. When she returned, she removed her rain-soaked blouse, threw it in the sink, and wrapped a coarse apron around her shoulders.

Jen took off her denim vest. "Here Mom, take this."

Gloria put the vest on and twisted her hair in a tea towel, placing it atop her head. "I hope it makes it. The storm is mean out there."

"Yeah, what about tomorrow, Mom?"

"We'll go. I've got the day off."

Jen and her mother sat quietly for a bit, and then spoke again with lowered voices. Earlier in the day they had butted heads over money; Jen had been crankier than usual, as though something was bothering her, yet she wouldn't tell her mother the nature of the problem. The discussion stayed on the surface – about money and her twisted tooth.

"If I'm going to make it, Mom, I need this stupid tooth capped," she said, rubbing

it so hard with her finger that it squeaked.

"Look, I paid for the head shots portfolio." Her mother sighed as she answered. "You have time for more acting lessons. As for your smile, it's cute. Unique."

"Stop it! It's not. I'm 16 now. Girls start way younger in movies. My skin is perfect. You said so yourself."

"You may be right, but lighten up, Jen! Do you still want to go tomorrow even though you're obviously in a bad mood?"

"Yeah. Sorry."

"Okay, I'm going to bed soon."

They decided to make their annual trip to Cedar Island Lake no matter what, even though Jen had begged for money Gloria didn't have. She wanted to tell her mother that she was about to leave, that she had already bought the plane ticket and had envisioned the possibilities of stardom, but there was a slim chance she'd stay if…

Gloria wrapped her fingers around the lavender grape leaves on her faded teacup and blew softly across the steam that floated a cinnamon smell into the air and she pretended not to see Jen's long delicate fingers covering her face in the drama of desperation. She pretended not to hear her mumble, "Ditch him, Mom."

"What?"

"You heard me."

"I can't," Gloria whispered, her eyes on the cup and saucer.

"You mean, won't."

"Shh, quiet, you'll wake him."

"That's just it. Who cares anyway if he wakes up?" Jen asked, imagining Ralph snoring with his mushy mouth open.

"It's late. Let's talk tomorrow," Gloria said, as bright flashes of lightning cut past the six-paneled kitchen window and a great snap of thunder shook the roof.

"Nite, Mom. Six a.m., right?'

"Sure, Kiddo."

The storm raged on into the morning hours, but it had broken just before they left. It was as though it would be bad luck to change their plans. Intuition may have led each of them to the conclusion that tomorrow would bring a defining moment.

The Canada geese were plentiful during this season when the leaves were beginning to turn bright crimson and autumn brown and startlingly yellow, like jewels. As girls Jen and her younger sister, Amy, had stacked them, tied them together, crushed them with stones, jammed them into bark dishes, playing house as smoky breezes flowed into their hats and gloves and pigtails. They gathered sticks that crunched underfoot along with mushrooms and toadstools, some that had oddly pink underbellies. Jen longed for those times when play took her away from her mom's face that sometimes bore sadness even when she smiled.

Scatterings of leaves and bulky branches littered the roads as they drove from their city bungalow to the lake area. Gloria swerved around the larger branches and piles of leaves and drove directly over the smaller ones that crunched under the weight of the tires. After pausing at Henry's One Stoppe, where they stocked up on bologna sandwiches, stinky Camembert cheese that only Jen and her mom liked, bread, chips, and Mountain Dew, they made their lunch right there in the car, placing the whole deal in the faded Black Watch plaid bag even after Jen wrinkled her nose up at the moldy smell.

Quiet during the last mile of the trip, Jen noticed her mother driving with her left hand, freeing the other to rub the lines across her forehead. *Intense.* Perhaps she had an inkling about her plan and that would be totally horrible, Jen thought, as she patted the ticket tucked in her skintight jeans' pocket. If she had left it in her room, her nosy sister, Amy, might have discovered it. She dug a cold drink from the bag and slugged down half of it while staring straight ahead, trying not to think at all.

Jen loosened the elastic around her ponytail, opened the window and let her hair fly in the fresh air. In a few minutes she pulled her head back in, flipping her head forward and back again, tucking the curly blond mess under grandpa's crumpled fishing hat that had a yellowed license secured by a rusty safety pin.

"Mom, didn't you ever want to leave Pontiac, break out of town?"

"Why?"

"I mean, this Midwest attitude people have – so freaking small town. Going nowhere. Not since Madonna, you know?"

"You're silly, honey. Always questioning, testing the waters. How come you're not like your sister?"

"Because I'm not. Amy's athletic and I'm not. And she hardly washes her face at night and doesn't wear makeup. I tell her she's pretty. She fluffs me off."

"Don't talk like that."

"Yeah, yeah, not about Baby-Amy," Jen said, screwing up her face.

"Come on, Jen."

"You baby her, Mom. You shouldn't!"

The sky ahead broke into light, filtered by the clouds. Jen flipped on the radio and sat back. She thought about her mom getting rid of Ralph and the daydream of her father returning popped into her head. *My father's out there. Maybe stuck, lonely at* some *truck stop.* "Mom, about my father - you know where he is, don't you?"

Gloria kept her sad eyes on the road, shook her head, and answered in a low voice, "He's on the road, honey. Checks come from all over." A slight flush rose up her freckled cheeks, spreading to her teeny earlobes.

"Like where?"

"You're bugging me, Jen. I don't know - Arizona, Utah, California. I stopped looking at the postal stamps a long time ago."

"Huh? I don't believe that."

"Damn it, Jen. Get off it. This is supposed to be *our* day."

They pulled onto the pebbled driveway of the deserted cottage – each neglecting to comment on the deaths of Gloria's parents during the past winter and the obvious need to see the family place sold at some point. Jen carried the bag; Gloria hauled along bulky fisherman knit sweaters and the threadbare lifejackets with loose stuffing poking out. Jen told her mom the lifejackets were ridiculous, that it wasn't cold and, old as they were, they'd be no help.

They passed clumps of shingles that had blown off the roof during the storm, a faded green and white striped lawn chair that had tipped over, and bits of twisted branches and pinecones that had flown from the surrounding trees during last night's wind gusts. Gloria righted the chair; Jen piled several branches and twigs to begin clearing the yard. Winding down the path through a tall gathering of pines, they sniffed the familiar spicy scent of the trees, kicked a few pinecones out of their way and smashed the smaller ones underfoot.

The first to reach the lake, Jen cried out, "Oh my God, Grandpa's boat!" She dropped the bag and ran to the water's edge. Gloria sped after her. They circled the fallen tree and knelt down on the soggy grass, wetting the knees of their pants, to see if the boat had survived. "It looks okay. Should we call the tree guys?"

"No," her mother answered. "Let's move it ourselves."

"You tough enough?" Jen said, already squatting, ready to lift the heavy section of the tree trunk aside. "Careful, Mom."

"Please, I'm not an invalid."

They yanked at the slippery wet branches of the treetop and then moved closer down, grasping the thicker part and lifting together. Once the boat was freed, Jen swiped the sap that clung to her hands onto the legs of her jeans.

"Don't do that! Those jeans cost big-time!"

"Yeah, yeah, money, money, always an issue," Jen answered, flipping her hat off, twisting her hair at the nape of her neck, jamming it back up under the hat again, and then she caught sight of her jagged fingernail. She bit at the torn part, thinking how she needed a French manicure. They do that stuff in L.A. She thought about Ralph's disgustingly weird nails, blackened with ink.

"Hey, let's do this thing," Gloria said.

There were no powerboats or pontoon boats or jet skis out on the lake. A family of ducks wandered up on a lawn, pecking at oak seeds in the grass. A flock of geese swooped down, surrounding them in a flash, taking over the territory. The ducks made a loud ruckus, squawking, waddling and flapping furiously until they reached the water's edge. The noise of their departure faded and quit as they swam away.

A V of birds overhead shadowed Jen and her mom, as though a black cloud that loomed had passed. Jen wanted to follow those birds, heading for sunlit beaches, the aura of success, dynamite clothes, the freedom to spend, spend, spend – be in the place where bougainvillea bushes bloomed all year long, where life was easier, exciting, where stars are born.

When had the birds traveled from Canada, Jen wondered, and where exactly were they headed? It caused her to question her runaway decision. With doubt in her mind, she thought about her wanderlust father, trucking out there somewhere – north, south, west, wherever...*Did he remember her? Did she get her long legs from him? Would he understand her? Would he even save her if she were drowning?*

Gloria sat in the front of the boat and Jen jumped in after shoving off. She grasped the oars and the boat moved smoothly across the shallow water that deepened within several feet. Tiny insects skittered along the surface of the lake and sparrows flew overhead. Jen loved rowing. She concentrated on the movement of her strong hands that gripped the oars as tightly as if she were balancing and swinging her body on high bars. With rounded shoulders, she moved back and forth; the oars dipped in rhythm, creating mesmerizing sounds. Her mother leaned back against the side of the boat, gazing and smiling into the distance. Jen's feet held fast. She licked her tongue across her top teeth, sensing the crooked one. Her thoughts returned to home and her problems. It seemed odd to her that her mother had settled on a man with a weak-sister chin, a scruff of hair under his bottom lip, and skinny arms popped with snaky veins. She'd had boyfriends before, but she kept distance between each one and her daughters, usually dating only on Thursday nights.

Jen looked directly into her mother's eyes. "You should lose him," she said.

"Come on, Jen. You're not old enough to understand. He makes me feel different."

"Different like what?"

"I don't know. Special, I guess - sometimes."

"That's bull, Mom. He baited you like a fish with ugly jewelry. Swap Meet crap worth squat."

"That's rude. Besides, he's teaching me accounting. He's got a good head."

"Mom, listen, you could take a class for that! You know the jerk weaseled his way into our home. Our home! Not his!" Jen stopped moving the oars to look her mother in the face again. "You know, I can't believe you're washing his gross underwear in with our stuff. I flipped yesterday when I emptied the dryer."

"I suppose that's how *you* see it, but…"

"Mom, he's gross. Those bulgy fish eyes!" *Always looking. She's blind to him.*

"I was lonely," Gloria answered softly, trailing her hand in the water as the soft chilly ripples rimmed her thin wrist and reached out in growing circles into the vast lake. "You're young. You don't know. All you think about is your pie in the sky movie star dream."

"Not so! Not so! I know enough. You can't replace my father," Jen answered, chopping the oar on her right side, turning the boat in circles, water splashing into the worn inside ribs of the boat with loud splats and across Gloria's hair and her face.

"Hey, cut it out," Gloria yelled, shaking water droplets from her red hair that had streaked dark-brown when wet and hung straggling to her shoulders. She tucked it behind her ears and dried her face with the sleeve of her shirt. Sheltering her eyes from the sun's glare with her cupped hand, she pouted, seemingly angry, and then burst into laughter.

"Yeah. Yeah. I know," Jen answered, grinning. "I can be a brat, huh?"

"You said it, I didn't."

"Yeah, but sometimes you don't hear me. Now, if I had a real father around…"

"Don't get on that," Gloria answered, glancing down at the diamond ring with the band she had worn thin. It reflected a prism of light off the sun's rays. She held it up for her daughter to see.

Jen had always lived only with her mother and sister after her father left. She'd been on a school-sponsored ski trip to Iron Mountain and a vacation up to the northern peninsula with her grandparents when Grandpa could still handle his old Pontiac. She depended on Gloria and mostly went along with her except for sneaking cigarettes from the kids at school and wearing a too-short denim skirt. One time she was forbidden to ride with a bad-boy senior who wore his hair blue-tipped and all kooky. She locked herself in her bedroom and lay there on the bed with her legs up straight and her dirty shoes marking the wall. She held out until dinner hour. The next day she learned about the horrific car accident. She would be dead now if she had defied her mother, yet now she was considering a bold move. *Do I dare? Yes, I have to…I'll tell Amy to stay miles and miles away from the perv, even though he doesn't go for her.* "No boobs," he said, last week. "Your sister got nothing in that department, but then neither does your mother."

"You know Mom, I kind of remember that day Dad left. It was wintertime, wasn't it? Me and Amy got home from the neighbor's, dragging clumps of wet snow over the carpet. We put our mittens on the heater like you always told us. The damp wool stunk. I thought you were sleeping until I heard things flying all over the place. You never talk about it."

"It was a different time. We were young. Your father was brilliant in his own way. I looked up to him. He couldn't wait to get this ring on my finger," Gloria answered, twisting the ring around, hiding the stone in her closed fist.

"You know I married your father quick-like. Then I got sucked in to life outside."

"You think it's your fault? That's bull, Mom."

"Jennifer, fault doesn't matter anymore. It's just how it is. I thought he'd come home, but he didn't."

Gloria stood and gestured for Jen to let her row. "I can't take this talking. You look for geese and ducks on the banks like we used to when you were little. You know where there's one, there's many. We can throw some bread."

"Oh sure, give it up. You're real generous with my lunch,"

As if she hadn't heard, Gloria stared up at the clean blue sky. "It might be too late for them." She steered the boat in a familiar pattern around a crop of land that jutted out from the uneven coastline that had individual docks and tiny beaches with leftover summer toys scattered about. Construction on a gigantic modern monstrosity, where a log cabin had been gutted and torn down, was nearly complete. "Your Grandpa would hate that," Gloria said as she gazed at the building. "City folk," he'd say. 'Go on back where you came from.'"

Gloria pointed out two swans, a notorious couple who had lived on the lake for years, gliding on the skim of water as though on a ballet stage. Jen thought their lovely white feathers reminded her of her first tutu.

"Hey Mom, look, the swans, faithful…"

"Funny, isn't it? They're smarter than we are."

They continued on in silence until they reached an island that sat on the western side of the lake. Gloria pulled hard, baring her teeth, as though she were racing. The bow bumped and scraped along the rocks near the gentle lapping waves at the water's foamy edge. Jen shook her shoes off, rolled up her jeans, and threw one leg over the side and then the other and stepped into the shallow water. "This is freezing!" she shouted, lifting one foot and rubbing her reddened ankle. "I'll get used to it, though." She loosened the line from the cleat at the bow, yanked it, and hauled the boat partially onto the shore. Her mother stepped across the middle seat and leaped out; the wet stones crunched together as she landed. They spread their sweaters on two large rocks, worn flat with time, and set their lunch bag out in front of them.

Gloria shucked her shoes and tucked her trim legs under her body and reached into her pocket. "Before we eat, I have something for you. Close your eyes. Hold out your hand," she said, placing a scarab bracelet squarely in her daughter's palm. The sun glinted off the amber and red and blue stones.

Jen pressed the pads of her fingers along the markings on the bracelet. "What gives, Mom? A good luck charm? You think I need it?"

"Keep it," her mom said.

Jen jumped up and gave her mother a crushing hug. "Keep it," she said. "The hug, I mean." They ate their lunch quietly, as though each was thinking of future days. The sun was lowering in the sky. The breeze quickened around their shoulders as they set the boat in motion.

"I love you, Jen," Gloria said.

"Me too, but really Mom, ditch him. I know he's offered to help you, but jeez, he's not even rich, not even famous, not even anything at all."

"I'll think about it…"

The lake mirrored the sky and the rushing clouds. The unblemished green-black water parted as the boat slipped along, leaving a wake, a memory of their path. Jen held her breath and placed her opened hand flat against her heart, her bracelet dangling from her wrist, as a bevy of birds flew high above them and across the middle of Cedar Island Lake, the deep dark part.

"The crows are gathering."

"They'll be leaving soon," Jen answered.

The next day while hurrying to retrieve her suitcase, plaid bag, and purse from the rack on the bus, Jen forgot the yellow envelope with her headshots. If she went to inquire about them, she'd miss the flight. It rattled her. Once settled on the plane, Jen had time to think. Her throat was scratchy, as though she had caught cold at the lake. She listed her plans in her head: get a cheap room for three nights, get a job, use the yellow pages to get the addresses and numbers for modeling agencies and studios. She removed her small pad of paper from her jeans and wrote definitively when suddenly the image of Ralph, standing in the doorway shadowed by the hall light, flashed before her. Pretending to be asleep but ever ready to punch his face if he touched her, her muscles froze. When he flipped back the sheets and snapped the elastic on her bikini underwear, she caught a whiff of his acrid tobacco breath. He laughed softly and left. She eased out of bed with the top sheet wrapped around her hips and tiptoed over to bolt the latch. She shivered, as the click sliced the silence of the night. Before climbing back into bed, she seized her water bottle off of the floor and, with her teeth clenched, she flushed the cold water against the skin on her pelvic bone that Ralph had touched, imagining his inky fingers on her once again. If she could only make her fortune in Hollywood and return to save her mom and sister, everything would be all right. She had warned her sister to stay away from Ralph. And, in her heart, she knew he'd hurt her family if she told about what just happened and other stuff. So, she'd go – tomorrow.

## Chapter 3
## Discovery: Onge and the Hollywood Squat

Onge's baptismal name was Oren Baxter Brown. Both of his parents had labored in the Florida fields before his mother was promoted into payroll and his father took off for Africa to find his roots. His mother had been a church-going lady who stressed the importance of being sanitary and literate to her son until she waited to hear from her husband and then accepted she got dumped. Onge's mother was fussy, insisting that he scrub his palms pink before and after meals. She said, "You eat so many you like to turn into an orange some day, a little Onge." She got to calling him that most times, except when she was mad and then it would be, "Oren Baxter, get on over here: make your bed, sweep the sidewalk, Clorox down the tile. Work on those figures. You'll make yourself banker one day." Somewhere in his head he knew that he'd leave out one day on his own, yet the possibility of wandering the whole distance to Hollywood didn't enter his mind.

After graduating Broward County High, he left, knocking around the coastline of Florida all the way to Jacksonville, working seasonal melon and orange picking and in coffee shops. He slept out in the open, rented single rooms and then, with a good bit saved, he took the plunge, trekking west.

Onge's hitch to L.A. took eight days. He had traveled along at a good pace, walking when he couldn't ride. He had the good sense to bring along three pairs of shoes and he kept on changing them. It was hard for him to tell when he might secure a ride. He'd thrust up his big thumb, peering into the windows of oncoming vehicles. Many folks who saw him on the side of the highway whizzed by. He could tell by the tilt of a man's head that he was afraid to look him eye to eye. Now at the age of twenty, he knew he was a big enough fella, and he certainly had grown strong over the years, building muscle at manual labor jobs. His clothing was not high style, but it was worn soft and clean. He carried a small suitcase and three books under his arm.

On the final leg of the journey, a hippie driving a rattletrap VW bus picked up Onge. The front was painted blue with stars all over it and the sides were striped red and white. It was a sloppy job. The man said his name was Rooster but he didn't say why. Onge told him his name and didn't say why.

Rooster kept one hand on the steering wheel while using the other to fondle his carrot-colored Kung Fu beard. He stopped in the middle of belting out *Born, in the USA. I was born...*

"I been where you been," he said. "Hitching. Got me to where I was going until I got access to this bus. Supercool, ain't it?"

"It is. Cool."

Onge had swung all the way up to San Francisco before heading south. This last ride took him down the coast. It was unlike anything he'd ever seen before. The jagged rocks plummeted down to the ocean. His eyes flew from the high-arched bridges down deep ravines that led to the ocean with all manners of blue and astonishing greens. In some places the water was so clear he saw brown bodies zinging along under it, and then, as they scooted up onto rock formations, he saw they were seals, loads of them. As he leaned out the window, sniffing the salty air, he heard their barking. Trees growing horizontally from cliffs spurted out in unexpected places. Some were gently curved by the ocean winds and others were bent violently, parallel to the ground. While spiraling along the open road, sports cars zoomed up behind the clanking bus then passed them at full throttle.

Judging the distance from where he was, he thought if a guy leaped he could twist and turn two hundred times in the air before he landed. *Man,* he thought, *crush to nothing but puzzle pieces.* Every time they went around a bend, they came up on something exciting: a fresh view of the blazing horizon, a mansion hanging out over the water, a tiny shack with half its roof blown off. It could be a place where a man pursued dreams of flying, where he'd build his own strutted wings, fit them under his armpits and go for glory.

Rooster pulled over twice, each time offering Onge lukewarm Jamba Juice and a jerky before they eased past Zuma Beach and then Onge spotted the Malibu sign. The place was warm like Florida, but not humid. The ocean breezes chased off the hot gusts. San Francisco was a place where a guy could blend in, but Malibu was full of females with blond hair and faces younger than their hands and knees.

"This is it," Rooster said. "I'm heading up Palisades. An old vet buddy got rich after Nam. He'll see me a couple steaks."

"Can I give you ten bucks for gas?" Onge asked, reaching to his hind pocket for his wallet.

"Hell, no. You paid your just dues some time or other. I was going this way anyhow. Peace, dude."

"Back at ya."

"Wait a sec. You look toasted, dude," Rooster said, staring at the half moon sweat marks on Onge's shirt. "Want to change in the back of the bus?"

Onge nodded yes and proceeded to change into a tank and shorts and the sandals he had bought in San Francisco. He wrapped his dirty things, shoes included, in a plastic bag and tucked it in his suitcase.

The Pacific Coast Highway cut a severe path between the brown hills lumping across the sky and the beach houses that teetered on the edge of the wide expanse of sand.
Sometimes their decks hung directly over the crashing waves that knocked on the home's pilings.

Onge imagined rich folk: the women, skinny sticks, and the men with man-tan faces, lolling about, sipping martinis, dreaming of their fat-ass bankbooks. He wished his lips were touching the iced rim of their martini glasses. If he owned one of those houses, he'd drop in a fishing line and let the sunlight rest his soul. And, of course, he'd take a good peek at the bikini-clad chicks on the beach. No harm there.

Winding roads led to estates with locations revealed only by the jutting points of their red-tiled roofs. Onge crossed the street to get a whiff of shade on his hot head and came upon a sign that read John Paul Getty Museum. He leaned in close to see the picture and diagram. It certainly looked like a Roman villa, the kind of structure he'd seen in books in the antiquities sections of libraries. His curiosity was fired up. Following the narrow driveway, he discovered a parking lot packed with big bucks automobiles; however, there was not a living soul in the area.

He entered the elevator and, when the doors rolled opened again with the smoothness of a rock beginning its roll down a hill, he stepped into the foyer and found he was face-to-face with a statue twice as tall as him. The sign at the bottom read, "Heracles, known as Hercules." Noticing that the man was carved from white marble, Onge thought it odd that Hercules had a cap of Nubian hair. *Could have been a black man.* Onge pulled at his shirt, dusted off his shoulders. There he was standing next to a full-sized replica of a man with his private stuff, a shriveled-up penis and a pair of balls unreal in their miniscule size, hanging out there.

A group of youngish women in teatime dresses, all with tiny purses that likely held lipsticks and fifty dollar bills, surrounded Hercules. Onge's face flushed when he saw the ladies staring rudely at the nude body. One woman looked him up and down, and back at Hercules several times, as though he was part of the display. She reached in her bag, proceeding to spritz herself with tart perfume under her pointy chin. He stepped back from the heavy smell and continued his tour of the Getty.

After wandering the halls inside and poking into the separate rooms with glassed-in cases that held golden vessels, silver bowls and ladles, he paused by the main entrance again, and this time he gazed down the steps to the shallow pool surrounded by mystical statues, men and women who were black with white marble eyes.

He was trying to imagine people back in history so far his math couldn't figure it. They didn't have dishwashers, TVs, jazzy cars, but they did have elegant homes like he'd never seen. He read that the whole place was designed after the Villa dei Papiri, which was only partially excavated, and other details realized from houses in Pompeii.

Outside the bees buzzed through golden trumpet honeysuckles, swirled around the tall lavender bushes that stood as tall as his chest. Formal rows of perennials in loud pink and white lined the sides of the pool. Older women, in plain dresses the same colors as the olive trees and artichokes, sat on the marble benches, speaking in hushed voices as though sharing secrets. One woman, with big square hips uneven enough to make her skirt hang crooked, leaned on a cane and the arm of a younger man who looked down when he saw Onge. *Caretaker. He's ashamed of his job*, Onge thought.

There was a lovely black woman sketching at the side of the pool. Her pear-shaped body had a long midriff and a round bottom. Her red hair, black at the roots and twisted back into a million tiny braids, joined together at the nape of her neck and then the whole clump cascaded down her back. She wore a single oblong silver bangle on her delicate wrist that moved along with her hand as she drew. She shaded the toga on the figure she was drawing; the delicate scrapings of the pencil were hardly audible. Her other hand wrapped around her skirt that she had tucked under her knees. When she glanced at Onge, her face opened up with a smile full of fantastic straight teeth that blossomed. Onge knew that their skin was nearly the same shade of brown, but surely, unlike him, this girl had breeding. She'd never get with him, yet he was drawn to her beauty and the soft continuous oval movements of her hand. She was surrounded by a pure sky of robin's-egg blue and nature's savory mix of fragrances: rosemary, olive, lemon, and sea grass.

Onge was still thinking about the smooth skin on the curve of her throat when he felt a gentle tap on his shoulder. He turned to find a man standing behind him who was impeccably dressed in a suit of fine material and a yellow paisley ascot.

"Excuse me," the gentleman with the clipped gray hair said. "This your first visit here? May I direct you to our special features?"

It was then Onge noticed his official badge with a photo of a young dude with a great shock of black hair curling past his ear lobes.

"I'm not usually out amongst you visitors, alas, but today is my birthday! I'm celebrating life. Being affiliated with this marvelous institution. An *everyman* experience."

Although he and this man were about the same height, Onge had the sense the gentleman was peering down his narrow nose at him, yet he was flashing an oozing grin full of blue-white teeth. *Blueblood.* He tried to look the man in the eye but he couldn't help focusing on his hands with manicured fingernails. They were as smooth as vanilla ice cream with fingers that surely wrapped around fine china when he had his afternoon tea.

"Observe this," the Getty-man said, pointing to the inside trough filled with water and the opening in the ceiling that was designed to allow rainwater to collect and be used for inside irrigation needs.

"Ingenious, weren't they, those Romans?"

Onge had been thinking the pool was too shallow for an indoor bath. Stepping down now and standing in front of the garden surrounding the pool, he took a fresh breath of air and breathed in the many scents from the plants and flowers.

The fellow gestured to Onge as though he expected to be followed. "The sculpture garden is a delight to many visitors," he said. "These exquisite tiles were imported from Italy; the clay affords the saffron and sapphire colors their richness."

Onge wondered why this dude was interested in showing him around. What did they have in common? This man had never seen a lick of hard work. He'd never ran barefoot through a field. He'd never been a daddy changing soiled diapers.

The sun was hot, shining directly on Onge, and, as he reached up to touch his hair, it was practically steaming. The pool looked so cool, refreshing, and he wanted to dip right in as he saw the blue sky and puffy white clouds reflected in the clear water and clear through to the bottom.

"Wow, some colors, and real gold, huh? Intricate designs," he said, staring at the tiles surrounding the inner parts of the pool.

"Superb observation, sir. I see you have an interest in tile. You might venture down to the Adamson House. It is merely a few blocks north. It was built in the twenties by an esteemed tile master. Divine, just divine. On the ocean, I might add."

Onge thanked the man for his help, walked around the pool portico once, and then took the elevator back to the parking lot. He walked quickly down the path to the coast.

Onge decided to take the bus. He sat on the bench, stretching back his shoulders, swiping his arm across his sweaty forehead, surveying his surroundings: the cars whizzed past in a continuous blur, the sun was gently falling in a dusky lavender sky, images of the clouds quivered in the rhythm of the ocean waters.

The bus stopped and he settled in the front seat as the driver turned and gave him a nod. He would ride until his gut told him to get off. The bus took him a few miles down the coast, then through Santa Monica up Wilshire Boulevard and out onto Sunset. The Los Angeles area was spread out with no definite delineation between towns; the city and street signs were obscure and sometimes missing. It was easy to tell that some folks had big money by the cars they drove, their sniffing attitudes, walking tall, and the size of their brick-façade houses. The others crammed into ratty apartment buildings, hanging on, trying to make it for their kids. Or maybe not, since drug money afforded the gangs hot vehicles and piles of gold they wore proudly. Young boys, and girls, too, rode skateboards and bikes, weaving in and out of traffic and right on the sidewalks, causing the pedestrians to move aside for them. Old men and a few homeless characters who rode bikes and pushed carts dotted the streets. Kids rocked along, mouthing rap. Cars, blocked up high, shook with banging sound from their speakers. The boys and their raunchy chicks inside juggled along with the magnificent volume surrounding the whole corner as the bus driver shook his head in disgust.

As Onge headed toward Hollywood, he noticed the billboards got bigger, the sidewalks more littered. He saw men he thought were Johns, queer boys flanking each other, dark-skinned gardeners at work everywhere on small patches of grass, clusters of maids waiting at bus stops, some young – letting loose their thick pony tails, flipping their voluptuous hair – some old, their hair bunched up under scarves, their bodies hunched over, plastic bags in their laps and at their feet.

Young kids were all over. Many were spindle-thin and some were fleshy, their pants sinking from fat bellies, the pants' legs dragging with mud-caked and frayed hems. The girls huddled together in groups, smoking, posing, their little asses wiggling with excitement. They were all putting on good faces, as Onge had growing up a black boy. He'd freeze his face with a blank look when he met strangers, looking straight through their prying eyes. There were people who might consider him invisible anyway, those who didn't know he was jack smart in school, and now a man who could be trusted to count money in a register and balance the sucker without pocketing a dime.

Underneath their bold clothing and cranky attitudes of bravado, Onge knew the youngsters had fears and angers the way teenagers did. They should be in school. Some were not even old enough to work. Hanging out will trouble them up. Alone is bad, ganging is worse. Cops notice. *Maybe, one kid at a time, I could help.*

Hopping off the bus in Hollywood, Onge went up the side streets, figuring there must be a hideout somewhere–same as cowboys head to the hills, must be people who hide out in Hollywood. He could.

Opening his pack, Onge removed his thongs from the tissue paper he had packed them in. He shook out his New Balance shoes and wrapped them, inserting them vertically in the side-pocket of his suitcase. Since he'd been on his own, he always managed to have three pair of shoes. He was hot on the latest. His heart stung when he remembered how he had to make his only pair of running shoes with frayed laces that smelled of Clorox last until his toes were squished and his mama went to the Goodwill to choose his suit and black shoes for church. Never new. She pretended not to notice every September when Onge's classmates were wearing Jordans and Nikes that first day of school. Sometime later each fall she scrabbled together the bucks for a new pair for him. He could see the shame in her eyes when she jutted out her chin and declared, "You'll be alright, Oren. Take up those books. Never mind what's on your body or your feet!" His mother tried to make things right, even when they weren't flush with goods. But when Onge turned seventeen, her priorities went wild; she indulged herself with men, champagne, hooker shoes that made much of her beanstalk legs. She grew round around the middle; the skin on her face blotched up with dark spots. She was hardly herself anymore, looking rotund walking up the street going both ways, but the men kept on coming. It was strange because the only stout woman his mother had ever admired was the singer she saw at Birdland before she moved south. Instead of white kid lullabies, she trilled be-bop notes to her son when he was a toddler, and now, years later, Onge found himself humming those jazz scales at the strangest times, like his subconscious was longing for his mama. She had told Onge that songbird-woman was fine-bodied up until forty and then she went to pot. And there was Mama following in her footsteps. At first Onge ignored the changes in his mother, then finally, after the third live-in guy, he left.

Now in Hollywood, the sun, going down, was a half-moon lazing against the horizon. On Curtis Avenue, the third street up off the main drag, Sunset, he came to a bungalow that was nearly hidden. He had stopped to dump the sand from his shoes when his eyes rose to view a fence smothered with fuchsia and orange-colored flowers and a small house behind it. The place was quiet with the exception of one bird loudly chirping somewhere inside the fence. Onge felt drawn to the bird and the house. The bungalow, painted purple with pink trim, stood among the beige stucco houses belonging to neighbors. He felt a strange sense of mystery about the place. It was different, like him, a bungalow that had seen stuff like he had seen life and, although tarnished, it was easy to see she had been a beauty in her day, just like he felt when he looked at his second grade picture of himself. He'd been all teeth at that time, but his eyes shined. That was before things messed up.

He lifted up and folded back a section of the fence large enough for him to crawl through and entered the yard. A peaceful rain of fragrance from the overgrown flowers caught his attention. Still for a moment, he listened intently and then tiptoed past giant tuberous jades, a flower garden and a patch of herbs clustered together near the garage. Green ivy climbed the walls of the tiny home whose windows were shaded with old drapery.

On the far side of the garage, Onge discovered a window with a sagging frame behind a violet morning glory bush. He hoisted it and stuffed a stick in to hold it up. He shoved one leg over the sill, straddled it and entered the garage. It was dark inside, but a band of light beamed through the open window and another light source at the top of the stairs allowed him to make his way to a large object on the other side. Flecks of dust flew through the light; moths flitted across his path. Onge stepped over boxes, under cobwebs, reaching a long low car.

"Whoa baby, what's this?"

He set his bag down, piled the books on top, and walked clear around the car. It was something else! It looked like it was hardly ever used, and now, it was abandoned.

As he ran his hand along the body of the car, it felt gummy; the humidity and thick dust had formed a pasty coating. *Fine body.* He listened and snooped around to see if anyone had seen him enter, but all was quiet.

Reaching into his suitcase, he retrieved his soiled shirt and proceeded to rub the whole of the car along one side. He placed his left hand on her trunk, planting a handprint. "Jesus, I branded you," he said aloud after seeing the outline of his out-sized hand, the fingers spread to a great width, having parted the dust on the metal. It was like a man leaving a mark on his woman's thigh. "That print. It will be that last to go, girl. You a beauty! A lion, but full of grace. Leontine."

Onge went to the front door on the driver's side. He cautiously opened it. The inside was spectacular. He marveled at the classy burnt brown leather, the swirling rosewood grain of the dash and the distinct smell, almost cinnamon, from the cigars in the glovebox. *Unbelievable. This thing just sitting, waiting on discovery. What else we got here.*

Beating back the cobwebs blocking him, Onge started up the stairs. He took one step and stood perfectly still hoping no one heard him on the narrow, creaky steps. At the top landing he found a half-open door leading to a room full of musty, unopened crates. With some effort he piled them against one wall and created a space where he could lie down. "Okay then," he said sighing. "This is it. I'll squat here awhile."

## Chapter 4
## The Streets: Starlet and Freddie Crossing Paths


The sudden thump of the airplane as it flew into a pocket of turbulence, dropping altitude, didn't help Jen's nerves. It was odd that this would be her first flight. She tried to think of the squeaks in the metal and roar of the engines as ordinary, but she found herself grasping the armrests and grinding her teeth. *Imagine it's a bumpy road. The clouds have hills, snow moguls...* As with other firsts and uncomfortable situations, she had put on her brave face, smiling inanely at strangers standing at the check-in line, asking only for Coke and a vegetarian meal and blushing only slightly when the stewardess told her those meals were to be ordered ahead of time.

"Vegetarian, honey?" the stewardess asked, her Twiggy lashes flicking.

"Yes," Jen said. "Keeps my skin clear."

"You are so right on," the gal answered, arching her dark brows, running her fingers across her coarse forehead and fluffing out her silly platinum bangs. "This pressurized air is so totally bad for my complexion. Wrinkles before my time, you know."

"You look nice," Jen said. "You live in Los Angeles?"

"El Porto, down the coast. Me and a hundred other stews and pilots. Beach living. It's happening. Hey, you want some of my stash, yogurt and apples?"

Jen told her that she'd make an exception and eat the lasagna with the orange tangy sauce that was only slightly flavored by meat of some kind.

After three hours on the plane, Jen arched against the rigid seat and realized that she'd been holding herself so tight that her tailbone ached and her muscles were stiff, as though she'd been at home painting her nails fire engine red, focusing on the backdoor knob, waiting for her mother and Ralph to enter after work. A girl in her twenties passed by in a glittery gauze dress ruffled to the ankles and immediately Jen thought she should have packed a dress, one that showed her body, the kind of sheath Farrah Fawcett slithered around in. Jen only had jeans and tees, the one skirt, and a see-through peasant blouse and her bracelet.

The pilot instructed the passengers to view the Grand Canyon out of the right side of the plane. Jen thought it strange that the terrain was dusty-brown and bumpy with a giant hole that was the canyon. And then, passing over Las Vegas, it looked so insignificant, not at all like on TV shows, as though it wasn't real, a toy city dropped in the middle of the dry desert. When the plane started its descent towards the L.A. airport, Jen squinted to see as much as possible; the city buildings crammed together surrounded by a yellow haze, the ordinary houses, some with tile roofs and pools and fences around them, and finally the tower of the airport itself.

As she prepared to exit the plane, the stewardess, who had sidled up next to the captain, asked, "Where you headed, honey?"

"Hollywood."

"Oh really? That place has its rough patches. Watch your back."

Jen began the long haul past the airport convenience shop, with its array of multi-colored Venice Beach and Lakers sweatshirts and big surf postcards, and down the escalator to the moving tram that took her to the baggage area. The mix of business travelers, families in all colors, moved along quietly. A couple of teenyboppers in skimpy skirts twittered, thumping their hips to the tunes in their walkmans. A boy with the beginnings of a beard and a hitcher's backpack chomped on a granola bar. His clothing reeked of weed. The whole scene at the airport seemed more open, airy, than the airport in Detroit. She had the sense that each person knew where he was headed. She didn't. Young and older people were in sandals, running shorts, and even tube tops.

Making her way through the sliding doors near the baggage area, she was hit with a blast of hot air. *This is it. California!* She felt out of place with her layers of clothing; her eye make-up dragged on her eyelids. In the ladies room, Jen peed and then stuffed her jacket and sweater into her bag. She flashed on the idea to roll up her jeans and knot her shirt at rib level. Still, she was so white. *So touristy.*

After finishing off her last bottle of water, she headed for a Hertz Rental booth and inquired about a bus. An Asian lady, with her hair in a stiff flip, immersed in a heavy-handed dose of musky stench that wafted out from the counter said, "This is car rental. Go up the escalator to the information booth. Can't help you here."

It was now noon. Jen stood back outside again, scanning the signs on the buses with black diesel exhaust puffing behind them. The sun's bright glow warmed the patch of skin showing below her knotted shirt. The sight of climbing jasmine and fuchsia bushes and tall clumps of Birds of Paradise set against the parking garage across the way amazed her. Even as the warm breezes tickled her cheeks, Jen reflected on how her mother would fuss over flowers, but she couldn't afford to dwell on her and Amy at home. The idea of securing a job, becoming a movie star, and eventually sending for her mother and Amy would work. *Keep on. Keep on.* She perspired under her arms; her hair stuck to the back of her neck. Lonely feelings crept into her head. Wait, she told herself. Fear would block her dream. Even though her heart seemed to be throbbing, she placed all of her belongings on the cement and shook her hands, as though they were wet with lake water, until her mood passed.

The night before she had hardly slept at all, considering whether to tear into Amy's room and abandon her escape plan, cash in the ticket or something, or even take her sister along somehow. Finally, she turned on the bedside light and looked intently at her shadow, twisting and angling her head until she could see the outline of her hair parading down her back. She scribbled a note, wrapped the paper around a pencil, stuck it in a water bottle, and hid it behind her headboard. The flight had been much longer than she expected, but she couldn't rest now. She had to get herself to Hollywood in one piece and find a place to cleanse her face and sleep, at least for the night.

As she stood on the median waiting for the bus, a man with a deeply grooved face bent his head out of an idling limo and eyeballed her up and down. A grass-green parrot, whose craggy talons clung to the man's forearm, beaded on her and unexpectedly attempted to fly at her face; his wingspan spread out humongously. He scratched furiously at the paint on the limo. The scritch-scratch sound caused Jen's spine to shiver but, before the parrot could take to the air, the man jerked it back with a leather tether strapped to the bird's leg. Startled, she lunged back, twisting her ankle in a pothole, and almost lost her balance. *Don't freak. It's just a bird.*

The vehicle, caught in traffic, crawled slowly away as Jen watched the parrot's furious flapping and heard strange guttural words that sounded like, "Girly, getcha girly, getcha girly..." emanating from the bird. *Weird.*

The sight of the *Hollywood/Vine* bus brought Jen relief. She shoved her suitcase and backpack on the rack above and settled in. The bus driver maneuvered The Big Blue past open car doors, jaywalkers, in and out of traffic, and halted within an inch of the curb at each stop. She scooted back against the seat and reached inside her shirt, adjusting her bra that itched her skin. She dug her fingers in, reaching for the hundred dollar bills stuffed in the tiny cups, but she quit when she sensed her seatmate's eyes on her. While smoothing her Tee shirt with her hands, she spoke to the lady next to her, "How far to Hollywood?"

"No speak English," the woman, dressed in a checkered uniform with a bulky plastic *Odd Lot* bag on her lap, answered as she pulled a file from her purse, blew on it and attended to her nails.

"Oh, sorry. Never mind," Jen answered, shrugging her shoulders.

The gentleman with granny glasses and a shabby leather briefcase who sat behind her leaned forward, nearly touching the back of her head, and said, "About 55 minutes. You have time to relax, young woman."

Jen shrank back. The man's putrid breath reminded her why she left home so abruptly. She managed to mumble thank you, took a deep breath and flushed her sweaty blond curls into a high ponytail secured with an elastic band. Twirling her bracelet around her wrist, she stared at the colors reflecting sunlight that bounced in the window. She stretched her legs out under the seat in front of her and her shoe slipped across the cover of a glossy magazine. The magazine was loaded with spa ads and Heffner-girlie blonds with plastic surgery boobs. Jen earmarked the "Dentist to the Stars" advertisement and the article about affirmations. *So California.* She would create one. *I'm an actress, an actress, a star! No, a starlet. That's it. I'm Starlet... Starlet Johnson. Perfect.*

A variety of smells floated in the open window next to her. Blackish dirt and grime collected in the grooves of the windowsill. A taco stand located on a street corner sent peppery odors into the air. *I'm starving*, she thought. *It's way after lunch back home.*

"Sunset," the driver announced. Jen, who now would refer to herself as Starlet, stepped carefully down, clutching her belongings, and gazed in both directions. She decided to wander a few blocks to get her bearings. A tiny boutique with glass floor-to-ceiling windows caught her eye. The sequined dresses on white-faced mannequins, their lips painted orange-frost and their wigs neon orange and blunt cut to the chin, were beautiful. Sucking in her tummy, she wondered if she was skinny enough to wear one of those dresses. *Like a size 2.* Would it cover her privates? Next door at the Blowfish Tattoo shop, a low whirring sound emanated from behind a stained curtain. Peering in, Starlet checked the gazillion stencils on the wall and the stained curtain where the sound was originating. *Trashy.*

It took Starlet two passes by the Sleepy Tunes Motel with its minuscule sign that flashed, "Day and Week Rates" before she made her decision. Expecting a sleaze behind the counter in the tiny office, Starlet was shocked to encounter a gorgeous girl focused on a coffee-stained bunch of crumpled pages that could have been a script. The girl's eyebrows were black and thick, her lashes were outstanding and she had a long slender midriff and little boy hips.

"It's totally hot, isn't it?" Starlet said.

"Santa Anas, crazy-maker winds. Get you some short or go on down to Diane's on Wishire and grab a polka-dot bikini. You're thin enough."

"I got shorts in my pack. No money for a suit. Later, maybe."."

"Okay then. I better study. Hey, don't drink the water. The pipes in this place are shit."

"No kidding. I better get going. See you around."

The room wasn't exactly filthy, but terribly old, out-dated, and even though the stench of Clorox permeated the bathroom, a huge black bug scooted from behind the toilet when Starlet entered. She took off her shoe and beat it to death, and then she hovered over the toilet seat to pee, as though she expected another bug, a spider, or a snake to emerge out of the rusty bowl.

Starlet peeled the thin bedspread and blanket back before placing her things on the sheet. The sandwich and fries were cold, but she was glad to have them anyway. Leaning against the pillow after her meal, she perused the yellow pages for a list of coffee shops and studios. After a while the stink of the food wrapper made her nauseous so she ventured out to a dumpster in the alley where a scruffy yellow dog leaped up out of nowhere and nabbed the trash in her hand without so much as touching her fingers. "Hey," she yelled.

"Cut it out, Harold," the desk-clerk girl called out. The dog high tailed it over to where the girl sat on the steps sucking a cigarette down to its last quarter inch. "Sorry. Harold here ain't no problem. He come from Kentucky with me. He don't bite none."

"That's okay. He startled me."

"He's half-blind anyhow."

"Oh, that's too bad. I'm Starlet. What's your name?"

"Bella."

"You're from Kentucky? You a model?"

"I'm not a model but I got Best Personality at Miss Mississippi last year, but my stinking grammar held me back. I'm studying though."

"So, you want to be in the movie business? You're so pretty."

"I ain't there yet, but I'm working my bod for a Diane's bikini. You seen her stores?" Belle answered, arching her back and sucking in her stomach.

"No, I haven't, but gee, that's cool. I better go. Jet lag's catching up. Bye. Bye, Harold." Harold ceased his lapping on the paper and looked up at Starlet, his eyes blinking.

There was only one straight up, uncomfortable-looking chair in Starlet's room so she headed for the bed again. She hadn't realized how exhausted she was until she awakened later and found that she'd fallen asleep. It was now nine in the evening. The clunky wall heater in the bathroom was out of order, yet Starlet braved the chilly air and hopped into the shower. "Yuck," she said when her feet touched the slimy bottom of the tub. It took forever to rinse shampoo from her hair with the pitiful dribble she stood under. "Damn it all to hell!" Starlet said. There she was, shivering in a crap shower in a shit motel. Still hungry, she broke down and cried, rubbing her hand across her soap-slicked belly.

She placed a chair askew under the doorknob and piled her suitcase on it, then went to bed. She squeezed her eyes shut, but they snapped open when she heard a loud thumping in the adjacent room and then scratching at the wall as though a dog was trying to break in. She wrapped the sheet around her body and moved towards the door that adjoined the next room. The lock was set, yet scraping sounds continued along with sniffing noises. She imagined occupants with a dangerous dog, maybe a pit bull, ready to attack her. *Calm. Calm. Get it together. Maybe heavy drugs were on the scene, a grey-filled, smoky bong, a hot spoon of drugs, a spoon with fiercely-boiling liquid, so it would burn your fingers.* She slipped on her jeans and tee shirt and threw her purse over her shoulder so in case someone tried to crash in or there was a fire, she could bolt. *Yes, positively, it's druggies next door smoking crack in bed, setting the mattress on fire...*

Starlet's thoughts ran wild. Her breathing was thin, she so wanted to call home. *No.*

Freddie left the diner disappointed with what he had discovered inside: faded movie star clips, garage sale notices, and lost dog pictures, all crammed up on the walls. A couple of anorexic dancers in faded torn leotards and wooly legwarmers sat in a booth sharing a salad; they would be no action for him. Freddie thought he knew what to expect from Hollywood. The girls would have balloon hooters like in *Playboy*. Their faces would be younger than those of the used-up women in Vegas. Soap stars would be tan from hanging on the beach. The guys would be hip and very rich, scoring big with hip-hop and Sundance flicks, with chicks flopped all over them on overstuffed red velvet couches. The place would be open season for straights and gays and crossers: a walk in the park.

Hollywood had a past where Tab Hunter and Rock Hudson lay around in Vintage tighties at the Beverly Hill bungalows; now there were chick stars, TV stars, boy bands sprung from garage jamming, all cool. Freddie might find a job at a studio taking stills. Freddie was surprised to find the streets narrow and plain, messed up with trash. The street people were skanks and, even worse, average looking. In Vegas the coppers kept the bums down and out of sight during daytime hours, but here in California, they were all over, slumped against buildings, staring dully down at their own chests.

Using one of his favorite trickster moves, he bent down, pretending to tie his boot. At that level, he could perceive a lot. He viewed some big-bucks leather on business dudes and crooked-toed women in sandals, but then he waved at twin boys in an elaborately painted gecko-green stroller and a big brother who dragged along behind the mother. *What if I had a brother?* Acting the clown, Freddie rolled his eyes back, stuck out his tongue while flapping his ears with his hands. The kids stared blankly at him. He stood up. A homeless, who came from nowhere, startled him. First, he smelled something rotten, the guy's mouth, and then he quickly stepped back from him. It was hard to tell the man's size, as he was wearing four or five layers of clothing in eighty-degree weather. His bare feet were swollen and blackened.

He lunged at Freddie yelling "Money!" He seized Freddie's arm.

"What?"

"Money, money, money, money!" he answered, his voice rising in fury. He poked Freddie in the ribs with a stick.

Freddie held him back with one arm, and grabbed the loose twenty he kept in his pocket and shoved it into the guy's hand, yelling "Hold up, hold up, hold up, man." "Aw     shit," Freddie said, running down the street, realizing that he'd been had. The lunatic had had him cornered, but he could have easily slipped away before giving up the money. When he did turn, he saw the man, with filthy gray hair sprouting from his head, straddling a crack in the sidewalk. He was licking the bill. *Whacko.*

*This ain't the Hollywood I expected*, Freddie thought. No Winona Rider, no Courtney Love. Hardly a limo around. His heart lightened when he spied a punker. The boy's black-swathed body was thin and speedy. He had a retro McCartney haircut, sapphire-colored liner rimmed his eyes. He wore a grooving fifties dinner jacket with rolled up sleeves, camouflage pants and rainbow string bracelets, like thirty of them. His hands flicked when he walked, his matching eagle tattoos on his forearms moved like puppets.

Freddie popped up behind him, tapped him on the shoulder as the kid waited for the light. He asked, "Dude, what's happening?"

"Dude? You nuts? Piss off." The kid flailed his arms in the air.

It wasn't the words but the kiss-off that bummed Freddie. He backed up, slipping down an alley to regroup. Dropping his pack and leaning against a brick wall, he caught a whiff of incense wafting from the open window above his head. The whine of a strange string instrument floated out. He pulled out his last Coke, slugging it down, hoping he'd get a little jump from the caffeine. He crunched the can with his boot heel, and kept stomping on it until it was flattened and then continued, as though beating on it. That bolstered him up. Gathering up his belongings, he crossed to the sunnier side of the street. He removed two bucks from his special envelope and bought himself a warm pretzel at Auntie Junes. He missed his mother. It surprised him.

The bus stop bench was close by so he decided to give his feet a rest. An old woman shuffled to the other end, plopping down while taking no notice of Freddie. Her moth-eaten blue beret stretched over her left eye. An ancient brown winter coat encased her body like skin, as though she slept in it many nights, her curves living in the cloth. The fur collar, once good mink, was threadbare and worn, gripping her neck with one outsized button. A rope tied at her waist kept the garment closed. Above the tattered red sneakers she wore, her ankles were scaly. She lit a cigarette, cupping the match with unsteady hands to protect the flame from a breeze that wasn't there. Once the tattered cigarette was lit, she shoved it in her mouth and immediately slumped over the wrinkly plastic bags in her lap.

Freddie watched the ashes grow and drop. He said, "Hey lady, lady, your butt! It's burning your coat."

Her craggy lids were still jammed shut as she batted at the fur and slammed her chest with a thump of her open hand. Then she took a deep drag and went back to sleep.

The mood on Hollywood Boulevard was changing. Streams of girls with lean midriffs, bare pelvic bones sticking out of their jeans, and hoops and chains hanging from their bellybuttons passed by. A gay couple passed him. They held hands, swung their arms playfully, stopping to eye shop windows. The younger one broke their clench to tell a story as though he was putting on a show with flirty-bird gestures. Then, nearly taking a bow, he listened intently as the older guy discussed a matter that might seem trivial to an outsider, perhaps just the right shade of his plum couch or the Crimini mushrooms on sale at Trader Joe's. Both stole glances at Freddie when they caught him watching. Freddie quickly lowered his head. *Not me boys, I'm not game for you.*

A bunch of kids he had seen earlier in the day camped out in a doorway where a big-bellied chick with pink hair and black lips strummed a guitar with a black widow painted on it. He considered approaching them, but then he chickened out.

They could have been his kind, he thought, yet he was bewildered as to how to even say hello. The homeless, with their "work for food" signs, had a better grip than he did. At least they had a clue where cops hung out, where restaurants trashed food, where to crash, where a guy could hide from dangerous eyes.

Freddie's thoughts were racing. He needed to scheme a place to bed down. He passed the Kodak Theatre and all its hullabaloo activity, decked out folks flooding down the massive steps after a bigwig event. *Time to do a money check.* He headed for an alleyway where two empty midsize delivery trucks were parked. Those drivers got no pull, he thought, or they'd both be hauling a big rig like Joe-Mack. Those babies let you rule the road, with their playboy mud flaps and wild pin striping. You could find desert sunset scenes, waterfalls, Jesus walking on water, everything possible plastered over those long haulers.

As his thoughts rolled back to his trip with the trucker, he sat down on the fender of the first vehicle that had the Sunbeam girl on the side of it, and pulled out his stash envelope. In the angle of light coming in from the street, he counted twenties, tens, and fives, placing the thick stacks of bills between his fingers; they flapped out like a fan. The cocktail waitresses back home used this method. He reached two hundred dollars and he mentally assessed what he had hidden in his shoes, the band of his shorts, and the hundred he pinned to his undershirt. He heard loud voices just before he spied three hard ass dudes wearing red and black doo-rags, crashing into the alley. His heart beat fast. He scrambled to stuff his money in his pack. With adrenaline rushing, he dropped a bunch of it on the asphalt. The guys surrounded him. He could smell their dirty sweat and boozy breath, and the big man, who towered over him, moved closer. "What's up?"

"Nothing."

"Like that green loot on the ground ain't nothing? Scoop it up, A-hole."

Freddie bent down to pick up the loose bills and someone pounced on him. "Ooof," he yelled when he got kicked in the ribs so hard it knocked his breath out. Sand ground into his face as he lay on the pavement, shaking, and trying to figure what to do. If he ran, he might be shot. He covered his head with his hands. The bills were yanked from them and he heard footsteps pounding the pavement. When he looked up, they were gone.

"Fuck," he muttered. "Fuckin' A."

He rubbed grit from his eyes and spit out the thick saliva that pooled in his mouth. Getting up on his knees, he gathered the loose money on the ground, the envelope, the bills he had fallen on, and as he checked under the fender, he caught a glimpse of a shiny object. It wasn't a dime, a gum wrapper, but links of a gold chain that must have come unclasped when the ganger beat on him. Freddie seized the chain, shook off the dirt and quickly jammed it in his pocket. He rolled it around inside his pocket and felt the heft of it, thinking it would go over big in a pawnshop. He figured it might bring enough to replace his money. He'd heard about karma; this was it!

Then Freddie panicked. *Jesus, what if they come back for the chain?* He grabbed his bag and took off. Outside the alley, he darted past an Indian restaurant where an intensely spicy smell wafted from the open door, causing a woozy feeling in his stomach. He stopped short in front of Blowfish Tattoos. Ducking in he reached up to touch the side of his throbbing head and his hand came back bloody. He used an old T-shirt to blot the wound. In all the rush he hadn't realized he'd been cut and now he was amazed to see a gazillion stencils and icons slapped over every inch of wall space in the tiny shop.

He focused on a creepy black widow with a red spot on her back similar to the one he saw on the black-lipped chick's guitar. The stencils included white whales, cheesy vampires, peace signs, and Goth girls with tits. Along another wall, he saw butterflies, gang tags, eagles and birds of every kind, and a green frog. The older pictures were yellowed; the newer Simpson heads and snakeheads were stenciled on crisp white paper.

At the rear of the shop, a makeshift curtain was set up. The once-white sheet, stained with brown spots, revealed the shadow of a tattoo man and his customer hunched together. Freddie, hearing the buzz of a machine and imagining the pain of a needle pricking skin, cringed at the sound. His mouth was dry. When the noise ceased, he heard a woman's voice say, "X, sure as shooting. Big bust at the *Coop*."

"No shit, the fuzz tags that dive, huh?"

"Any dope around here knows that!" the lady answered.

"Yo, Louis. That you out there?"

"No," Freddie answered.

"Okay, have a looksee. Don't touch nothing."

Freddie's head banged. He was no chicken. He wouldn't wimp out like the time his dickhead father shoved him down in the driveway at home and he bloodied up his knees. He'd been caught spying on dickhead puffing weed out back near the Joshua tree. Freddie fell when he was slapped, white pebbles stuck in the skin on his hands and knees, along with confetti from his parents' wedding chapel. His elbow had that same roughed-up skin now. That day he vowed not to cry again. No matter. And he would run away! Now, here he was. *Get a damn tattoo. Toughen up.*

Pressing his palm against the wound, he plopped down in the only chair in the place, the kind left out in alleys on trash day, the wicker loosening around its joints, the gold spray worn off on the seat.

*Tattoo it is.* Freddie skimmed the boatload of choices. He was caught up with the animals: wild tigers, sharks with multiple rows of teeth, and then these birds, mates in stunning colors, kissing beak to beak. The pair had purple heads with bright orange beaks, lime green rings around their necks. Their plumped-out breasts were red and black, striped like casino rugs. Freddie wondered if they were both males, if their cries in the jungle were raucous, if he might find some in a California zoo. *Radical.* They could sit on my shoulder or ride across my back—impressing the hell out of everyone. *Too much cash.* After circling the shop three times, he eventually honed in on a frog. He'd pretty much made the decision to go with it, but he continued glancing back at the birds. He fished out his camera and took their picture. He had committed them to his collection.

Emerging from behind the curtain, a beefy woman around fifty with a testy-looking, "don't even think about it" face zoomed past Freddie. The proprietor of the shop wiped his big-boxer hands with alcohol from a gallon jug. The tart smell filled the room.

Turning to Freddie and extending his hand for a shake, he said, "Rocko, body artist. Tat?"

Freddie shook his fingers out after Rocko squeezed them, answering, "Yeah." Of course he had no idea what a tattoo man should be but was set back by the guy's size, his missing left pinky, and his lumpy shaved head. Tattoos ran from his collarbone down both the guy's arms. In contrast to his comic book arms, his whale-belly white legs poked out from khaki shorts. He had one crazy American Beauty rose, its stem winding around his ankle.

"Saint Theresa rose," Rocko said. "My mother, from Italy. Pray to her every day."

Rocko bent down on one knee, blessed himself. "The day she die, I crush a dozen roses, put the petals in her casket, a fancy golden job. I quit the fight game."

The tat man told how he'd been in the same shop nineteen years. How people wear lockets and stuff, but the rose brought him luck. He told how his poppa had been a barber, the only one in his village. He lathered and cut, listening to town gossip. He could have been a damn psychologist he put so many marriages back together. Always, he'd tell the men, "Go home. The grass ain't no greener on the other side of town. What you gonna get, another set of chi-chis and bush like you already got."

"Yeah, I guess."

"Okay, what'll it be. I seen you eyeing them birds. Birds of Paradise. Crow's cousins. I did them only once. Back-breaker. You got money?"

"Not a whole lot."

"Okay, then pick your poison. Under four inches. Forty bucks."

Freddie chose the frog and Rocko sat him down, grabbing his arm before he could change his mind. After the alcohol swab, and at the first jab of the needle, a jump of electricity in his skin, Freddie winced, saying, "I can't do this!"

"Shut up. Breath deep."

Freddie's eyes were running, his whole body sweating, yet he'd come this far; he knew it was now or never with this deal. It didn't help that Rocko stunk like a swamp.

Biting at the thumb of his right hand to distract himself, he also concentrated on the tattoo on Rocko's back. "That Texas?" he asked.

"Shhhhhh. I'm focusing," Rocco said, turning up the opera music on his boombox.

When it was over, Freddie swiped the sweat from his face, looking at the swollen red mess on his arm. "That it?"

"Here," Rocko said, as he layered on gauze and tape. "Keep it covered. Leave him alone. After the scab falls off, you'll get your green. Twenty-five smackers. You get a first time discount."

Freddie reached down under his pants to his white jockeys, slipping bills from the elastic waistband. Rocko held them by the corners, avoiding the perspiration that had seeped onto the numbers.

**Chapter 5**
**Loss: Joe-Mack and Frenchy**

While Joe-Mack made short stump trips from Arizona to
Nevada and California, he wondered what had happened to
Freddie. Did he survive the Hollywood streets? Along his
travels, he viewed strange red rocks, as if painted with sour
blood, and their plundering shapes against orange skies.
Landscapes slid past his eyes like a movie setting, screen to
screen. He half expected the hills and formations to crumble
like parched clay. Billboards flashed by advertising all kinds of
junk: cell phones, Las Vegas, crap movies, coffee beans. He
figured the Michigan highways were not so clobbered up,
although it had been forever since he'd been there and the
memories of his home state were skewered with pain. He once
had family there.

One clear recollection haunted him–the vision of his and
Gloria's first night together. Hell, it was practically sanctified.
He'd been older at the time, but not by much. They had
declared their love and held back from doing the deed in order
to make it more meaningful. Closing his eyes and burying his
face in his hands, he nearly went into a trance, remembering
how she felt, his hands exploring her body's terrain, its curves,
how he nearly exploded when his body entered hers. Her skin
was hot and wet, unbelievably silken and lustrous. Afterwards,
she clung to him. He had to pry her fingers from his shoulders,
setting her back to rest on the pillow.

Gloria, a girl who looked better with her clothes off than
on, dressed simply, a little prudishly, but when she took off her
dress and her luscious auburn hair spilled down below her
shoulders, teasing along her pink nipples, she was dynamite.
The powerful combination of her lemony scent, her touch and
her generous little heart beating under his caress sent him
straight to heaven. At the mere sight of her, he longed to seize

her breasts and hair, the curling locks floating on her salty freckled skin, all of it, immediately into his mouth.

Joe-Mack had watched other men linger around her, eyeing her an extra long minute, and he imagined them fantasizing about her, but she didn't seem to notice. She'd snuggle up next to him and run her hand along his arm as she listened to others' talk. He hadn't seen the affair coming. He missed the damn clues. Her scent changed from the fresh lemon spritz to Obsession. When he asked her what was wrong with her old perfume, she told him it was okay to change.

Cheating was for ragged old marriages, for couples who never truly loved, he had thought, yet when he found out, he was speechless. His mind went wild. *Run the bastard over.* He wasn't up for forgiveness. It must have been his fault. He'd been too busy working overtime, volunteering with kids at the recreation center. He trusted her… He had lived for her and his little girls, who were only three and five with chubby cheeks and golden hair as fine as silk thread when he split. Sometimes he wished he had been shot dead. Death would be sweeter he had read somewhere. It was true.

Just as sure as he was up with the sun every day, when his thoughts went to Gloria, he thought about his daughters. He left in a fury, without thinking, intending to go back and see them. They'd be strangers now. Hang-up calls were made to Gloria; thousand dollar checks were sent intermittently. The day to return never happened. A drunkard now, he was not a good man for Jen and Amy to know.

Joe-Mack swiped his hand across the hot dash and checked his fuel gauge. The dust of the desert clung to his palms. His rear-end stuck to the leather seat as he shuffled around, trying to ease the aches of the road. Sunrays flooded in his side window and he thought how wholly sick he was of the sun, in his eyes, at his back, on his left ear and frying his arm hairs, the road that never ends and the white line that snaked in his dreams, the entire damn chaos.

Perkins Truck Stop was humming. The facility began as a roadside vegetable stand run by Bill Perkins's daddy. The younger Bill, Jr., with riches up the ying yang, was a regular Joe, who kept the farm going in honor of his pop. The troublemakers, Rob and Rich Hunt, left their wagons parked askew, apparently anxious to put the hit on the loose girls.

Checking his watch, Joe-Mack realized he was late, yet again. Timing off, he'd been running too fast or too slow lately. *So, fire me. Who gives a rat's ass?* There had been a time when deadlines counted; now he wrote a lot of crap in the liars' book. The big-ass companies looked the other way, no damage control there, as long as they scored profits off the drivers.

Joe-Mack jumped from his cab, anxious for a fresh cup of java. His pants were hiking down. Belting them in a notch, he thought he simply couldn't take more road food.

A bowl of Campbells tomato soup Gloria used to fix along with a toasted cheese carefully cut into fourths would do him fine. Of course, it wouldn't taste the same without her fixing it. She used to perch by the kitchen counter, swinging her curvy hips while humming a Dylan song. Joe-Mack observed truckers who started out skinny bulge at the waist and guys who started out fat waste away on uppers. It was a lousy game. The losers jack-knifed or flipped or merely rolled down the soft shoulders of the road when they fell asleep–like the pull of a soft-shouldered woman in the night. More than one truck bounded out of its lane toward the middle—could be black ice, rain-slicked roads or sun creating illusions on pavement, swirling patterns jumping sideways as though they were alive. Some guys got jumpy as all hell. They'd swerve to the side to avoid a mere mouse skittering across the road and then, shoot over the divide, wiping out a couple of passenger cars.

He spotted Frenchy's rig and then a buxom gal being shooed out of his cab. She tugged at her blouse buttons while gazing up at Frenchy. Joe-Mack could practically hear her cooing, as his bud threw him the high sign.

"Let's eat," Frenchy said dashing up beside his friend's rig. "I'm all charged up, man."

"Charmed the pants off her, huh?" Joe-Mack asked, slapping his friend on the shoulder.

"Better believe it. Like it was the last supper."

Inside they settled at their usual booth. The two men had a couple of laughs, dinner, more coffee, and then Joe-Mack got serious. "Man, you're on borrowed time. You got to cool it."

"Haw, what do you know?" Frenchy asked, whipping out his hanky, dusting off his penny loafers. "You and I cut from different cloth. This gig's a breeze and a half."

"Alright. Stick close. I see you drifting, you're toast."

Once back in the truck, Joe-Mack blasted the Dolly tape through the CB. "You okay?" he'd ask every ten minutes.

"You my nursemaid or what?"

"Shut up! Stay alert."

A few loud raindrops splattered on the windshield. In a matter of minutes the rain pelted the glass hard and fast. It was impossible for Joe-Mack to see anything but a blur of red splotches in front of him. He rammed the horn with the flat of his palm, attempting to signal Frenchy to pull over. *No dice.* His buddy's rig took a wide swing from behind him, and passed, inching in between Joe-Mack's vehicle and the car in front of him.

*Christ.* "Pull over, Frenchy. Jesus, pull over! I'll follow suit," he said, thunder cracking overhead with a loud boom and lightning spitting a wide swath of light directly in front of him. More flashes cut through the sky off to the north.

"Slow up, damn!" he yelled into the radio. *Candy ass is blowing me off. Drunk on life, the fool.*

The rear of Joe-Mack's trailer started swiveling, a pull of its tail. Momentum was building. *Control it.* He could feel disaster in his tingling soles. The load was shifting, banging inside the trailer. Joe-Mack pumped the brake, quit, and pumped again. *Whoa girl. Whoa baby. Jesus.*

He jerked the steering wheel frantically to avoid a tire that had spun off Frenchy's truck, and ran up on the shoulder. The whole thing shook to a stop. Joe-Mack's head jolted toward the windshield, the seatbelt dug into his shoulder. His chest heaved, his breath was rough, as though air was scarce. The truck didn't jack-knife, but his heart was beating like it had.

Just in front of him, Frenchy's vehicle had flipped on its side, having scraped its way off-road and into the trees. A mass of black tire dust surrounded the rig. The stench of burnt rubber filled the air. As Joe-Mack ran towards the crash, he caught sight of the guy's front end wrapped around a mutilated tree trunk. The engine was smoking-black, the side door crunched in. Joe-Mack scrambled up the side of the cab. The first view of his friend nearly put him down. Blood dripped down Frenchy's forehead, into his eyes. Joe-Mack reached through the break in the shattered window and held his hand against the wound to stop the bleeding, saying over and over. "You're okay. You're okay. Hang tight. I'll get ya." Somehow he was able to retrieve his cell from his pocket and call for help. He started to pull on the door handle, trying to remove him from the wreckage. *Don't. Don't.*

Tears were rolling down his face, dripping off his chin, but he lifted his arm and brushed them aside with his shirtsleeve. While still holding his hand against Frenchy's forehead, he swabbed his friend's eyes delicately so as not to rip any skin, with the other, and then, he realized that he was holding Frenchy's head up, and getting no response to his actions. "I love you, Bud. I mean, I really love you."

*A friend is a guy who knows your gut and doesn't spill it.* Frenchy had been known to lay his last fiver on you, but now he was gone. Dead. Irreplaceable.

Joe-Mack envisioned him – a man up there on a gold-plated throne with fawning angels, one prettier than the next—his kind of heaven.

The men of the road had their escapes: the usual, drink, porn; and the unusual, knitting, oil painting, cross-dressing. In the last eleven years, Joe-Mack had seen it all: women making the most of their men at the wheel, broads flirting all over the truckers, their skirts up around nowhere. He was flashed tits, propositioned over the squawker, and, like him, even the guys who weren't looking for it, got a bang out of the road show.

Joe-Mack's rig rolled under fiery red skies, the hum of his engine so much a part of him that he no longer even heard it – rolls of cotton clouds back-dropped with sizzling blue and gray mist, as though there was an artist in the sky, loving, angry, but always there — golden dinosaurs reaching for heaven's gate, raucous thunder in bold black and blinding lightning before flooding rains to drown out a man's thoughts.

Weather aside, he picked up all manners of folk who ran out of gas or broke down in the middle of the steaming summer desert, yet one kid stuck in his mind. There had been something oddball, even helpless, about Freddie's silhouette shadowed against the pink cirrus-mottled sky, his weak frame curved under an overstuffed pack that he could hardly balance on his back. He stood alone amidst the sounds of crickets buzzing, dust roiling, lifted by desert winds, and the intermittent sound of a truck cranking on the rise of a hill. When the boy climbed into the cab, and Joe-Mack got a good look at the kid, it was his big eyes, yielding and shy, yet startling in their pathetic beauty that grabbed him. They were dry, but Joe-Mack imagined them dripping tears. The eyes that attracted lost souls on a pilgrimage to see the miracle of a crying virgin. The kid had given up precious little information. It eventually came out that he had a nutty family that lived in a chapel.

His Jen would be about the same age as Freddie. *What about her and Amy? What were they up to? If I can't guide them through their first crushes, their lovesick years, I could reach out to Freddie, who is still very much a child.*

Freddie's skin had been clean, as were his clothes, but he was about to face a dirty side of life that Joe-Mack knew might break him. It was possible the teen was smarter than he looked. The irony that Joe-Mack himself was a runaway of sorts, hit him.

Over the years Joe-Mack had one-nighters, mostly with barroom gals when he was juiced up. Then, he settled in with regular visits to Lucille, a gal whom the fellas would call a road wife, a soft spot in the hard road. The night he met Lucille three years ago, she was flirting up her customers. The Hunt boys were eating it up. Frenchy immediately worked his smooth-talk on a new waitress who had just moved into town.

Lucille had come over to take his order when a song popped up on the jukebox. No sooner had the first stanza of "Can I Have this Dance?" started, when she grabbed his hand, yanking hard, saying, "Come on, Mr. Paul Newman eyes, let's do this thing."

It started as a joke for his friends — him clutching her tightly around the waist, pulling her body to him, swaying to the music, the whole place guffawing, and then, he found she tickled him, this little chick, who clung to him like crazy.

The song quit. Lucille broke free and rushed to pick up her orders.

"Whoo, whoo," Frenchy chanted, "Whoo, you got it, man."

"Cut it," Joe-Mack said. "Just humoring the chick."

He left that night, but a week later he asked her out for coffee. She said, "Coffee? I got coffee up the wazoo. Got a better offer at my place." That first night was the beginning of a long thing with Lucille, yet Gloria never left his head. It didn't make sense after all this time that Joe-Mack had this need that flew around his heart, as though he had no control at all, an eagle fallen from his nest, his wings paralyzed. The desire to hear Gloria's voice became unbearable. He'd made hang-up calls before, usually when he was ready to pass out in the twilight alcohol haze — before he knew the hangover, the cotton mouth, shaky fingers would kill him the next day.

It had been exactly twenty-four hours since his friend's crash. He was numb yet it seemed he could still feel his hands cranking his own wheel, his consciousness ground into his mouth. The moment of premonition right before the flash of light slivered across his shocked eyes haunting him. *Jesus! God, what could I have done different?* A pompous dresser, Frenchy would hate the stains on his starched shirt. *No goodbye. No so long.*

Out of habit Joe-Mack headed for The Red Tide. After three shots in three minutes at the bar, he left, feeling no better than when he entered. He searched the sky for a glimpse of the angel on his way through the crowded parking lot. She had never appeared again after that first time. And, indeed, he was certain it was Gloria's spirit. The mesmerizing vision, so beautiful, had been seen through the glaze of first sun. The profile and iridescent hair had almost healed him, consoled him and, although burnt into his memory, it wasn't enough.

It had only been three days, but seemed like eons since his last call. He discovered the new area code from the operator. *The old city's population must be expanding*, Joe-Mack thought. *Prospering even.* A few bungalows might be still standing amidst tall buildings and condo complexes and strip malls and perhaps an endless line of convenience stores. Craft and discount shoe shops providing work for teenyboppers and welfare moms – those who could only earn a pittance without losing their housing certificates and stamps.

Gloria had not moved. His support checks were received and cashed promptly. He wondered if the *Dove-gray* paint job had held up through the icy winters where the ponds froze up overnight, icicles hung from eaves and telephone wires snapped. He sent money enough to cover the tiny mortgage, the dentist and doctor bills and, of course, enough for books he imagined Gloria would have chosen for the girls. He imagined them as young ladies now, at fifteen and seventeen, and likely looking like their mom.

"Hello," Gloria answered in a sleepy voice.

Her voice brought him a mental picture of her rising from the pillow, leaning on her elbow as she reached for the phone, her nightgown slipping down over one shoulder revealing her breasts–the freckles on her skin as mere soft dots in the skimpy light from the streetlamp. He remembered how her hand touched his cheek, as his own trembling hand gripped the phone. Her fingers used to find him beneath the sheets, her nails tickling him as she caressed his thighs. He remembered how she'd blow her sweet breath on him, teasing.

"Who is it?" she said.

The last time he called, he heard a recording and he had expected it again. She had changed her message. "Hello, nobody here. Not me. Not the kids. Leave a message. If it's you, Jen, call me. Please." Her voice shivered at the end of the message. "It's okay, Jen. I love you."

This time, she answered, "Joey?"

"Wait," Joe-Mack said aloud. Was that Gloria? Was he dreaming? Was he hallucinating? Had the booze finally fried his brain? He abruptly held the phone back from his face, staring into it as though it was human and then, realizing she might have heard him speaking, he hung it up softly, delicately, as if he had been listening in on a private conversation between two lovers.

## Chapter 6
## The Gathering: Freddie, Green, Onge, and Starlet

By Wednesday, the day after Freddie left, his Dead shirt stunk under his arms. It had a twenty-four-hour smell to it, a couple of coffee stains, one mustard blotch and a few dirt patches from clumps he had picked up while sleeping under the overpass. He felt his underpants sticking to him now: the more freaked he got, the more he sweat, especially between his legs. His birthday pants were crumpled. He remembered the look on his mother's face when she had handed them to him, all wrapped up in a shopping channel box and old, frayed purple ribbon. She was proud. The sorry-looking waitresses hung close by ready to sing a weak refrain over the one white candle, the one chocolate cupcake.

"Eighteen. Some day you'll take over the chapel, my Freddie," his mom said.

"Crap," Freddie answered, twisting the ribbon around his ring finger.

"What did you say, sonny?" she asked.

"Nothing."

At the time, he knew he was a born loser. Who else would have the misfortune to have a father like Frederick and live in a sleazy Lily of the Valley Chapel?

As his mother, Rose, watched him eat every speck of the cupcake, he plotted his escape again. It had to be on a Tuesday. His father banked on Mondays, gambled all that night at the Crocodile Pad, the local slot joint that had a stuffed crocodile with red- painted rocks for eyes that sat guarding the front door. He'd always say, "Going to the Crock for a quickie," and didn't return until Tuesday at noon. Who he spent time with Freddie didn't know, but he was sure they were creeps.

It would be cool to wake up in Hollywood away from his mother in her orange crushed velvet Mumu and his father, who hogged the bathroom, working on his comb-over, leaving the floor tile slicked with the stink of him. But Freddie would send his mom cash just as he had stuffed twenties under her pillow every week. After all, without a few dollars, she'd go nuts — without the shopping channel and her favorite TV dinners, she'd explode, he just knew it. *Zingo — bits of soft flesh and shards of velvet confetti dust the floor.* No. When he returned, he'd have enough for his Mom to start over.

He'd stashed away what money he could from his regular raids of tourists' hotel rooms. Freddie now had very little cash, but he still had his bag, camera, and the blue silky dress. For good luck he removed it from the bag, smoothed it out, and folded it into a square pillow. He wasn't even sure why the dress was so important to him. He had stolen it, squirreled it away in his closet, and a part of him that knew he would use it in Hollywood. Perhaps it had something to do with the woman who had worn it — perhaps it had something to do with its quality, so high above the junk his mother and father wore and made him wear. Perhaps it was a symbol of his future. It was a mystery, but one he had chosen as his destiny.

Freddie ripped yellow pages from a phone book and placed them on the ground in the shape of a body  With his pack under his head and the blue dress nestled under his jacket, he lay down. There, under the freeway bridge, he spent a fitful night, listening to the traffic and a few birds that nested in the rafters of the bridge, twittering away to each other.

It was impossible to calculate how many hours he slept. The noisy birds and his fearful thoughts of being robbed, beat up, or killed there under the overpass kept him jerking under his blanket. Just as the sky was lighting up he dozed a bit. Finally, he shook himself up, took a pee by the fence, gathered his things and went on his way.

The last twenty-four hours had been a super-long time without a TV and a mom telling him to do her errands. He was free and the freedom felt nothing like what he expected. The days were interminably long, his stomach talked to him practically every hour, yet he was scared to spend the little money he had left on food. He wasn't used to bagging food from dumpsters; the idea of it made his stomach turn. He saw normal folks, even one man whose body was built like Joe-Mack's, but when he stopped at the light and turned so Freddie could view his face, he was much younger with a dumb beard rimming his chin. It wasn't him. Freddie was at loose ends. He hadn't had enough sleep or food to settle his jerky self, to help him think straight, yet he wasn't busted enough to head home. He'd stick it out.

He was heading back to the diner when he saw a girl dressed in baggy clothes with slops of green hair hanging down one side of her face; the other side was shaved close over her ear which had at least ten or twelve piercings. He had stared a little too hard because she noticed and walked straight up to him, challenging him with, "What? You don't like my hair?"

"No, no, it's okay," he said, but he openly gawked at the long cellophane-green strands of hair that splattered down past her shoulder almost to the pocket of her man's shirt.

"What's up with you, kid?" she asked.

Focusing on the cracks in the sidewalk, he answered, "Just hanging. Got here yesterday."

"You still got your mother's Tide smell on your clothes?"

"Huh? I don't know," he said, turning away, hiking his bag up over his shoulder.

"Wait," the girl said. "Where'd you crash at?"

"Down that way," Freddie answered, pointing west.

"The bridge?"

"Yeah."

"You made it out of there with your shorts on? Shit, the pervs had an off night, then? Hey, I'm Green," she said. "Who are you?"

"Freddie. From Vegas."

"Okay Freddie from Vegas, you lost or what?"

"No."

"Then, where you headed?"

"I don't know. Looking for work."

"Sure, and lost."

As she said this, Freddie looked into her eyes and knew that she knew what *lost* was. Both he and she were lost before they even set their miserable feet on Hollywood Boulevard.

"I'm considering something here. You a trouble-maker?"

"No," he answered, trying to see beyond her swagger. Her camouflage pants were crusted with dirt; she had to be a runaway like him. Not local. She might know *struggle*, the ropes.

"You got cash?"

"Not for you, I don't."

"I ain't asking for myself, stupid. Heh, if I wanted big coin, I wouldn't target you. Lighten up, man." It was then Green mentioned a crash-pad. "You interested?"

"Might be," Freddie answered, toeing at the tuff of grass between the cracks in the sidewalk. "Where?"

"Never mind location. You chip in, stay straight?"

"Yeah, maybe."

"Okay, you got to pass with Onge," she said, circling her earrings one at a time. He noticed a touch of a smile, which could mean that she was teasing him, sizing him up, or setting him up.

"Wanna go for it?"

"What's in it for me?"

"A place to sleep."

He was going to ask about Onge, but the girl was already hightailing it down the street. He tagged along. Joe-Mack had warned him, but this girl, who wore yellow chamois work gloves and walked like a guy in hiking boots seemed okay. *Nothing risky so far...*

Following Green to Sunset and then up the hill at Curtis Street, Freddie stopped close enough behind her to smell her sweat. The yard, teeming with bushes, flowers and squat palm trees, nearly hid the house behind them. Three jade plants hogged one corner of the yard. Green raised a section of the wire fence that was bent and re-twisted together. She hunched over, exposing a crudely tattooed initial L on her back. She climbed through. Freddie hesitated.

"Come on. Hurry up."

She walked down a cluttered path overgrown with grass and weeds, passing a small garden with tiny plants that smelled sweet in the airy sun-shiny space. The small bungalow out in the front of the lot was beige stucco that had faded to white with wooden casings around the windows that were peeling and bare in some places. The wrap-around porch was freshly swept; it had a vase of long-stemmed white orchids set next to an antique rocking chair. If a lady sat in it, he thought, she could lean over and caress, even get a whiff of the flowers.

Freddie asked Green who lived there. She told him the house supposedly belonged to an old lady, who used to be in the movies. "She don't bother us none."

Halting by the garage, she said, "This here's secret. Don't open your yap. Onge don't like you, you're history."

"Who would I tell?"

"Nobody. I figured."

Before following Green into the garage, Freddie turned around to see the way he came in, in case he had to take off fast. He followed Green down an overgrown path to a garage window blotched up with fingerprints. She rattled the window open and he followed her through. The light was dim but he checked the place out. The interior was loaded with musty cardboard boxes, old clothes hanging on racks with spiders drifting from sequin to sequin and an antique car set up on blocks, the only shiny thing in the garage.

"Wow! Is that a Mercedes? Cabriolet?" Freddie asked.

"How'd you know?"

"Car shows are a big-shit deal in Vegas," he said, moving close to the vehicle.

Green shoved him away. "Don't touch her. Stop right there."

"Alright. Alright," Freddie whined, zipping his hand back.

Green headed up a set of narrow steps that led to the second floor storage area. A triangular window sent a shaft of light into the dim room. Once his eyes adjusted,
Freddie got a glimpse of the people inside. A black guy with long arms that hung down past his knees and an American Indian nose sat on the second rung of a stepladder that was perched in the center of the room. The others were slopped around on blankets and an old easy chair.

"That's him, Freddie. Onge," Green said approvingly. Freddie leaned back against the wall close to the door while Green went up to the man on the ladder. "Onge, this is Vegas. Found him on the street. Newbie."

Freddie rubbed his palms along the sides of his shirt, glancing down at the clothes he'd so carefully thought about before he left home. Now they seemed all wrong. He might well have been butt naked for all the mileage they gave him.

Onge said, "Come here."

The man's voice was commanding; it rose from his massive chest, his thick neck. Freddie immediately thought: radio announcer. He took a couple of steps, moving closer to Green but still hovered behind her. He swung his head around for a quick check of his surroundings. The kids appeared to be busy but listening. Freddie knew how kids could mess around, glancing out windows, shuffling papers at school, but all the while catching the drift of the teacher's voice. Here they were paying attention in their own individual ways. The blonde was brushing her hair that streamed down past her shoulder on one side, catching the sunlight from the window. The black girl was filing her nails.

Onge crossed his arms, overseeing the whole operation, Freddie thought. His hair was combed through, his nails clean and white against his dark skin.

"Look Freddie from Vegas, we got no indolents here. No slackers. Teamwork is required."

"I ain't lazy."

"Alright then, you brought yourself to the city of angels. What for?"

Freddie looked down at his feet. "I hitched."

"Speak up," Onge said.

"This guy, Joe-Mack, dropped me off. Drove a massive truck. A powerhouse. Brought me all the way in from Vegas. It was cool," Freddie said.

"Over the roader?"

"Yep. Says I can call him if I want."

"Beautiful. I say you start alone. Then providence shows up. Out of nowhere. What did he have to say while you riding high up in his trucker cab? What manner was he?"

"Clean-cut. He told me to be decent."

"Alright, man. You said it right on the button. That's what you got to do in this place. Be straight. Your heard me say it, right folks? Right Pepper, right Stripe, right Starlet, right

Green?" Onge said, pointing to each one. "We got our messes, but we working them out."

*Joe-Mack would be stoked that I remembered his advice, but what would he think of this place? Of Onge?*

"I myself spent a good deal of time hitching. I seen truckers, everyone odder than the next. Truckers not no stereotype. You go thinking you got a tough guy, and bingo, he melts down over his cheating wife. There's roadies like this Rooster fella. He'd give you his last buck and then there's mean-ass mothers cut you down quick. The run of the pavement gone to their heads."

"My guy was good. He fed me. You know," Freddie answered, feeling his skin redden up, afraid he showed on the outside the meek and terribly needy feelings he was swallowing down.

"Yeah. But you know about *sin,* being where you're from. There's big time depravity out there, but you made it this far. You looking for some kind of gig? Here?" After pointing to his own chest like he was part of the squat, he then piled his orange peels one on top of the other, like a stack of tiny dishes.

Although Vegas' mom hardly ever fed him fresh fruit at home, the idea of a juicy orange suddenly cranked up his hunger. *Better than dumb fruit cocktail with faded cherries.* He was starved.

Onge saw Freddie clutching his stomach and said, "Hey, you want one?"

"Yeah."

He rolled an orange around in his palm and tossed it to Freddie, who bungled the catch, but quickly retrieved it.

"What's your business here?"

"I don't know."

"Look, you – just not saying is how it is."

Freddie considered an answer that would be acceptable. "Work. Photography."

"Photography? You know it ain't easy like jack to find work. First you got to stabilize. No due process here. You in or you out when I say so."

The squat was only one room above the garage, but it appeared each of the kids had a space. Onge took the dominant spot in the middle and up on the stepladder.

Freddie glanced around. This man, Onge, had a folded-flat stack of bedding, a rain-stained red plaid suitcase, a tottering pile of books under the ladder and a red rusty cooler behind him. The black chick had her arm flopped across a Kmart shoebox. In it Vegas imagined, after looking at her curling purple nails, a line-up of nail polishes, maybe cigarettes and matches. It was the seriously dark circles under her eyes that made him think she was a druggie - that and her twitchy neck. Her pile of rolled-up clothing secured with a bungee cord sat next to her. On her lap she held a denim jacket that appeared to have a doll rolled up in it; Barbie-sized feet stuck out from one end.

The other two were unlike any kids he had seen so far in L.A. The blond girl was a complete babe. Her eyes were as blue as the deep end of a pool and she had some amazing body. Although he hadn't seen her standing, he could tell her legs were long. She sat with her arms wrapped around her knees. A silver leather motorcycle jacket hung by a nail on the wall behind her. She stopped brushing her hair to choose a ribbon from a bunch that streamed from the back of a weathered deck chair. Light from the ceiling window hit her hair. It was almost glowing. A dark skinned guy with long black hair, reached up and smoothed out a Phantom of the Opera poster that had started to curl up. His wooden crate contained paints and brushes, and brown grocery bags. Behind him, a cracked mirror from an old medicine cabinet was taped to the wall with duct tape.

Just as Freddie gathered impressions of these squat members, he noticed that they were eyeing him. He was shy, embarrassed, lame, but relieved not to be alone, yet his stomach was shaky.

He turned and caught sight of the doorway in the corner of his eye. He could bolt if things got hot. He bounced on his feet, ready to spin out. Then Onge said, "You looking restless, man. Settle down. You don't know squat."

"Yeah," Freddie mumbled, yet when Onge looked at him, right through him, he panicked. *Loser.* How could he possibly belong with these street-wise kids? He had wanted freedom from his lame family, but he hadn't counted on being so fucking lonely every minute up until now.

"Sit down. Ease up," Onge said.

Freddie set his pack down. He wound the strap over his arm for safety sake. He slid his butt onto the scratchy wooden floor. Green perched on top of a messy pile of clothes next to a Life cereal box cut out like a tray. It was filled with piercing needles, a few single earrings, a stack of old photos and Vaseline hair lotion.

"Listen here, first off, this ain't no shelter. No rip-offs, no bugs. You might have heard the expression, 'Earn your keep.' You be doing precisely that."

Freddie stared at Onge's square jaw, his straight up posture and the glare in his eyes of a boss-man. His Polo shirt had folds in it, as though it had just been removed from its plastic wrap. His cutoffs stopped just above his huge knees that were identically scarred vertically down the whole of his kneecaps. The only surprise about him was his neon orange flip-flops that hung off the back of his heels.

For an uncomfortable few seconds there was quiet in the squat. Then Onge slurped juice from the orange he'd been tossing in the air. At once a clatter of voices erupted from the gang of kids, jeering and hooting—words like *whussy, bling, bling.* Vegas' hands flew up to conceal the gold chain he had slipped on after the robbery. It had tangled up with his safety pin necklace.

Then he heard voices in unison, "Who, who, who." The bodies in the small space mixed sweat with the heavy stench of paint, garbage and perfume. The sudden noise was deafening.

Onge raised both his arms like a referee, "Whoa. Whoa."

There were a few murmurs, rolling eyes and elbow jabbing.

Again facing down Freddie, Onge said, "What we got here? Fresh from the street?"

He seemed to want an answer so Freddie said, "I guess."

"What you gonna do for me?"

Freddie shifted closer to Green. "I don't know."

"We ain't gangbangers. We're streeters. You know anything about living on the street?"

Green said, "He got here yesterday. Not enough time to get wasted."

"Appearance wise, you okay. Can you contribute, Freddie?"

Freddie was paying close attention to Onge out of the respect for him as the leader, but in the periphery he saw Pepper glaring at him, the beauty twirling a bracelet, Green picking at the threads of her frayed pants and Stripe painting his face.

"Money?"

"For one thing, yes," Onge answered. Leaning back, he told how, in mighty California, a kid had choices. "You can slide on down by the railroad station with all the other bums, skirt along upside hills with the mountain lions, the pumas, like that, or hunker down under freeways and you crashing with strange bedfellows. Druggies and sex monkeys leave you bare-naked without a cent and a decent set of clothing. If you think you up to it, you dumber than blow."

"So you want money from me?"

"Don't make no assumptions! You up to appreciating a roof over your fool head?"

"I am," Freddie answered, as though it was a vow—unlike most of the chapel couples who woke up with cigar bands or cheap cubics on their fingers. His father had told him you can tell a rock is real by the way a woman holds out her hand, her fingers quivering with delight, her smug smile lighting up her face.

"Don't be shooting your mother-mouth about this place," Onge said. "Squealing is for pigs. Kindness ain't the only rule I got. Secrecy is paramount. Be careful comin' and goin'. No lights at night, and don't draw attention. Someone still lives in the bungalow, and there are neighbors."

Onge jerked his head at Green. She went to the cooler and fished out a donut and juice bottle for Freddie. "You up for the name, Vegas?"

"I think so."

"No guessing where you spent your first night. With amateurs under the bridge, right?"

"I froze my frigging ass off, frigging cars drove me crazy. I thought L.A. was tropical."

"You lost? It ain't tropical, it's a Mediterranean climate. You ain't noticed the humongous lemon trees in ordinary front yards, black-skinned avocados at Third Street Market? Nights, like people, can turn cold. Air is ice on tired skin. You're worse off if you hungry. Keep something in your stomach, a damn piece of bread, a carton of milk a child ditched in the parking lot at McDonalds. Full stomach gets your cells pumping."

Vegas was asked if he'd ever been arrested. When he said no, he was directed to shoplift a bag of oranges for Onge who said, "You see, my main fixation is oranges."

"No sweat," Vegas said, telling how he lifted stuff in Tinseltown, sneaking into rooms, but only from rich people, drunks with lots of scratch. As he spoke Vegas cut a look at Starlet to see her reaction. She had the shiniest lips he had ever seen on a young girl, as though she had just licked them, yet she was carefully applying a fresh coat of clear gloss. It occurred to him that she didn't belong with the others. She could have been a cheerleader with pigtails flying and her skirt flaring up above her panties, showing her goodies off. His heartbeat jumped.

"Okay then. Let's see what you made of. Get on to Lucky's. Green, take him." Onge instructed, flicking his head towards the door.

Although dazed by the whole squat experience, Vegas focused on the girl. *Those shiny lips. Like she's been licking them. Those smooth legs.* The activity outside Lucky Market was typical L.A.: a scratchy old dude was devouring a cigarette, his crusty lips nearly inhaling the filter, a long-haired gray dog tied to the newspaper stand lapped a messy taco on the pavement and two women employees in square-shaped red vests were talking down their men. It could have been any market, anywhere.

For a minute Vegas forgot he was in Hollywood. A well-toned mom with buff calves threw her kid in a basket and slammed ahead of Vegas and Green. Her chunky-faced boy wrapped his fingers around the cart and rocked back and forth as his mother stopped abruptly to scan the circular. The little boy pointed at Green's hair. She threw him a peace sign. The mother noticed and gave her a filthy look, swished her freshly snipped hair aside, jerking down the aisle. Vegas entered while Green lingered outside, pretending to choose a flower bouquet from a gang of them jammed into pails.

His insides were zinging and with his fingertips almost tingling, Vegas made fast work of his job. He wrapped a bag of oranges in his jacket, slipped two pre-wrapped packages of roast beef deli meat into his pants pocket along with a stash of red licorice. He planned to hold the candy aside and, if he had the balls, and in a couple of days, he might hand it to Starlet. He whisked a small bottle of peroxide off the shelf and paid for it at the counter. Whistling *Glory, glory, Halleluiah* all the way out, he practically skipped up to Green who was waiting in the parking lot.

"Five minutes! You're good, man. Now let's book it in case some jerk saw you."

Vegas followed Green. She turned to ask, "Got anything good?"

"Oranges and other shit."

As they hustled up the hill, she brushed against his arm.

He winced.

"What?"

"Careful. Tattoo," Vegas said as he removed his jacket.

Green told Freddie she wanted to see his arm. He said to watch it. "Done this morning. It's fresh."

She signaled Vegas to follow her to a patch of grass behind a row of white oleander bushes. Vegas sat down and began inching off the tape. A crew of dark-skinned day-workers stopped at the other end of the lot. They started mowing the grass and trimming the bushes, ignoring the kids, used to people in their way.

"You want to see it?" Vegas asked.

"Yeah, got mine two years ago. Kept it covered so my father wouldn't see it and beat the crap out of me." She pulled the waistline of her pants down, revealing a butterfly on her hip.

The dried blood on the edges of the stained gauze patch was stuck on Freddie's skin.

"Close your eyes," Green said. She reached over and ripped it. Freddie yelled, "Ow, Jee-sus." Then he and Green looked at the red swollen mess that covered most of the green color.

"How does he look? Like it should?" he asked.

"A frog?"

"Yeah, you dig it?"

"Hey, I do. A frog tat. Major cool."

After Freddie took the peroxide from his bag, Green told him that she would clean it. She and Lily used to fix each other's cuts with peroxide after wandering through broken down barns and abandoned cellars. They got pretty good at digging slivers out with their fingernails and doctoring scrapes back then.

"Who's Lily?"

"Never mind." Green poured the peroxide into the cap, then directly on the tattoo. It fizzed white and stung like hell. Freddie lay back against the grass, blowing quick breaths from his mouth. "Hey, where you live at, like before?"

"On a farm. Most families back there had a load of kids, for working the place, you know, but we only had me. Other moms had legs that bowed and backs that rounded with toting feedbags and from lifting bushels of turnips, but my mom was different. She didn't belong in Iowa. Me, I got my father's stubby legs, but Mom, she had movie star legs and ankles. That Burke and Sweetzer, who both lived down a ways, stared bug-eyed at her big-time on market days. It wasn't like she was a flirt or anything."

Green stopped talking and put her hand up over her eyes, as though she didn't want to see anything in front of her. She didn't cry, but her whole face dropped down.

When she spoke again, her voice was weak. "She got frail, like an old lady, but she was only thirty-eight. She had to sit down peeling onions. She tried to hide her crying, blamed it on the onions. She turned yellow. She died." Green sat up stiffly, as though she had reported an accident. "So that's that."

"Jeez," Vegas said, rubbing his head as though what she said had given him a migraine. "Sorry."

"My father wigged out after the funeral service at Johnson's Parlor. A creepy place that smelled bad. The fool sprawled out on the cemetery grass, pounded the fresh grass. Bawled like a baby. Screwed up the stupid black suit he bought. A total whack-job. He moved me and him to the Barkers, a trailer camp. What about you?"

"Me. Nothing."

"You shitting me? You ain't here on holiday."

"No, but... My father, Frederick was a dickhead - mean. My mother, a space-cadet, and me, nowhere, so I left out. I can get a job. I know I can. Here's my Nikon. Check it out," he said digging it out from his bag. "I take portraits, weddings mostly. Here. I'll take you."

As Vegas lifted the camera to focus, Green quickly covered her face with her hands. Vegas snapped it right when she peaked out between her fingers. "Don't," she said. "I'm ugly."

He had captured her and, as he peered at her face through the lens and she thought he was through snapping, he clicked again, catching the drift of an open-lipped smile as if she were about to bite a fresh-picked strawberry. There was an inkling of sweetness, perhaps shyness, in her demeanor, perhaps a memory that she tried to keep hidden, like some folks carry in a locket. He pretended he didn't see it, but he did and she knew it.

"You still got a mother..."

"Yeah. When I get my shit down, I'm busting her out of there."

"Good luck with that. You hungry?"

"What about Onge?"

"He can wait. He's testing you. Anyhow, they got supplies back there. Once you're in, he don't kick you out, except John-John. The dude thinks he's hot just because his father was loaded. Onge put him on probation for hooking up with some rich fart, showing up three days later, drugged out. He cleaned up and got back in, but he comes and goes."

Vegas had been stamping down thoughts of home, but now Green's questions triggered thoughts about the chapel with its indoor-outdoor plaid carpeting, and how he never even had a real living room, a TV room, being it was loaded with wedding crap. He wondered what it was like to be brought up in a different place, another state. He couldn't picture himself on a farm with giant bugs and spiders that bit and stung and animals that stunk. Thinking back on his mom, his whole body seized with sadness. It wasn't her fault he was so screwed up. The woman was a misfit, living in a weird world of her own making: wearing costumes for the weddings her husband performed, talking to the shopping channel girls on TV like she knew them and acting blind to the fact dickhead left every night for the casinos. And that bastard scammed the money. *Money was God to Frederick.*

"Let's move, Green," he said. "I got business to do. I mean, after Onge gives me the high sign."

Gently lifting his arm gently so as not to disturb the fresh bandage, he asked, "That girl, Starlet, she like tattoos?"

"No, she's into virgin skin, unblemished."


An hour after he left with Green, Vegas re-entered the garage and this time he had bounty under his belt. Music drifted down to the first floor. He stopped, cocked his head, trying to identify the song or at least the name of the group. Was it The Hole? The Sex Kittens? He had listened to a mother-load of sounds at home, but once again, his insecurities flared up. He was clueless, like his mother. Vegas would scope out the CD covers when no one was looking, but he, for sure, wouldn't ask anyone.

Entering the room he saw Onge reading, Pepper slumped over, sleeping, and Stripe and Starlet were both gone. Was it a coincidence they were missing from the squat at the same time? Would that girl be interested in Stripe? The guy was bizarre.

"Hey, you back? Bring the loot," Onge said.

Vegas handed him the bag of oranges. Onge ripped the bag open with his teeth.

"He did alright. Slippery dude," Green said, high-fiving Vegas.

"No trouble?" Onge asked.

"Nope," Vegas answered.

As he spoke Starlet came in with a six-pack of Coke she placed in front of Onge and then sat down cross-legged in her place, hugging her perfectly rounded shiny knees. Vegas stole a sneaky glance at her and under her skirt, but he couldn't scope out her panties. She caught him. He looked down, pretending to loosen his boot.

The successful gambit of shoplifting encouraged Vegas, but Green discovering him and then Onge giving him a chance to join this group of kids was unreal. Wary still, he was on alert. After all he didn't trust these kids. Danger could flare up, spreading like a desert brush fire, ragweed crackling, white dune primrose blossoms curling brown, stinking, disappearing into carbon, hot and uncontrollable. As for his own behavior, he thought about how he was providing for this stranger, Onge, even when he had no hint as to how his own mother was surviving. Had she run out of TV dinners? Had she run to the police after he disappeared? He must send her a few twenties soon, but he had so little of his own money left. If he could raise some bucks and then run into Joe-Mack again, the trucker could mail the cash from another town or actually make a drop-off. He thought he could trust Joe-Mack. The guy was honest. He had plenty of money of his own and he was straight up. He'd keep the secret of where Vegas had landed. She'd tell him her name was Rose. She'd ask about her sonny. But then this Joe-Mack, who was a respectable dude, would see the chapel, his dumb home and might even run into *dickhead.* Anything could happen and yet it was an excuse he could use, the mother thing, to hook up with Joe-Mack. He reached into his pocket, fingering the card with the trucker's number on it.

As Vegas was drifting in his thoughts, Onge was filling up on oranges, their scent permeating the small room. After the others ate, Onge tossed a water-stained roll of paper towels to Vegas. Then, looking blissful, he leaned back against a roll of bedding, glanced full circle at all the kids' eyes, drawing in their attention. He began to talk, his voice low and slow, as though he was a father telling a bedtime story. "Sometime you only get one piece of beauty in your life. That girl-car, Leontine, she's it for me. Ain't no piece of pimp trash. She's genuine. If Leontine be jacked, it would be like somebody stole my soul. Yes sir, she's my salvage and refuge, a symbol of what was back when. Beauty that lasts. I seen, in books and movies and in a blue moon, on the street, a cherry one, same as her up there in San Francisco. Them vehicles were spectacular in their day, and still are. You got your Rolls Royce Phantom, '47 Tucker Torpedo, '29 Auburn Speedster, and Leontine, a '37 Mercedes Cabriolet. Now that I found that girl, I can take care of her, touch her paint like it was skin with my own unworthy hand.

"It's all in here," he said looking down benevolently, pounding the book on the top of his stack. "That vehicle could reach one hundred and five miles, supercharged. She's the picture of good times, a time to reflect on—when there were stupendously rich men in every country: African kings, Hawaiian Buddhas, black aristocracy, Louis
Armstrong and Billy Holiday, her voice smooth like silk pajamas sliding over your behind. Real kings and queens in Europe on thrones and not on no spaghetti can neither."

Onge reached down, lifting up the top book, then he opened it to a dog-eared page. "I seen this car a long time ago. Studied them all. Facts: a mere pittance of prosperity in books. You can do the same. Educate yourself! Keep the hounds away, away from your door. Think big, young ladies and gentlemen. Work hard."

He told how there was a time when the population of America respected each government, had pride in country. "Money was real, not no deficit piling up. Work was respectable. You could shine shoes, run factory machines making welting for Leontine and her like, and then came a time when Negroes could attend college, not just a few of them. Opportunity, my friends. Opportunity!"

Vegas listened, rubbing his eyes as though he was trying to see the picture in Onge's mind, as the man's face went bright when he talked.

"Life is a picture show. You kids are shooting stars, a sparkle in the mysterious dark, but you got a chance. It's called *hope*."

*Maybe*, Vegas thought, but he wondered about down-deep problems that made the kids flee, end up in the squat and, like him, they must have brought crap memories with them. As though Onge had read his mind, he said, "You all bring your tribulations with you. I say dump them outside this door. Ain't doing you no good to lament the past. Look forward."

When Green saw Vegas staring at Stripe, she said, "Watch it with that one. He's cold. No matter how arrogant the dude is, he's pure genius when he wants to be."

*Stripe had the kind of looks that appealed to girls* - smooth russet skin, black shoulder-length hair that he flung around carelessly, a tight body. He appeared to be into himself. The others kind of fit in a weird way, but he stuck out. When he caught Vegas staring at him as he removed his gear, Vegas had to look away from his gray eyes. He sat apart beneath the cracked mirror, deftly removing the mask from his face, washing the paint delicately with a smelly turpentine mixture he had in a pop bottle. The line was gone that had divided his face. A chick could be taken by Stripe, who had the free-styling attitude of a boy, and a look of abandon.

## Chapter 7
## The Real Deal: Starlet and Victoria

Starlet rose before the others, including the new guy, Vegas. She was unable to sleep after all the kids had finally settled down or passed out. Vegas, spending his second night in the squat, made shushing sounds in his sleep, his breath in crazy rhythms. Passing him in his spot near the stairs, she looked at his face. She thought how juvenile he appeared when deep in sleep, perhaps dreaming as a child would. She tiptoed down the stairs and out to the fresh California morning. Crossing the yard next to the garage, she reveled in the privacy, safety actually, of the fenced-in yard. It was neat how she could discover a spot that became special with natural things around—the feel of prickly bushes as she passed, the smell of dewy grasses and the sounds of a bird's early morning chirpings. Perhaps he felt the same early dawn quiet and safety.

Starlet recalled the time she dipped under the broken fence, leading with her head, careful not to let loose wisps of her blond hair get snatched by the wire like the time she ripped chunks of it out when she was twelve. Back then she and her sister knew the barbed wire was meant to keep her and the neighbor kids from entering the vacant lot, but they found it a perfect place to play and act out stories. That one day her long hairs escaped from her loose pony tail, flouncing on the wind that rushed down the alley; they were as fine as silky webs abandoned by spiders. The tall pale grasses and wild daisies multiplied each summer, rubbing together in a wavy dance in the vacant lot next to the factory. Standing deep in the grasses with stiff stalks swishing her calves, she inhaled the familiar smell of paint that filled the air. Spying through the factory's beat-up windows, she saw masked workers who sprayed reds, silvers, and metallic greens on the automobiles that would soon be hauled across the country. She imagined touching their stickers with the pads of her fingers that were still hot with glue and flinging them back yelling, "Ouch!"

Starlet gazed up and down the street. She remembered Detroit and its suburbs and how important the auto industry was to her grandparents, and how many families depended on car sale numbers. There were bulky Pontiacs and Buicks and Ford trucks — all those American cars that flooded her local streets. Later in the day a slight number of these would roll down Hollywood Boulevard, as they'd be outnumbered by hotshot Porsches, screaming yellow Hummers, and the latest Mercedes models. These cars ruled, along with the Rolls Royces that were usually angel white. These *Rollers*, as Onge called them, seemed to glide mystically along, without the least bit of a rumble. Starlet knew the people who owned them had to be big-time money; they lived in mansions behind ornate gates that were bugged with alarms. She had seen the yards and fence posts with carved white marble lions and gargoyles, all that over-done rich stuff along San Vincente Boulevard. The day she took the bus down that street the coral trees were blooming, dropping petals on the runners who streaked along the mid-island — a sight no regular Midwest kid would see, even in summer.

Once at the fence, she hunched down, passing through carefully, one leg at a time. Turning back she took one last look at the yard, her stomach tweaking like it used to when she was a hungry child. She remembered scraping her heel when she and her sister climbed down the rocky sides of a deserted well. She had lost her grip. Once they were back out, her sister played the nurse, removing Starlet's sock, blotting the cut as they sat amidst violets that grew every which way along the paths and miraculously lined the inside walls of the well. She still had the scar that ridged across her ankle; it had blended somewhat into her normally summer-tan skin, but every time she shaved her legs, swerving the Daisy razor to miss it, she recalled how both she and her sister had sneaked into that lot, how she was the one left with the white zigzag patch of skin.

Alone and deep in thought, Starlet was startled when a frog inside the fence croaked. She hadn't realized she was so jumpy. A fresh blister on the back of her heel buzzed. She favored that foot, mincing down the hill with a hiccup gait in red spikes that flattered her legs. Her shoes were way too loose, like the pair of her mother's Keds she wore running through that lot back then, dirtying them up in mud puddles bigger than the ruts in these city streets.

When Starlet reached the corner, she slipped her heels out, tamping down the backs of her shoes, and clicked along to the bench. She could have brought her sneakers in her carry-bag if she'd been thinking, but now it was too late to worry about that. Taking a deep breath, she glanced up at the butternut-colored sky, hoping the smog would burn off as it usually did.

At the bus stop in front of the diner, she sat down with her back against the real estate man's face in the ad. She picked up a wrinkled page of *The Hollywood Reporter* and blotted her bloody heel with a Madonna headline. As Starlet fussed with her foot, she heard a swishing sound. It could have been a shoe-shiner's stained cloth rubbing against leather, but it was thigh-high boots chafing together. The woman who wore them shimmied her hips as she crossed the street. Her perfume was sickeningly sweet, a fragrance that hung over a sweaty smell but didn't mask it.

"Girl, you gonna infect yourself good with that dirty old paper. Use this," she said as she stuffed a Kleenex into Starlet's palm. "Victoria here, help you some."

"Thanks. These," she said, pointing to her bloodied shoes, "are killing me."

"I know *that*," the woman answered, sitting herself down as though she owned the place.

Starlet tried to check out this woman without all-out gawking. Her short leopard print dress wrapped her tightly and when she sat it bound her middle section into three small rolls of fat, the only fat she appeared to have, and her skirt rode up her thighs. Starlet thought she caught a glimpse of the woman's black underwear in the space up her skirt, but it could have been a shadow of her privates.

"You new on this block?"

"Waiting on my friends," Starlet said, inching away from Victoria.

"Don't go shy on me, honey-bucket. I been where you be."

Onge's warning popped into Starlet's mind. "Watch out for them *ladies* of the night. They mostly on something. When they got the itch, ain't nothing stop them. They streetwise, and you ain't."

Yanking the hem of her mini-skirt past the beauty mark on her left thigh, Starlet caught her silver polished nail on a loose thread. The nail bent back. "Ouch," she said, immediately thrusting her finger into her mouth, sucking it. Then she stared down at the cracks in the sidewalk, focusing on the tiny sprouts of grass that grew between the slabs of concrete. She tucked her hair behind her ears, wishing she could give it a good shampoo. Catching a glimpse of Victoria's amazing nails, the color and shine of bloodsuckers, curving like a hawk's talons, she thought, *those suckers could do a lot of damage.*

"You like these?" the woman said. "They look evil, but they break easy." She rubbed each nail with her opposite fingers, blew over the polish though it was already dry.

Stifling a huge yawn, she flicked her hair extensions over one shoulder and then stuck out her chest as she breathed in the early air of the new day. "You say you waiting on friends. Don't screw my mind. I been on this here block since two A.M. Ain't nobody you interested in cruise by here. A couple a lookers is all. Plenty of the man, though. Bust at the Palimino last night. Rich dudes. You figure money dudes to be intelligent? They plenty dopey when they get their high on."

Starlet left the Kleenex sticking to her foot and put her shoes back on. "I'm splitting."

"Hey wait, Miss Down-home. You awful skinny. You on something?"

"I'm not a junkie."

"Maybe not. Not now, but… Anyway, I'm Victoria."

Victoria was close up. Starlet had passed hookers on the streets of Hollywood but now she could reach out and touch this woman. From far away the young chicks looked like models, only dressed trashy — some with fuzzy-fur baseball jackets, cleavage popping and wild hair down to their asses. Victoria's face had an odd sheen to it; the sandy-colored make-up base tinted her skin vanilla. Her neck and arms were shiny brown. Heavy charcoal liner circled her eyes. The crack between her breasts was deep and wrinkly.

Comparing breasts, Starlet realized how shrimpy hers were. She looked straight down her V-necked blouse at the natural space that separated her next-to-nothing tits. Up to now, she'd only met a couple of college boys who picked her up, going for her hair and legs, she guessed. They took her out to The Hamlet, offered her booze in their cars, but no money, and when they got slammed on cheap beer, she ran back to the squat—too ashamed to tell anyone. She stayed away from older men, older than her father would be. They creeped her out. So far she had used her money from home, begged a little cash, but hadn't given up more than a feel, even though she knew the boys wanted a quick blow. Victoria was in the know; she wouldn't waste her time with flaky college kids.

Sucking the space between her bottom front teeth, Victoria crossed her arms over her chest, looked Starlet up and down, sizing her up. "What you doing, anyhow? You ain't got no home?"

"I do, but…"

"But nothing, you ain't cut out for the street. Blind man see that!"

Starlet *was* planning on heading home but on her terms. She wasn't going to discuss her plans with Victoria. "I love your choker. My mom bought me one once. My dog ate it."

Victoria cracked up. "You got to watch them dogs. Had one myself, Crackers. He'd eat the legs off the damn chair if you let him. Give him an 'ol rib bone, he fracture it with them choppers of his. He lay all spread out on the kitchen floor, not a scrap left when he done. I fed him a whole sleeve of Saltines to aid those bones going down."

"Did he bite?"

"Haw. Only white folks. He don't like white folks, no-how."

Starlet couldn't help laughing. "Discriminating dog, huh?"

"You bet, girl."

Victoria stuck two fingernails under her lace choker, stretching it out. "You like this frilly dilly, this cheap piece of crap? Elastic. Don't be wearing no gold chains round your neck. I seen a dead chick once who don't know no better." Clucking her tongue, she shook her head. "Enough about that. Call me Vicky-O. O. O."

Her voice went low, mimicking a ship's horn, when she said "O."

She busted up at herself, but Starlet didn't get the joke. "Hey, do you have kids?" she asked.

"Yeah, one time, I did. Cute little buttons. Hey, you hungry?"

"Yeah. Starving, actually. Hey, I'm Starlet."

"It suits you, kid." Vicky led Starlet up the worn but freshly swept steps of the Over Easy. The regulars never lifted their heads to look at the two females. The out-of-towners, sporting their Hard Rock T-shirts, google-eyed them, tip to toe, then rolled their eyes at each other. A woman with an out-dated taffeta dress that once had been elegant sat at the counter with her chin held high under a red hat. Vicky said, as she passed the lady, "Hey Mama, how you doing? Church-going hat you got there."

She swung her head in the general direction of Vicky. "Why, bless your heart."

Once situated in the last booth, Starlet twisted her leg back up on the seat and carefully removed her shoe. Vicky grabbed a napkin from the holder, wet it with her
tongue, and handed it over to Starlet. "You'll live. A girlie can get those mother blisters from them dyed-satin jobs, shoes chicks wear to proms."

"I missed my Senior Prom," Starlet said

"Like I say, you'll live. I quit long before then. But hey, it's okay. We both alright, right?"

"Yeah. I used to dance around in a pink tutu when I was a little kid. With all that netting and stuff." In that moment Starlet could feel the pink foam curlers in her hair, the slippery-slide she made in her socks with lace ruffles on the polished oak floors. Her mother's hands worked her hair, setting it at night, and then combing out the ringlets the next morning. Her mother smelled fresh with a soapy smell after her shower. She would kiss the top of her head. Starlet grew up but her mother insisted on playing with her daughter's hair. Although Starlet was a head taller than her at fifteen, she'd bend her head down and smack her hair, saying, "Honey, I could find you in the dark. You smell the same as the day we took you home from the hospital. Your dad, so proud." Then she would pull back. Tears forming in her eyes, not dropping but glistening Starlet told Vicky, "Mom was cool when I was a kid, encouraged me to perform, but ahe got crabby as I got older when the boys came around, flopping on the couch, calling at midnight."

"A mother's got to do what she got to do. Give you some shit when you busting out all over yourself. You thought you were some kinda star? So what. Everybody wants to be a star. *Babylove, my babylove.*" Vicky broke into song, shoulder rolling until her black bra straps showed.

Starlet's face reddened. She quickly looked around to see if anyone was listening but only the counter boy was smirking. Vicky went on about how she had a voice back then but didn't get the breaks. She swung her legs into the aisle. "I still got me some great legs."

"No shit, you do," Starlet answered.

The bright sun suddenly spread across the cracked Formica table. What was once a strong gray color was faded to white in spots. Someone had taken a knife and carved initials next to the napkin holder. Starlet's gaze drifted past the sun-washed table, out the window to the street sign. She wondered why it was called Sunset Boulevard when she would have named it Sunrise Boulevard. Home to rising stars.

Facing Vicky in the stark daylight, Starlet noticed her scars, one angling up the side of her nose, another slashing down her hairline in front of her ear. Her hair frizzled black at the roots and flew out in sunset colors, flaming orange on the ends. *She was tacky,* Starlet thought, *but somehow true to herself—not trying to be anything other than what she was.* Starlet imagined this woman would tell her the whole story of her life if she asked, but she wasn't ready to ask.

"What you looking at, girl? My hair? This good-dirt black? These extensions cost me big bucks, but underneath I got soul-making hair. I say, 'Black is back!' but alls the johns want is bottle-yellow or high-red. Now honey, you got

Cinderella hair. What you doing in big old Hollywood, anyhow?"

"I don't know," Starlet said.

"You know alright, not telling is how it is. Okay then, let's eat." Victoria signaled to the young man behind the counter. "Two Tuesday specials, heavy on the chorize."

Starlet thought about home. How odd it would look to her friends if they could see her with Vicky. She bit her ragged nail; Vicky dug in her purse and came up with a nasty purple lip gloss. She smeared it on her lips, running her tongue over top and bottom, "Got to keep the color going, girl." Glancing at the lady seated at the counter, Vicky yelled over to the boy behind the counter, "Hey Greenjeans, give the lady more jelly. Can't you see she likes the stuff?" She turned to face Starlet, "The woman likes jelly. Probably never got enough when she was a kid."

"Got it," he answered, fishing under the counter for more jelly packets, placing them on the counter and several in a to-go bag. "Here, Missus," he said to the woman.

"Thank you ever so kindly," she said, her eyelashes flickering, her head bowing slightly.

Starlet giggled, "That's his name?"

"You got to hear this." Vicky said, brushing her dreds back over her shoulder. "One night I pop in for a bite. I order eggs, same as now. Gonzalez is fixing them. Then he starts struggling with this humongous jar of mint jelly. He drops it. Next you know, the whole damn place is green—his chin, his pants, the floor, even the ceiling. I tell him, 'Nice play, Greenjeans.' He humors me."

"Oh, I get it now."

*Bet she was a funny kid.* Starlet realized that she hadn't been laughing much since she left home. It seemed like a long time since she was silly. There was the time her sister took up packing Styrofoam balls and after drawing red veins on them, she scrunched them into her eye sockets, wandering, tripping all around the house making ghost howls. It was so dumb, it was funny. She was a goofball kid—knew how to have fun. Vicky must have had some fun, sometime.

Once the coffee was set on the table, Starlet's stomach rumbled. Vicky-O said, "Hungry tiger in there?"

"Really!" Starlet said, using the tip of her pink tongue to test how hot it was. "I never drank coffee at home. Only Earl Grey." She remembered her mom in her scruffy robe, the tea on Saturday mornings with a ton of sugar and milk. Early risers, the two of them sat at their kitchen table, gazing out the six-paneled windows as wind spun the leaves and the sun rose up, sometimes a neon-orange ball in the sky. They talked or they didn't talk as the noisy whirr of the clothes dryer in the mudroom sifted in..

"You want tea?"

"No, this coffee is great. Hot."

The lady at the counter in the dented straw hat *was* drinking tea, using both her blue-veined hands to steady the heavy mug. She had left nearly half her food, a whole muffin and poached egg, on her plate.

"She's something," Vicky said. "I seen her before. She don't eat much. Listen kid, old people don't eat a lot. My granny was strong as an ox; she had trophy muscles under her sad-looking housedress, but she never ate 'til everyone had something. *You* know there was nothing but nothing left, but hell, she could shine a mean-ass floor all the while singing. Got my voice from her."

"Do you think that lady lives alone?"

"Could be, but she got memories. I know that. She might've had people, but life can tumble down, girl. I mean, check those locals," Vicky said pointing her fork to the men seated at the end of the counter. "Looks like they got nothing and nowhere to go, a full set a teeth between them. Not enough bucks to buy a decent Sirloin. Life is messy."

Starlet wondered if the lady was a spinster like her back-home neighbor, Mrs. McNamara, whose hand shook when she spooned out peanuts at Halloween time. Then again, this woman was in Hollywood; she could have been in the *silents.* It was hard to see what she had for beauty in her youth, but she had a good movie star nose, small and upturned. It seemed to Starlet that old people all looked pretty much alike –tiny, wrinkled, sad until they smiled. And they talked about when they were young.

Victoria poked Starlet. "Where'd you go to with them thoughts, girlie girl? Thinking's dangerous. When you a hottie, folks don't expect it. Eat while you can!"

"Sure," Starlet said, picking up a piece of sausage with the tips of her fingers. "This is good." She thought how stupid it was that she and her sister used to horse around, watching TV, letting their macaroni gum up. They didn't give the slightest whit about food then, only squeezing into tight jeans, but now, her stomach was empty a lot. When she lay down, her ribs stuck out. This meal would last her a whole day.

"You know sweetie, them brains, I had them. Ain't no good if you don't have back-up."

"I know what you mean. This one kid at school was bright in grammar school. Totally messed up in junior high. Shitty parents."

"Okay, listen," Victoria said, checking her watch, "my time is up." She reached inside her bra and lifted out some bills, threw a hundred on the table. "Give Greenjeans a tip. Keep the rest."

Starlet said, "Wait, I mean, thanks."

"Go on, finish. Stay off the street today. Listen girl, I know my city. It ain't for you." Victoria was halfway down the diner, when she turned back. "You got some kinda home. Go back, make amends. Be cool."

And then, Starlet was alone. Out the window she could see Vicky with plenty of thigh and butt showing as she stepped into a yellow cab. At a distance now, she could have been a stranger, but she wasn't. Vicky, her gaudy bracelet flashing, waved out the open window as though signaling Starlet. Starlet remembered how she and her girl-scout friends used to message each other with tiny mirrors at day camp, thinking they were all that, but Vicky's the one who's something else, Starlet decided.

A man entered the diner. He wore a Red Wings hat backwards and one gigantic gold chain hanging halfway down his chest. Up in Gonzalez's face he said, "You seen a black chick here this morning? Damn orange hair, big honker tits?"

"No. Coffee?"

"Don't do coffee. Milk," he said, slamming his money down then reaching for a toothpick.

Starlet noticed his nails were the same color as Vicky's. She bent over to pick up a dime on the floor and when she sat up, he was gone.

## Chapter 8
## Stalker: Starlet and Onge

Starlet left the circle before Onge, heading for a tiny movie house, the size of a rich man's living room. The ticket counter was inside a cubicle where the vender sat up on a stool, reading a *Star* magazine. Wavy lines crossed his forehead as he glanced up over the paper; his granny glasses slipped down his nose as he took Starlet's money and punched the ancient cash register. The hand-scrawled sign on the glass had layers of tape that had yellowed with time. It read "Open $2.99 all day." Two men who wore their hair in ponytails ran the place. Starlet named the taller one Grey-Stringy and the other Black-Horse. Were they brothers? Lovers? She didn't know. She only saw them together, counting tickets and money on Tuesday evenings or Saturday afternoons going about their business in silence as though each knew his job. Their bodies were close in the rigged-up enclosure, Grey-Stringy sitting and Black-Horse standing next to him, acting as if they had worked together all their lives, perhaps in a factory sorting screws. Their hands had the same rhythm.

This evening Starlet paid her money and then passed through the worn velvet curtains, walking across the lobby's speckled linoleum floor that reminded Starlet of a kitchen floor. Her eyes adjusted to the dim lighting. She passed through the double doors into the theater itself. After counting five heads in the small space, she carefully chose a spot apart from the others in the back row. She dusted the seat off with her hand and placed her backpack next to her. If Amy were there, they would make it a "discovery," guessing who might have sat there before, guessing what stories the four walls could tell and perhaps what stories the men who owned the place could tell. She pictured her sister and her as younger kids, whispering secrets and elbowing each other over the last greasy handful of popcorn.

The tears came unexpectedly. They were warm against her fingers. Starlet blotted her lower lids with her forearm and wiped her cheeks with the straps of her blouse. *Suck it up.* She was counting on getting home soon, but for now she had to find a job and plan things out. Onge would help. She was lucky to have a friend like Onge. The rest at the squat were sketchy, but okay. Onge kept them in their places with his rules. It was in the squat or out on the street. Vegas might turn out to be a friend; at least he wasn't scary.

The little theatre allowed Starlet to escape her worries. She could act like a child, leaning back with her head against the worn leather, her knees up, her feet against the back seat in front of her. The first time she had seen Grey-Stringy he introduced himself as Mort, and after deserting the ticket station, he popped up a fresh hot batch of popcorn behind the makeshift candy counter kitchen table. The next week she ordered from Black-Horse, whose eyes were bloodshot and squinting and who hadn't told her his name. He asked her to wait a minute. He delivered the steaming king-size bag, which smelled so good, better than any food she'd had in California, and, as she inhaled the aroma, it reminded her of back home. Black-Horse served it to her with a little bow, and definitely wouldn't take any cash for it. He said, "Beauty is as beauty does, my dear."

The movie actresses on the screen were big-eyed with skinny-penciled brows. They slinked across the screen, lay on fainting couches, and charmed their leading men with fluttering lashes. *Oh my God, thin waists!* They never broke from character, always perfect in their looks, even high dramas: the loss of a beau, the rich girl gone poor, the villain chasing them down with menacing music in the background.

Rumor had it that the owner of the bungalow was an old gal who starred in films. Carefully scrutinizing the car scenes and the young women in convertibles, especially those with movie-star dark glasses and polka dotted silk scarves tied under their chins, Starlet searched for Leontine and the mystery-lady on screen.

After the show Starlet stood in front of the theater picking through the last kernels from the popcorn box, crunching those few that were half popped between her teeth. Her mother always said this habit of hers would ruin the enamel on her teeth, but she didn't care. Her mom *did* care about little stuff like that. She then brushed the front of her skirt before throwing the box in the trash barrel by the front door. Taking a minute to breathe in the night air and get her bearings for the walk back, she decided to take her usual route up Sunset. The sidewalks were crowded with teens lingering in doorways and on corners and older couples dressed for big bucks restaurants.

While waiting for the light to change, she felt someone standing up way close behind her, almost breathing down her neck, and at the same time, she heard a strange clucking tongue sound. Before she could take off, she felt a poke in the small of her back and a delicate slide down her calf, like an itch or tickle. Had she watched *Psycho* too many times?

She slipped into the street before the light changed and ran in front of a car full of teens partying it up in a convertible. Change jingled in the man's pocket as he hustled after her. She turned to see the guy in a crazy black hat that shielded his eyes. His hands were shoved in the large lumpy pockets of an old man's plaid overcoat, but it hung loosely; his body could have been slim, young boned. She dashed across the street between the oncoming traffic, entering the closest store, a music place crammed with teens. The place stunk of their perspiration and Fritos and lip-gloss. They milled around the aisles throwing CDs to each other, teasing, yelling, making out, as the clerk tried to ring up prices on the disks. Over her shoulder, she spied the man outside the front door. She sneaked out the side exit and sprinted around the block until she reached Curtis Street.

Her heart was beating now just as it had when she was twelve years old playing with her younger sister. She had pushed ahead to be the first one in the vacant lot. Passing through itchy tall weeds and masses of violets, she headed to the section of trees that protected them from prying eyes of the factory workers next door who took a lot of cigarette breaks. It seemed that each time the girls came to the lot, she noticed something different: an old beat-up roller skate, a couple of Pepsi cans tossed away by someone who didn't need the dimes, a condom near a flattened patch of grass and a stack of crunched Black Labels.

The time she spied the condom, she quickly picked it up with a stick, and, stabbing it like it was an old balloon, she hid it under a moldy pile of leaves. "Snake, stay back," she warned Amy, and now she thought again, *snake, stay back.*

Having reached the squat, Starlet hesitated by the window entrance, while she was still puffing from the run, to reach down and touch a slender cut along her leg that hardly bled at all. It stung a little, but she was too flustered to worry about that. Once inside, she tapped Leontine's window glass three times signaling Onge. She peeked in. *Whew. He's there.* Usually she headed up to bed, but this time she knocked a second, and a third time, she pounded, without the telltale rhythm.

Onge awakened, shoved back his serape, shook his head back and forth, and ran his fingers through his matted hair.

"Onge, you awake?" Starlet asked, opening the door of the car.

"Now, I am. What's up?"

Starlet's voice was shaky as she leaned in, her hair brushing against the open door, "Nothing really."

"Not nothing," he said. He had known without looking it was Starlet by the almond odor coming from her legs, the oil she used to make them shine. "Get in, sit down."

"I'm scared, Onge."

"I see that. What's up?"

"Coming home from the movie, this guy was all over me at the stoplight. Then he followed me."

"Here?"

Starlet told Onge that she lost him by ducking in a store and running home.

"What's that," Onge asked pointing to Starlet's leg.

"I thought it didn't break the skin when it happened but it did. It's nothing."

Without speaking, Onge yanked two paper towels from the roll he kept in the car and dabbed at Starlet's cut.

"His body was real close. Disgusting. I could feel his body on mine, and then the leg thing."

"A crazy-head?"

"I guess."

In the slight light Onge saw Starlet's face crinkling up, her voice choking.

"I was spooked," Starlet said. She bent her head and cried, her shoulders shaking.

"You're okay."

Starlet continued telling what happened–how the stranger-dude wore a flea market overcoat. "He made a funny sound, his tongue clicking, something like that."

"You seen him before? Is he local? A stalker?"

"I don't know. A lot of kids wear those coats. Maybe at the diner or somewhere…"

"I'll handle this tomorrow. Go on up."

"Okay, but you'll be here, right?"

"Right. Now go, I need to think on this."

Her shoes in her hand, Starlet tiptoed up the stairs.

*Just a kid,* Onge thought. *She ought to be home with her mother. Wonder will I ever have me a kid?*

The Los Angeles sky was never dead black–either the bright lights of the city reflected up or the yellow moon played in the distance, reflecting on a smoggy haze. Cool air breezed in the open window, and by the next day the haze would burn off, the sun shimmering its hottest at noon. A police helicopter shadowed, whirring above the Sunset area, sending its cone of light down onto the street, the back yards and the hilly backdrop thick with underbrush. A siren screeched in the night, sounding closer and closer and coming to an abrupt "wrupt." Voices from a near-by house rose in pitch. High on their own arguments. *Fists would be next,* Onge thought. Several young men, gangers maybe, high maybe, hooting in the night air, cruised by, bantering in rude voices.

Onge walked over to the window in his socks. A fresh spider web surfed across his face as he raised the broken screen and poked his head outside. The helicopter made another round, swooping close enough for him to see the flashing lights and the men inside and feel the swish of wind as it bent the bushes and blades of grass. While leaning out and attempting to spy through the fence, Onge heard some chatter from the officers, who had exited their vehicle. After noisily clomping up the steps of the rattletrap porch next door, they announced their presence with a loud rapping and their voices in unison, "L.A.P.D." The cops entered the house. There was a lot of commotion and yelling, the woman's shrill voice above the others. After a short while, the squad car left. Ten minutes and the feud ended. It was quiet enough to hear a cat meow under the sweeping fronds of the palm tree.

The helicopter took another swing around the area. *Skycop jacking up there, playing flyboy.* Onge shuffled back to Leontine shortly before the pink dawn rose under the sky of the new day.

Settling back down wasn't easy this time. He slammed his back against the backseat, rolling over again and again, changing the position of his pillow. Finally, he took off his socks and fell asleep.

The next thing he heard was the slam of a car door. He sat up with a start. It had been a difficult night for him, but he best get moving. A lot goes on while innocents sleep and the trash comes out.

## Chapter 9
## Hit: Onge, Starlet, and Vegas

"It's a good thing I decided on the Keds today," Starlet told Vegas. Onge moved with purpose, as a father would, stuck with his kids tagging along. The pace was fast. The three were on a mission. The day seemed ordinary, mellow, as they passed familiar shops, and people, the sunshine warming their bodies. Angelinos read about the dangers in the *L.A. Times*; they Lojack their cars, alarm their houses, but once outside surrounded by the city's beauty, they lull themselves, forgetting about danger. It's easy to be sucked in by the sun and the proximity of the beach, the Malibu Coast, the flash and dash of the bistros and bejeweled women. The absolute beauty of the place, its rhythm. The people themselves are gorgeous, manifesting every combination of skin colors – a million J-Los prance by in stacked-up sandals, a Mel Gibson look-alike delivers Fed-Ex letters, his knees tanned and shiny, a busty babe flashes cleavage at the local country bar steeped in city slicker authenticity, drink after drink, all grit and sad song.

Starlet and Vegas each took an extra step, skip actually, stretching their strides to keep up with Onge. He openly eyeballed the folks walking towards him, a curious, confident black man, taking it all in. He scanned the car windows as they passed by, the shop doorways, stared into the strangers' eyes, and looking back at Starlet, it was as though he could read the intent of men who glanced her way.

Two children around eight years old stood in the middle of the sidewalk, hand slapping, "Ching, ching, my playmate, come on and play with me."

Onge paused next to them. "Hey, Babycakes, how about school?"

The taller one in humongous Jordans, perhaps her big brother's, called out in a sassy voice, "Vacation day. Inservice meetings." Her ankles, tiny above the shoes, were perfectly formed, like polished brown jewels. Double orange elastic hair bands held the over-sized shoes on. Her heels made a squishy air pocket sound every time she bounced. The shoes were new, unlike Starlet's that had been broken in by her mom. The day before Starlet left home she hand-washed them in a bowl of Clorox and Tide and water. Then, she sat on the top cellar stair with her chin in hands, waiting for the clunking in the dryer to stop and the bell to ring. After ten minutes, Starlet's insides were jumping. She couldn't sit still anymore so she yanked them out while they still were damp and the stains remained as light grayish spots.

The girl playing on the sidewalk giggled with her friend, a stocky little thing, likely not a blood sister, unless mom had two dudes fathering the kids. She stood proud with a jutting chin, wearing a stretched-out yellow tube top that exposed her puffy belly and outie belly button.

"Alright, little sister, keep tight with them shoes," Onge said, high-fiving each of them, their tiny fingers dwarfed by his.

Moving along, he turned back. "Watch yourselves, hear?"

Starlet wondered if he had a sister. She'd never asked him. She'd been so into herself. Now was not the right time, but later today she'd find out. He was concentrating on the looks of strangers. Interrupting him wouldn't be at all cool; he hated being interrupted. She would wait to ask. His temperament was even, but he was totally aware. Always, it seemed. He could sniff out trouble, sense it: when it was time to douse the light in the squat, when the copters were overhead, and when Pepper and John-John were about to screw up.

When Starlet heard the first snap, and then she saw the alarm on Onge's face, as he whipped his head back toward her and Vegas, she was confused. *Pop, pop* – sounds cracked the air. *Firecrackers? Tires?* Then Onge's mouth opened wide, as though a scream was on his lips, but she only heard, "Un, un," like someone had punched his voice out of him. Immediately, his right leg faltered. A genuflect. Clutching his chest with both hands, his other knee dropped and he went down on his side and then his knees curled up fast, like he was a puppet and someone pulled the string too tight.

Starlet crashed to her knees. She seized his elbow, rolling him, trying to sit him up, hold him, hug him. His weight dead, he flopped back, his spine jellied. Red liquid oozed out from his shirt between his fingers. "Help me," she screeched at Vegas, who stood frozen still. "Come on," she yelled, and he bent over to help her lift Onge's shoulders up.

Onge gasped, "Hit. I been hit," coughing up the words and a clod of blood.

The outside world gone, Starlet knew it was only he and she. She bent her face close to his, his acid breath hot on her one second, and the next, she reached up, violently ripping off her T-shirt, her breasts shaking. She balled up the cloth and jammed it against Onge's wound, holding hard to stop the bleeding. His eyes were speaking to her. They were child eyes, but blank. Suddenly calm. *Where is his fear?* Seeing him so helpless, flat-lined, she was filled with terror.

Gravel dug into her soft skin as she knelt. Suddenly aware of the strangers gathering around her, their body heat stifling, she screamed, "Get back, get back!" She grabbed Vegas, pulling him down. "Vegas, do mouth to mouth."

"I can't," Vegas yelped. "I'm sorry. I can't."

She hated him right then. "Jesus, never mind, I will."

Placing her hands on Onge's cheeks to steady his face, she stretched her small lips around his swollen mouth. His lips were velvet-soft and salty with blood. She pulled back as though she shouldn't have touched his lips. What did she know about resuscitation? Nothing! It was like she was kissing her father on the lips, the father she hadn't seen for so long. *Oh God. Help me.*

*Fast. Fast.* She pulled back. His lips lay there, quiet, his mouth slacked open, defenseless. This man of words had fallen silent.

*Do it.* Starlet breathed into his mouth twice, then again, and waited. Taking a huge breath, she blew it into him, her own chest thumped with fear, and then she pressed her shirt against the wound with one hand, while banging on the other side get his breath going.

Vegas turned to a woman standing on the sidewalk watching. "911," he yelled, "Somebody call 911. Fuck! Hurry."

Onge's eyes, big balls of white lined with red, were flipped back. Starlet was straddling him now. Her legs squeezing, her whole body on him, breathing. *Hope.* "Don't leave me, Onge. I need you. Don't." Before she could tell if her mouth to mouth was working, someone wrenched her off him. She lurched from the grip, turning and kicking the cop in the crotch. "Save him. Do something!"

As if in a dream, she heard a siren whining in the distance, coming closer, and then a second one in the opposite direction. "Let the paramedics through," he said, stiff-arming Starlet. She looked up at the gathered crowd and saw the two black children they had just passed. One said, "I'm sorry, lady."

"Yeah, I know," Starlet answered sobbing, and she cried harder when she saw her sadness reflecting back at her in their little girl eyes, so innocent a minute ago…

Onge's big body was jolting, his feet shaking, involuntarily, and then, he stopped moving. His shirt was so messed up. *He'd hate that.* His eyes jiggled, his legs splayed, his feet turned out, as if someone had OD'd him.

*Not Onge.*

Throwing herself on Vegas, she nearly knocked him over, crying, "Oh God, Vegas. He's going to die. It's my fault." She wiped her mouth on her wrist and saw, in horror, a smear of blood and saliva that was Onge's. Her eyes went to Vegas, but she didn't see him. She envisioned the squat. Out of the blue, it fell apart, a sand castle disintegrating. She imagined her and Vegas, Green and Onge as mere dolls, tumbling, crushed under foot. *The king was dead.*

It was four in the afternoon the same day Onge was gunned down when Vegas and Starlet hiked back to the squat. Hollywood had been as hot at twelve noon as it was now. The Santa Anas dusted hot gusts of air into their faces. At the police station they held hands, one hand shaking as much as the other, squeezing for comfort. After each was questioned separately, they sat on the scarred leather bench, their hands entwined, their eyes looking mostly down at the cracks in the tile floor, the ruts and black marks from shoes and boots. When Vegas finally summed up the courage to look directly at Starlet and she back at him, it was hard to believe hers were the same eyes he had seen that first day: sparkling, dazzling with joy, and now, fearful, almost turning down at the ends. The charge officer finished his paper work and handed Vegas his card. "Listen, pal," he said, scratching the side of his freckled temple, "you remember any details, call me, pronto. We're thinking here, novice gang-initiation thing."

"Okay, but we need to know."

"Sometimes inconclusive. A lot of shootings go unsolved."

When they found out they wouldn't be incarcerated, they both started breathing normally again. The minute they closed the station door Vegas let go of Starlet's sweaty fingers; the crisis had passed. Now their bodies nearly touched during the long walk back as they stepped in a rhythm, their angular hips bumping intermittently. Vegas wanted to slide his arm around Starlet and walk with her, the way he'd seen lovers around town walking when the girl's hand would slip down and brush against the guy's butt.

After they entered the garage, Starlet sidled over to Leontine. She was stiff and quiet. Vegas assumed she was thinking of the last time she spoke to Onge and how his belongings remained there in the trunk, but he was rotting bad in the morgue. He could still see the desperation on Starlet's face when she tried to save him; then her skin had gone pale and stayed that way. Her rock was gone and the conflicts she and Vegas could face in the future were scary. His own thoughts were running fast and fierce as he imagined hers were. *What would happen to the squat? The kids, letting loose. What would Joe-Mack say? Where was he? What if he had a boy and the kid bolted?*

Starlet opened the back door, slipped onto the seat, leaving empty the space where Onge usually sat. Vegas took off his shirt and rubbed as much of the car as he could reach, the long sleek sides, the trunk and hood ornament. His armpit curved over the hot roof. Starlet sat inside, pulling at the ends of her hair, sucking her top lip, rocking a little.

Vegas leaned his head in. "You freaking?"

She shook her head yes. She pushed over just a little, as if inviting him to join her, but leaving the space for Onge, his ghost. She bent forward and rubbed her cheek along the back of the driver's-side front seat. She spoke softly, "Onge loved this leather, the smell, Leontine, herself. She had a past all her own he told me. You know, Vegas, I could hear him sometimes talking to her, asking her questions about where she'd been, what she'd seen. You think there were places Onge had dreamt of, maybe, and now, he will never see."

"I guess so."

She dropped her chin onto her chest, as if in silent prayer, and then, she apparently remembered the crusty blood on her blouse; she blotted it gently at first with the pads of her fingertips, then she madly swiped her palm across the stain. "Look," she said. "I hate this mess, but this mess is a part of him. Oh God. Oh my God."

Vegas thought he could smell Onge's blood, just as though he was standing over him; he'd never seen Onge so much as cut a finger, even when he was slicing oranges with a butcher knife.

A loud sob burst from Starlet's lips. Her shoulders bounced, her chest squeezed out the crying sounds, as though they were reluctant to leave her, as if she were remembering every bit of his death—the shots, the sounds splintering the air that weren't even that loud. They were surprisingly quick, and then Onge fell.

"I couldn't. I couldn't damn save him. I wanted to. So bad," she said, punching at her knee. "Really bad. I'm such a loser."

Vegas grasped her fist and held it against his own leg. "No don't, Starlet. Don't. Hit me, if you have to hit someone."

She shook her head as if to say, "No, no, no." She swallowed her sounds, and then sniffled.

"You're not a loser. Come on, Starlet. Don't cry," Vegas said, squinting back tears.

"But what about his body? Where is it?" she asked.

"I don't know," Vegas answered, shaking his head, rubbing his forearm over his eyes.

"We could do something, if they would let us bury him. They got laws. Next of kin stuff. Do you know where his mother is?" Starlet asked.

"Miami, I think," Vegas said.

"Hey, we're talking big cash here? I could call someone," she said.

"Who, your mother? No, I was thinking Joe-Mack. He carries a hefty wad of money. I seen it."

"Why would he help you, Vegas?"

"I don't know, but maybe…. He's a loner, you know. Like me."

Starlet ran her fingers along Vegas' jaw line, "You mean you used to be."

The whole day had started out simply. Onge told them they would scour the neighborhood and identify Starlet's stalker. Vegas trusted Onge and so did Starlet. He would protect them. Uncertainty prevailed in Hollywood for kids who needed shelter and food, and danger lurked everywhere. What if the bastard who stalked Starlet had traced her to the squat?

"I can't believe he's gone," Starlet said. "What an indecent way to go with not even a chance to face your murderer. Blasted down…"

Vegas hunched his bony frame, cupping his fingers under his fishbone ribs. He and Starlet were silent. The sound of a cricket chirping under the car broke the quiet. For Starlet and Vegas there was nothing to say. Summoning courage, he patted Starlet on her shoulder, gently as though he was touching something that might melt, the transparent whitish skin of a water lily. Starlet fell back, her body like jelly, the crook of her neck resting against his arm. Her neck was damp and warm. She lifted her head as though speaking to Onge somewhere up in the sky, to God, or even to Vegas who sat as still as he could, giving her a chance to talk.

"You know, I big-time trusted him."

"Yeah."

"He was a huge guy, but he didn't freak me," Starlet said. "He was on my side. Did you ever notice his eyes, the way they looked when he would glance up from reading? It was like his mind was working full time. He could really talk, too. Philosophy."

"Remember how he lectured us?" Vegas asked. "About the past and thinking big?"

Nodding her head, Starlet sat quietly for a moment and then, asked, "Why, Vegas? Why him? He protected me. I can't believe he's gone. I expect him to be upstairs or coming in the window. Do you believe in ghosts? Maybe in the night he'll come to us."

"That would be cool."

"It's my rotten fault. I wasn't even thinking about him or danger really," Starlet blubbered. "My sister said, 'All about you, Starlet, all that, that's you.' I'm clueless. I was actually looking for Vicky, then bam."

Vegas' mother had called him gangly, her voice oddly proud, but he wasn't strong and he knew that, but here next to Starlet he felt solid. She was delicate with a body full of air and sweet water, moving with a natural grace. He thought she probably always did even as a child, tucking her toes into dress-up shoes, pretending to be a ballerina. Onge had known she was special.

Once Vegas got past the shocking blue of Starlet's eyes, the zillion stars in them;, he puzzled as to why a stunner like her was stuck in the squat with him and the other losers. Onge was adamant. "Stay off the street," he'd say, harsh-like. "You going home, princess pie, if I have to get me a motorcycle with a sidecar. Jaunt you there myself."

Starlet leaned forward, starting to whisper. Vegas could hardly hear her. The words seemingly floated, falling soft, not into his ears but to the air in front of her. He strained to listen, moving just slightly closer to her, into the realm of her scent.

"I had been here one week and one day," she said. "I managed to hide a roll of cash up in a tree. My first week was a bitch. I was killing inside, but I wouldn't give it up and go home."

"How come?"

"I had reasons."

"So, then what?"

"Get this. I spoke to three girls in the Gap. They totally ignored me. I was bummed. The guys were always looking. Some dufus picked me up. 'Let's go eat,' he says. Free food, yeah, right. He picked up burgers. Wanted me to sit in his dumb Jeep and eat take-out. How stupid! He thought that was a tremendous deal, big wow, buying crap food gave him access, like shoving his greasy fingers down my blouse. I got out of there fast."

"Dumb ass."

"I was going to waitress, but you know applications require a phone and address. No go with that. The boy behind the counter sent me to the squat. He knew Onge. Sometimes Onge slipped me money, Vegas. There was nothing going on. Honest."

Starlet pressed her knees together like she was protecting her virginity, if she still had it. Vegas had no idea if she had ever done it.

Starlet cupped her hands on her forehead, shielding her eyes. "Vegas, I'll tell you something, but don't interrupt, okay?

"Okay."

"The place where I'm from. It's not all that hot. My mom worked at Realbrite Cleaners. She was smart, could have done better, but she tried to control her hours away from us. Me and Amy were regular kids. 'til Lowlife shows. Funny how one prick can ruin your life. I mean, it was terrible not having a dad, at least, not around, but…"

"Yeah, but what if you do and he's a pig?" Vegas chimed in, telling how he blamed his father for getting his mother in the chapel business. She only liked the dressing up part. Overdressed and covered with make-up, she'd wrap her pudgy arms around the slender brides, wishing them happiness, but when Vegas looked in her eyes, he saw they were hurting bad.

"Once, I asked this kid over. I was seven. His mom comes to pick him up and says, 'No place for *my* son,' when she spies my mom in her black slip and whiffs the pot outside the building. It was tough. I guess you know about tough stuff, huh?"

"Are you through with your story?"

"Oh, sorry. I'll be quiet."

"So, my mom got me this job at the cleaners. I hung clothing, sorted boxes, hangers, and then I was supposed to learn the register. The lady manager said I had initiative. People don't take me for smart, but I'm good in math. Me and my mom and sister were doing okay. One day she starts dating this man. He's obnoxious, but she likes him. I mean, why? He's accounting management at the Dome. Big deal!"

"Moms with men, go figure."

"I mean, she was sick of work. So what. The guy promised her pie in the sky, but he's conning her. Believe that!"

"I do."

"The jerk is looking at me funny. I hear him jiggling the bathroom door when I'm showering. I picture his hairy hands on the knob. He goes away and I watch TV, but the big shit comes in and plops on the living room rug positioned where he can spy up my skirt and, all this time, he's fingering his mustard cowboy string tie. It happened so fast," Starlet said, squeezing her eyes shut, her lids fluttering. "He's in my space. And more, if you know what I mean. I love my Mom."

"Sure. Yeah."

"I couldn't tell her, Vegas. He raped me. I left."

Starlet held the bottom hem of her skirt cupping the flakes from her nails. She got out of the car carefully, dusting down her skirt onto the cement floor. Fluffing up her hair, then taking a deep breath, she said, "Let's go up."

"You okay?" Vegas said, puzzled as to what to say. He was not sure he had heard her right, but if he did, he knew he couldn't handle the details.

Without answering, she started up the stairs.

They bumped into Green who had been sitting on the top stair. "Spying?" Starlet asked.

"Shut your trap," Green answered.

## Chapter 10
## Dress Up: Starlet, Vegas, and Katha

The day after Onge died, the big hype on the California scene in the *L.A. Times* was about a white man who had supposedly murdered his wife, dumped her body in their Catamaran, and shuffled it off to Catalina, where he moored for two days. It was rumored that forensics had DNA samples and blood drops that showed up under ultraviolet. The body hadn't been found; the woman was apparently set afloat, amongst all species of fishes, giant turtles and all, to be bumped by sharks, and to finally sink, weighted down by an anchor, to the bottom of the Pacific. Green read the article to the others in the squat. They immediately blasted the killer with epithets: "scum" and "son of a bitch." Green scanned each page, searched on into the second section for notice of Onge's death. She discovered it under the fold on the left side of page twenty-two. Taking a deep breath, she read, *"Gang-Related Death in Hollywood, Unidentified Black Male."* After a few non-descript lines referring to the victim's probable age and the lack of ID on the body, it ended with the common request: Call the 800 tip line. No reward was listed.

"As if anybody cares," Green said.

Starlet let out a sob, hiccupping her words. "Not a gang! We told the damn cop who he was. They didn't even care. He wrote our facts down like a grocery list. They're for sure lost in a paper pile." Starlet told how the detective looked down on her and Vegas, calling them "unreliable."

Vegas swiped away tears with his forearm, rubbed his forehead with his hand, slipping his face behind his arm, holding back his desire to sniffle. Then he reached over to pat Starlet's hand. "It's okay. It'll be okay."

"Sure, Dweeb, like you know," Green said.

As if the mood of the day wasn't dark enough, it was raining. Heavy sheets of water pounded the grass and the herb garden, pelted the glass of the triangular window set in the roof of the room upstairs in the garage. At first, droplets from the leak along the windowsill sounded in splats on the floor, then they ran in a regular line, like a faucet. Green stuck a pail under it, but soon the leak streamed so heavily, the pail was soon full. She dumped out the meager contents of the rusty cooler, two Cokes, one box of stale donuts, and scraped it across the floor to catch the rain. Puddles were circling outward, seeping into the kids' belongings.

"Hey, pile your shit up on the chair, on the stairs out there. Hurry up," she said.

Starlet hung her bag on the nail, rolled up her blanket, shoving it out the door. When she started to sit again, she jumped up. "I'm going outside. I can't stand it here." She ran out and stood with her mouth open to the rain, drinking it. Rivulets ran down her cheeks. In two minutes, her clothes were soaked down to her underwear, everything clinging to her body. She plopped down, with her short skirt hiked up, her wet underpants against the wet grass, her tears mixing with the rain. *What do you want us to do, Onge? We're crap without you. What next?*

Starlet took off her skirt and blouse and the soggy sneakers. She wrung out the clothing and slogged up the stairs. Crouching behind the door, she peeked in, yelled to Green, "Hand me something, will you?"

Green yanked the plastic tablecloth off the pile of clothes on the chair. Even though Starlet's body was drenched and shivering, she recoiled as the damp oilcloth touched her skin. Quickly, she slipped on her jeans and dry sweater, crossing her arms against her hard nipple buds. Her clothes felt looser. She was reminded that she hadn't eaten a thing that day and barely a thing the day before.

The rain stopped. The birds outside were quiet. Backed-up water sloshed over the eaves, taking leaves and crusty dirt clods along with it. It ran down onto the lawn and garden, where the daisies flopped over, their white petals splayed in the brown muck. The sky brightened. It had become an umbrella of mottled blue with dashes of pink sluicing through it.

The ladder where Onge always sat was empty. Most of his books were water-logged before Green could salvage a few of them. She took the dry ones and piled them on her sleeping bag that was rolled tight, sitting in a corner.

"Listen, everybody. We need a plan," Green said.

"Duh," Stripe mocked her.

"Look, we had a conversation. He told me some stuff."

"What?"

"If anything happened…"

"He had a premonition? That's bull."

"We need revenge," Vegas piped in.

"Onge had rules. Can we just follow his rules? Anyhow. Leave Leontine alone, at least."

As Vegas inched over towards Starlet, he caught a dirty look from Green. He was tight with Starlet and it pissed her off. He'd seen Green come unglued at Pepper and Stripe, but she was touchy around Starlet. It was as though she couldn't handle Starlet's beauty and Starlet's pure ease with her looks, but perhaps she was reminded of another time, and her friend Lily from back home.

That night, Vegas and Starlet went out to scam pizza from the trash behind Uno's.

The busboy wrapped orders that weren't picked up and leftover whole pieces in a plastic bag for them. Onge had worked out a deal with him. On their way back, they paused at the bottom step of the stairs leading to the squat, and they sat close with their hips touching.

"I feel screwed over," she said. "Don't you?"

"Kind of."

"You going to give it up? Go home?"

"No. My parents suck. My father will pound the shit out of me if I go home. You know, I was a dirt bag to him, a cockroach he could corner in the kitchen and wham," he said, slamming his fist on the banister, "crush." He treated me like crap, but now he has to deal with my mother. Do her errands."

"What a bastard."

Vegas's mind spun with garbage, the sour details regarding his folks, their quirky life. How could he explain them to Starlet without turning her off? He found he was again thinking again about the Rodney incident. He could still feel the bite of Rodney's mother's dirty look and her screams still rang in his ears when he thought about it. Starlet seemed to accept him, but she might lose interest if she knew his past.

"You'd hate my parents, for sure."

"Why?"

Vegas looked down at his fingers, squeezing them in and out. He made the decision not to tell about the time his father slammed the piano lid down on them. He had turned nine years old, but he was still such a stinking ball baby. As he looked down he could swear his pinky finger on his left hand was still redder than the others, dented in. When Rose ran the water on his fingers, it made the pain worse. She didn't get it. He thought that might have been his first real thought of running away. But he felt a little better when she gave him a huge bowl of macaroni that he had to spoon out with his good hand.

They were eating and talking. Vegas folded his pizza slice over and wedged half of it into his mouth. Starlet first sniffed the cheese and said, "Yummy," and then licked it from the slice. With her mouth still full, she asked, "Tell me, Vegas, why would I hate them?"

"He was a jerk, a jerk-off."

"Jeez, tell me what he did," Starlet asked, placing the soft tips of her fingers on his wrist, leaving a spot of grease on it.

"Well, he put me down. Put me down, even in this dream, see. It totally was his putrid mean face, his body in a purple tux, tails and all. His fly was unzipped. It was gross. In real life he lorded over me and Mom. What a shit-head. He scammed all the loot from the weddings!"

"He took all the money?"

"Yeah. The first time I picked a pocket was because my Mom needed cash for her shopping. That's all she had, the shopping channel. One day I got this idea. I'll fucking leave. Then I did it to get the hell out of there. Otherwise, I'd still be the Loser Vegas kid."

Starlet said, "So you're not a criminal just because you took stuff. You needed it."

"Shit, the whole thing was bizarre. The man had friends or so he said. They never came by, but he'd mention some asshole, Billy, and Henri, a French dude, after his bar trips, but who the hell were they? No clue. He wore outdated tuxedos that Rose brought home from the second hand store, as if he could impress the customers, but if you touched them, your hand would slide right off, they were so slimy with cruddy sweat. They had purple silk linings and gold cummerbunds. You never know in Vegas, they could have been some dead star's duds, like Liberace. And by the looks of my father in them, he could have been a limo driver or a croupier or a lounge lizard. He bounced on his feet during ceremonies, couldn't wait to bust out, booze it up, get laid, whatever."

Vegas went on to say that after the wedding couples paid and left, zingo, he'd drop his pants, suspenders, right there on the living room floor and slip into the same pair of shit-hole Levis. "Afterward, he'd re-do his comb over and head out to the Joshua tree for a few tokes. I smelled the grass. I was kind of hoping for a contact high. Man, I wanted to get my hands on one of his joints, but I thought he'd kick my ass good if he caught me."

"Did you do it?"

"Yes, yes, the night before I left, I smoked a whole joint. I was reeking of weed; my throat burned like a mother, but I couldn't stop laughing. Can't you just see the bastard hunting for his bone?"

"That's cool. You're funny. So, the tuxedo was part of his act?" Starlet asked.

"The whole deal was so phony. Mom was in charge of color coordination—he gave that to her. She fussed with ratty wrinkled flowers, paper, like you get in Mexico, and the clothes we wore. I took the pictures. Sometimes I raked in decent tips when the creep-o wasn't looking."

There was the incident when Vegas nosed around in his father's closet and discovered a business suit. The pockets were still stitched up, and when he squeezed the fabric, the cloth popped back. No wrinkles. There was a new pair of loafers with fruit-bag tassels. They were stuffed with cedar blocks that smelled. "He was gone a lot, you know, so I could have the run of the house when he was out."

"It's funny, but," Starlet said, "but all I got is memories. When I was little my dad, his fingers around my ribs, would hold me with my head nearly touching the ceiling. I can sometimes feel them now just before I fall asleep and dream. They were strong, and quick as anything, he'd swoop me down and toss me up like a ball and pretend he wouldn't be there to catch me, but he always was. My head could have hit the floor, but it didn't. He left when I was five. And I guess you know just this year things went totally bad."

"But what if he'd been an asshole like mine?" Vegas asked. "No great gift. I was totaled with him by ten years old. It took me a long time to bolt. When nobody loves you, you feel dead, especially when you're a weakling, a dumb fool."

Starlet leaned over and put her head on Vegas' shoulder. "Don't say that. You're my friend. That's something."

He blushed, looking down at his scrawny body in disbelief that this girl could be close enough for him to smell her spicy skin. But next to her, he felt like a scumbag. His pants were stained with mustard; his shirt smelled like days-old B.O. and he didn't have clean clothes.

"If you could have one wish," Starlet said, with a silly grin on her face, "what would it be?"

Vegas said he didn't know. In the past he had wished to get to Hollywood and now that he was here, he was dumbfounded. Yes, he wanted to fit in. Yes, he wanted friends. He wanted to cash in big. And, as he went over the large wishes, he narrowed them down to wearing the blue dress.

He said, off-handedly, "Did you ever dress up?" His thoughts were taking humongous leaps here, but he went for it.

"On spirit day at school. Halloween, of course."

"We worked every Halloween. These dinks would show up at the chapel smashed. Would you believe they wanted to hitch up in cheesy maid's uniforms or wooly King Kong costumes, that kind of shit?"

"That's too funny. You didn't dress up for Halloween, I mean, everybody does that, don't they?"

"Nope."

"That stinks."

"Naw, it's okay. I don't care."

"Do you think we can make it without Onge?"

"I don't know."

"It's bad. I'm scared."

Vegas didn't have the slightest idea how to soothe Starlet's fears, but he could plan an escape from Hollywood, just like he had planned and executed his way to Hollywood. "Want to go somewhere else, like Malibu? Onge was hot on it. Or San Diego? We could surf. We could sneak into the zoo. See the birds of paradise."

"It takes money, you know. I'm down on cash. At least we can sleep here while we figure things out."

Starlet talked about her mom and home. She said, "Maybe, if you help me, we bust Ralph. I mean, if you go with me, I got backup. I miss my mom."

"You would take me there?

"Yeah, but not for a while. 'til we get traveling money."

"We could sell some of this stuff in here. Hock it. Nobody uses it."

Starlet did not answer but she went to peruse the clothing on hangers. "I bet those trunks are full, too," Starlet said, pointing to the trunks lined alongside the back wall. "It's got to be vintage. We could sell some of this junk in Venice. Anything sells there." She opened a trunk and pulled out three dresses, holding them up to her body. First a crinkled up red silk and then a faded beige long gown that had sweat marks under the arms and hung straight to her ankles and finally a flirty, fringy Twenties dance-dress.

"Want to fool around with this stuff?" Vegas suggested, digging through a box of wigs and hairpieces.

"Yeah, it's like shopping."

Vegas knew that Starlet would expect him to choose a costume from the garage haul but he knew exactly what he would wear. It was risky. "I got something."

"You holding out on me?" Starlet said twisting her knuckles into his ribs.

"Hey, that tickles," he said. "Listen, this is secret, right?"

"Sure, now give me some privacy," Starlet said bouncing over to the racks of clothing, brushing away the spider webs. "Let me check these out. Tomorrow night we meet, like in the movies. Nine o'clock. Here."

Vegas had the sensation that something good was going to happen. His mouth kept breaking into a smile as though his secret was bursting out; he wasn't exactly sure why, it was a kind of expectation. Underneath all this excitement with Starlet was the thought of the blue dress. When he'd lifted it he'd had no idea why, but now, it was clear. He was going to be in the spotlight under the California moon. He wondered if teenagers all over were gazing at the same moon, searching for answers. Were they contemplating a runaway move? It hadn't been easy leaving home, but tomorrow night, and maybe just for one night, he had destiny on his side. He would reach for a thread of happiness.

That night Vegas lay awake, his armpits wet, his back sweating; Starlet was sleeping just a foot away. He could reach out and touch her forehead, run his hand along her hair, but he didn't dare. His own skin was crawling with excitement. With all the fear around someone stalking Starlet and the reality of Onge dying, he still had hope. It was distant, but there, in his far-away mind.

When Vegas awoke the next day, he thought it was about five o'clock. He rolled his spine around to loosen the stiffness, licked his dry lips. The early morning light was trickling in the window, laying a stripe across the floor. He eased out of his sleeping bag, grabbed two garbage bags and headed out to nickel and dime it. He had them full and cashed in the bottles and cans within an hour. This was a harder, slower process than picking a pocket or stealing a purse, but somehow he didn't want to rob anyone today. It might bring him rotten luck, bad vibes. Back when he did those things, it didn't seem at all criminal to him, and even Starlet wasn't shocked at all, she said, because he helped out his mom. But he was way far off from calling himself a modern day hero, a Robin Hood, a Spiderman. His mother was probably still sobbing all over her velvet duster, looking for him in local shelters, the jail, somewhere close by, but she'd never assume he would have made it all the way to Hollywood. His father was probably glad to be rid of him; he might be abusing his mom worse since his punching-bag kid wasn't there to muddle things up and take the brunt of his cruelty. *I might call her. But then, she might send someone after me.*

After the bottle routine, Vegas wiped his hands on his pants and carefully removed the blue dress from his pack. The folds were imbedded and would certainly need a cleaners to get them out. With the garment over his arm, he sped down the street in his black boots, stopping in front of the One Hour Cleaners.

"Can I get this back today?" he said to the clerk.

The red-lipped lady said, "Yeah, four buck deposit."

"How much for paying all at once?"

"Eight bucks."

"Here."

"Your mom's night out, huh?"

"Something like that."

"Forget it, ain't got time to run my mouth on this job," she said, flipping the dress on top of a pile of white shirts in the cart behind her and giving him a once-over glance with one raised eyebrow.

"Hey, watch it," he said. His dress had landed on top of a stack of men's foul shirts, their cruddy collars circled with dirt. He knew if he lifted those shirts to his nose and took a whiff, he'd barf. They were dress shirts like his father wore over and over under his tuxedo. His mom didn't seem to notice as long as the jerk's cummerbund matched her dress that was some loser putrid purple or gold-garbage glimmering color.

"Be careful," he said, but the woman with her bulbous butt had already headed to the back of the shop where she fished out a cigarette from her pocket, popping it between her lips.

Starlet avoided him during that day. He was left to wonder if he had fantasized the whole plan the night before. Maybe he was going bonkers, or maybe Starlet had changed her mind, realizing that he was a complete fool. Yet she'd been teasing him the way girls do to guys. He took a walk, took his sweet time eating a pretzel. He wandered into a bookstore, looking at books Onge might have liked. There was one called Orange Horses and another with gigantic pictures about that museum Onge had grooved on. He was a smart man. He didn't deserve to die and yet he was gone. One day alive and gone the next. Life is change, Vegas decided. When you get relief, someone you can depend on, the world spits on you. *Tonight will be different.*

After picking up the dress, he went directly to the garage and hesitated by Leontine. He opened her front door and lay the dress over the leather seat carefully so as not to wrinkle it. He hopped in the back seat, cranked open the window and listened to the outside sounds, the same as Onge used to do. A couple of dump trucks rumbled by, a cop car's siren wailed in the distance, and piano music floated from the house. Joe-Mack had played a CD of classical tunes during the ride and now this music sounded similar. Vegas moved his fingers nimbly through the air on an invisible piano, creating rushes and flourishes and grand pounding movements at the end of his would-be concerto.

Finally he rolled the plastic up from the dress and removed it from the hanger.

After pulling off the cleaner's tag, he dropped his pants and shirt on the cold cement floor, an echo of his father. A shudder skimmed through his body as he slipped the sparkling dress over his hips. It landed just above his skinny ankles and bare feet. The Harlow wig he had found covered his black hair where the dye job was fading. He stood next to Leontine, attempting to get a good view of himself in the side mirror. His fingers tingled, his eyelashes fluttered as he raised his chin to grasp sight of the chunky rhinestone necklace. At first it chilled his skin; it was set just an inch above his Adam's apple. The necklace bounced as he swallowed with anticipation.

Vegas stepped up on the running board, standing on his spread toes, as though he was surfing in Malibu, moving forward on a speeding board, riding a raging wave. He examined images of his torso in the mirror. He bent the mirror up, checking his rose-colored lips and white teeth. He twisted the mirror down to see how the dress drifted along his slender body and long legs. *Oops better fix this.* Placing the mirror back, Vegas breathed on it and polished it up with a T-shirt that belonged to Onge. Stepping down he V-ed his arms out like the wings on the hood ornament, feeling free, as though riding currents of air. *Body prison, gone!*


Upstairs Starlet saw Green sucking on an empty pop bottle, popping her lips on and off the end, creating an echo of sound and then playing with it, blowing in it, tossing it up and down. She sat on the sawhorse watching Starlet dress. "What's up with the get-up?"

"I've got plans," Starlet answered.

Green flicked aside the long section of her hair, "You opting for a movie or are you in one?"

"I've got a date."

"You know how it was with Onge. Him scouting you out. You want me to watch out?"

Starlet ignored her. She stood in front of Stripe's mirror, twirling. The beaded fringe on her dress clicked as she checked her slight hips side to side.

Pepper whistled, "You go, white girl."

"Shut up," Green said flipping her off.

Downstairs Vegas circled the car, nearly skipping. He was free. Set loose from his mind, his conscience, his father's disapproving voice, cut loose from the confines of his pants. When he saw Starlet at the top of the stairs, he panicked, the screws in his mind tweaking. *Freaky. Why did I do this? How can I be a blue lady and love Starlet?*

"Vegas!" she shouted as she ran to him. "Look at you!" Slinging her fair arms around his neck, kissing the skin over his collarbone, slicking her tongue under the necklace, she nudged it around. Her breath stung his neck.

Vegas's insides jumped. He looked down at her. The sadness came up in him, a shriek coming forth. It was all the worse when he heard the sound, like he was outside himself, but couldn't stop his voice. His shoulders shook.

Starlet wrapped her arms tighter around him. Then she placed her fingers gently under his chin, lifting it up, "Come on. You're okay. You're my little boy blue. Honest, you're okay."

"No, no. I'm not. I'm lost. I'm not even Vegas. I'm Freddie. This blue dress – as strange as it sounds – is part of who I am. It's my chance to be free because I don't need to be me when I'm wearing it."

"I don't care."

"Let's dance."

But he had never danced. It was outside the realm of possibility for him, yet there he was. He felt Starlet's body, tits and tummy and thighs all pushing up against the blue dress and his body under it. Blood was surging through his veins. He was on a precipice, ready to jump for pleasure, wanting the moment to come and yet not come. He was bulging out the dress and she kept moving under him, his hips involuntarily thumped, and she kept swaying as though she didn't notice, or as if she was into this change in his body. He let out a yelp, pushing back from her. "Oh shit, Starlet."

"Freddie, it's okay. Come back. Hold me tighter. It's okay."

Then, after a couple of seconds, she pushed away. The break in their touching helped him gain control. "I'm alright," he said as he took deep breaths. She stepped back up to him to continue the dance.

Starlet and Freddie moved gently as if surrounded by an ocean breeze while floating in the moon's first light. It was so warm.

Inside the bungalow, the cat pawed at Katha's arm, then he brushed his raised back against her hand, and finally, switched his tail across her face.

"Simon, Simon, you naughty boy. It is the dark of night. Must you? Must you misbehave?" He continued taunting her until she flung back her blanket and carefully rolled up to a sitting position, waiting for the dizziness to go away. She pulled her robe together, tied it and slipped on her slippers, and headed for the back door, as Simon ran through her legs nearly tripping her.

"Ah look, Simon, it is a lovely gracious moon, lighting up the yard," she said,
cautiously stepping off the stoop. It shined behind the line of trees, the fence and silhouetted the roofline of the garage. Katha took a moment to breath in the scent of the night-blooming jasmine bushes. Simon hunkered under the bushes, scratching and clawing at the hanging branches, as though he expected to find a sleeping bird there he might toy with. He meowed back at Katha, letting her know that he'd be just a minute.

It was a clear night, the smog having been lifted and blown away by the Santa Anas. There were several stars, some brighter and closer than others, scattered in the sky. In a moment of daring Katha shucked off her slippers and dug her feet into the dew-covered cold grass, giggling a bit to herself. It was then she noticed a light shining through the garage window, muted by the presence of hanging branches wandering across the upper part of the window.

"Simon, what in heaven's name? The garage light is lit."

Katha made her way to the window. It was open. She leaned in and saw two young women dancing. The taller one was wearing a horrific-looking wig; the other wore a black dress as close to her skin as a seal's coat. It appeared to have a similar silhouette to the frock Katha had worn to a spectacular celebration ages ago.

"Simon, that blond hussy is wearing my beaded gown." The cat brushed her legs, and when she scooped him up, she wore the loose-skinned cat like a fur wrap; his soft fur caressed her arm. Simon clawed at the tassels on her robe
loosening threads that hung past Katha's wrinkled knees.

Katha listened for dance music. There wasn't any. *Were they pantomiming*, she wondered. She swayed in tandem with their movements; the cat remained over her with his four paws swishing against her frail body. As the two youngsters separated, Katha said, "Hello. Hello there. What in the world are you doing?"

Starlet looked, and when she saw the old woman, she froze.

"Come here," the woman said. "What is happening?"

"Nothing. Really."

"Come closer," Katha said. "Why are you wearing that dress? It is mine. I'm Katha Willis."

Vegas yanked on Starlet's arm trying to take off, and, as she pulled away, she said, "Come back, don't go."

"Hi," she said, to the woman. "It's a nice dress. I was just trying it on."

Starlet climbed out the window. Vegas caught a clump of hair from the wig on the rough wooden window casing and it fell off. He grabbed it, but didn't place it on his head.

"Why, you are a male," Katha said. "Here, make yourself useful. Take this irascible boy." She handed Simon to Vegas.

"Whatever."

"Excuse me, my name is Miss Willis."

"Hi, I'm Starlet and this is Vegas." Starlet then apologized for being in the garage. They were not trespassing just having fun-times. "We didn't hurt anything. We didn't touch the car."

"Oh, that old vehicle. I hardly think about it anymore." With that said, Katha
turned and walked toward the house, as though expecting them to follow. She stopped in
the middle of the yard, turning to say, "Excuse me, what are your names? I didn't catch them."

Starlet said, "I'm Starlet." She pointed to Vegas and said, "This here is Vegas. He's my friend."

"Yes, I'm aware of that," Katha answered. "Come now, I'm chilled to the bone. The night air is dangerous for an old girl like myself."

## Chapter 11
## Old Hollywood: Katha and Starlet

Vegas trailed behind the two women noticing that they had the same size hips, about the breadth of two hands with spread fingers, and although the old lady was a foot shorter, she might have been tall in her younger years. Her spine curved, but it appeared she was attempting to hold her head high. Her pride was visible in the clench of her uppers on her lower teeth, the rakish tilt of her chin. Onge was like that in his voice and upright mannerisms when he expounded; Stripe was like that in the way he parted his black shoulder-length hair exactly down the middle, framing his long face, and the slick of his nearly russet skin.

Starlet and Vegas waited for Katha to lift the skirt of her bathrobe. She wobbled up the dew-dampened back step. As Vegas and Starlet followed behind her, passing through the tight kitchen, it was easy to see Miss Willis had narrowed the use of her house and garage down to the kitchen and adjoining living room. The two rooms together were actually about the same size as the squat. The heavily-pilled and stained chartreuse blanket, the vintage couch with a body-sized dent along the middle, and the pillow covered with a pillowslip woven throughout with torn lace, clued him in. The old lady slept on her couch. The kitchen walls were plastered with curled and yellowed posters. The mahogany dining room table set against the wall in the kitchen was way too large for the room. The three of them had to suck in their tummies to ease by it. The living room, too, was crammed with furniture much too grandiose for its size. Every surface was covered. End tables were stacked with dusty movie magazines, striped and paisley silk scarves and an assortment of cups with the dregs of dark liquid and bloated tea bags floating in them. The women on the covers had fluttery eyelashes, stenciled brows, and

Veronica Lake hair. Stacks of clothing that might serve as costumes in local theaters were adorned with bits of ribbon and frill and odd-colored petticoats. A black and white pony-fur vest, man-sized, hung on a hanger jutting out from the front door. Books and photo albums and framed pictures lay about, some face down.

"Come in," Miss Willis said, entering the living room. She swiped the mix of gray tabby hair and whitish fluff from the faded maroon brocade love seats. She spoke to her cat, pointing her finger at it, "Naughty boy! Simon, I've admonished you to stay off my lovely pieces. They are my best, you know."

The cat settled in on top of the antique oak sideboard where he had landed after speeding ahead of his mistress and leaping to the perch that was obviously his favorite spot. He blinked his green eyes. The sun slipped in through a crack in the closed drapes and warmed his back.

Starlet walked over to the cat. She petted his fat fur and he reached his head up under her hand as though asking for more touch. After scratching his white neck, she grinned at Katha, and sat down, wedging a pillow against the back of the loveseat. "Nice kitty."

"Independent fellow, my Simon. A gift from a fan, I might add."

Vegas stood around, drumming his fingers against his thigh.

"Please sit. I'll make tea," Katha said, crossing her arms over her chest with a dramatic bow.

It was then Starlet spoke up about one of the posters. "Is that you?"

"Back in the day my hair was lustrous, wasn't it? Yes, it is I."

Once a curvy sized twelve, the woman had lost height and weight over the years and used less space in her home. The skirts of her robe and nightgown swept the floor as it had the grass outside. Her hair was the same length as in the pictures, but it had thinned and gone gray. Now she wore it close to her scalp in finger waves that sprouted into ringlets, which looked kind of ridiculous to Starlet. She slanted a little to the left when she walked, reaching out with a shaky hand to lean briefly on an end table or the wall, but she stepped around the oddly placed chairs and tables, the ottomans, piles of clothes, a box of laundry detergent, and paper grocery bags filled with more magazines. It was as though she was blind, not looking down, but sensing where she might place her feet without tripping — exact precision executing a path through and aside the total mess.

She stopped at the leather-top coffee table with rolled carved legs to adjust a bowl and two ashtrays. "Boehm," she said, focusing on the object with milky eyes. "German china. Superb craftsmen. Ronnie Regan loved these bowls."

Starlet thought the china bowl's colors of green and yellow on a background of white were spectacular and the edges so fine she could almost see through them. Nothing like the milk-glass hobnail bowls her Grammy Stevens had let her run her tiny fingers over, again and again, as a toddler. This bowl was paper-thin. She leaned over to look at it and spied the crack that ran straight across the base. It made her sad and she wasn't sure why. It was no longer perfect. She wondered if Katha had knocked it over one night while sleeping on the couch, perhaps she slung her arm forward in the midst of a dream. Starlet's mother still had her grandmother's vases and bowls long after the woman died.

Starlet had tired of playing with them, but now she missed the ordinary ease of gliding past them as they rested in the maple hutch—there to remind her of her grandparents.

She sat on the loveseat, patted the place beside her. "Come here, Vegas."

He ambled over and balanced on the very edge, his knees jiggling, as if ready to cut and run.

"Jell," Starlet said. "Be nice."

As Katha rummaged around the kitchen, she moved with purpose, with the dignity of someone who had once commanded a great deal of attention. She wore a long necklace that sparkled against her drab robe. It made a pinging sound as she jostled it against the table while setting out three cups.

When she saw Starlet gazing at it, she said, "Diamonds. A lavish gift, the last of any consequence. My Blake was insanely jealous. I still have the Tiffany box around here somewhere.

The enthusiast was not a man of means, but a true devotee and a lover of nature. Those were splendid days."

It was then Starlet heard Katha whisper to herself, "Drove them wild I did." After a little chuckle, she turned to Vegas and started firmly, "That era has past." Her face brightened for a brief moment. And, looking aside, she said, "Sometimes I feel I am still young, inside, at least, in my thoughts. Desires."

"Desires?" Starlet said, sending a puzzled look to Vegas. His eyes were fixed on Katha's necklace. Starlet sent him a severe "don't even think about it" look.

"What did you say, my dear?"

"Nothing. Nothing. Really," Starlet said, flashing an expression of embarrassment.

As though Katha forgot she was making tea, she came back into the living room and passed the sideboard, glancing in the mirror that was opaque in the corners, silvering along the beveled edges. She leaned forward, squinting. With great purpose, she yanked several bobby pins from her hair, allowing the last of her curls to flop down, shaking her head as she did so. It was then she mentioned that she never removed her necklace since it was her good luck charm.

"I'm terribly sorry you caught me unawares," she said, burrowing through a pile of scratched lipstick cases in a pressed glass compote dish. When she discovered the exact one, she drew a scarlet mouth up and over the lines of her mouth into a bow on the top lip and swung the tube down beyond the true line of her bottom lip. "There, now, I'm not so pale. Gracious me, let us visit."

She offered them a dish of hard candy wrapped in Christmas paper. "I don't indulge in these but reserve them for guests." Starlet chose one and used her nails to scrape off the paper. It left her curious as to when Katha last had company in her house.

The living room had an arched doorway that led to a narrow hallway with a wall heater that had vents on both the hallway side and the living room side.

Katha straightened up and summoned Starlet to follow her. She took Starlet towards one of the three doors, stating that she couldn't face it alone. It had been years since she entered.

Starlet halted, as the layers of perfume and powder Katha wore sizzled up her nose, and she was about to sneeze. "Was Blake your husband?"

"Oh no, paramour. The studio wanted it that way."

The older woman looked up and down the hall as though she expected someone to walk out of one of the doors. *A ghost*, Starlet thought. Katha leaned forward, thinking, listening, perhaps to her own voice, making a decision.

"Come with me, Starlet. I shall bestow a gift upon you. One that will remind you that you are a gracious woman. Something many women of today forget. You will stand apart if you remember to have dignity. Value yourself. There was a time when I forgot, gave it all up for a man, the bastard. Oh my goodness, there I go. I mustn't blaspheme. Pardon me, dear."

It tickled Starlet to hear the lady cursing. She covered her smile with her hand to hide her reaction so as not to insult the woman.

Starlet found Katha quite unreal. Katha, her teeth quite brownish with age, grinned at Starlet with the enthusiasm of a girly-girl – being eighty-eight had not dampened her awareness of beauty. She turned back to the living room as though she had forgotten something and then continued giving Starlet a tour of the bungalow filled with curling movie posters and piles of faded costumes. She paused, frowning as she lifted one of the two fancy filigreed silver bowls, now tarnished, that sat on her sideboard. The collection of silver spoons in the bowl clinked in a soft chime as her wobbly fingers shook the tiniest bit. Setting them back down, she lifted the second silver piece.

"I'm a collector," she said, lifting the bowl, grazing the contents across her nose, sniffing with an air of snobbery. "These are the remnants of the final gift he bestowed upon me. I cherish them."

Starlet dipped her head down, her blond hair mingling with Katha's scratchy gray ringlets, close enough where she, too, could smell the dried orchid petals, as delicate as tissue paper skin. "Orchids?"

"Yes, my dear. The remains of a pristine, perfect, faultless angel-white orchid. The most delicate, the prettiest of a multitude. I truly cared for it as best I could, but then, it died like all the rest.

"Come," she said, shuffling Starlet down the narrow hall for the second time to a closed door. Starlet stood behind her, pushing, helping to loosen the stuck door. The saccharine yet bitter aroma hit her first, then she noticed the bedspread that was covered with orchid petals, yellowed with age—much like the shriveled skin on the back of Katha's hand, as crinkled as the woman's lace collar that poked out from her robe.

"It has been seventy years – not a lucky number for me, but never-the-less, it is so. My Mr. Tanaka was devoted to me, my talent. He understood the importance of fragrant fresh flowers in a young *brilliant's* life. Even after the studio dismissed me, he afforded me great attention with his respect and gardening prowess.

She told how it was all Anna Maria's fault. "That horribly-freckled Anna Maria." It was beyond comprehension that Katha could have been replaced with the bandy-legged woman from Italy with her overbearing breasts. "And they bought me off with tawdry trinkets and makeup cases and a stipend not worth mentioning. Why, she could hardly carry a decent wardrobe on her frame. It was said they had to shorten all of my frocks!

"Starlet, can you possibly imagine my despair? In my day, the fans adored my dramatic black hair and sterling eyes, but time changes all. This woman, with an atrocious mole above her lips, who murmured throaty foreign love songs, replaced me. Me, with perfect diction. You wouldn't know this, dear, but I feel I must warn you of the pleasures and evils in Hollywood."

Katha set the bowl on a Rosewood lingerie chest, pushed aside a flurry of orchid skins, and perched on the bed. "I was a young bird in all my feathered glory. The men would gather and pet me and feed me, and their universal arousal was new to me. I got caught in Blake's web of desire, until he fancied Anna Maria."

"That sounds bad," Starlet said, her hand holding Katha's with a soft touch.

"That slut planned it all, to wrench him from me. She knew secrets. To bloom, to be seen, to die in glory. It was all I asked for. Blake returned, fell to his knees, but, as I sobbed with the agony of it all, the mystery revealed itself. The camaraderie he had with the producer, Steven. How they sported their knickers and jaunty plaid caps. He deserted my tainted body, but not before he handed me a fine linen handkerchief with a bold 'S' initial.

"If it weren't for the orchids, I should have flung myself out the window." With that said, Katha flopped onto a pillow. One arm graced her forehead, as though she was posing; her tiny ribs heaved up and down under her robe like the miniscule chest of a robin who'd fallen from a tree — an overplayed gesture, yet she did appear to be sobbing.

Starlet was reminded of her and her sister acting like drama queens with Mom in order to win arguments. She could hear her own voice now whining, "Mom, Mom just 'cause she's younger, why do I have to share? It's not fair. Not fair." *All that boo-hoo about nothing. Was Katha playing her now? She did look pretty forlorn.*

Just as Starlet was wondering what to say, Katha stretched out a wobbly arm, asking Starlet to help her up. "You, my pretty, have viewed a performance. Grand, wasn't it? Open the left top drawer, and take out my gloves, please."

Starlet found a Lord and Taylor bag full of gloves: leather, silk, and lace.

"Take the red mid-length ones, darling. Put them on. They suit you."

Once back in the room with Vegas, the actress decided that Starlet would be her ingénue and that they should arrange for a party at the diner the next day. It happened when, out of the blue, as though musing to herself, Katha said, "My little lovely, Starlet, you could learn from me. There are tricks to this trade of acting. For example, you might wear wonderfully gaudy rings right over those gloves. You must know that I am well aware of the hush-hush secrets to success and, listen carefully, my dear, your fans will presume jewels to be the real thing rather than fakers; some of these little deeds are as old as the infamous Hollywood hills, like me. I'll see to it there's no Anna Maria in your life."

Starlet stood next to Vegas yanking at the gloves that reached up above her elbows. She watched him snicker at the sight of her wearing them. "Cool it," she whispered, "these are a gift."

"If you say so," he answered, still smirking.

"Now my dears, let us plan to meet at the diner just down the road a bit. You know the one I mean, don't you? The name eludes me at this moment."

"The Over Easy?" Starlet said.

"Yes, we shall have a small gathering to celebrate the opening of The Katha Willis Drama Academy. Starlet, you are my first pupil. Vegas, you can assist Starlet, I presume."

"Sure."

"Now alas, I must resume my beauty sleep. Do not forget. Do not be tardy. Meet me at precisely eight-thirty tomorrow morning. Invite your friends if you wish. Good night now. Please see yourselves out."

As Katha turned toward the couch, Starlet noticed a curler the woman had missed, when she'd ripped the curlers from her hair earlier. It was still entwined with gray hair and perched in the middle of the back of the woman's head.

"Excuse me," she said, "there's a curler in the back that you missed. Let me get it for you."

"No, don't," Katha answered, reaching to nab Starlet's wrist and gripping it for some time. She lifted it, caressing her surprisingly soft and loose-skinned cheek with Starlet's hand.

"It's alright. I've slept many nights with my face plastered with Ponds and curlers in my hair in preparation for the next evening's gala."

As she said this, while still holding onto Starlet, she beamed. That's when Starlet realized that this poor woman had no human touch, her only attention being from the meowing of Baxter and his whining to be petted or from her gardener and the lovely flowers he left on her porch. *It was a humanity thing,* she thought, feeling the woman's bones through her wafer-thin skin. Then Starlet went crazy with missing her mother so much, the way her mom would peck her cheek good-bye as she and her sister left for school, the way she brushed down Starlet's messy hair, smoothing it out after a rough day of play or school or tumbling around in her dream-filled sleep.

She took a hold of Katha's hand in both of hers, leading her to the couch. "Let me tuck you in," she said, as Vegas looked on.

On the way down the steps, Vegas said, "Hey, that was a surprise. She likes you, Starlet. I don't know about letting the others in on her house and her stuff though."

"Oh Vegas, you don't trust anybody. And you're always thinking money: how to make it, how to steal it. Not all life is about money!"

## Chapter 12
## Snatched: Starlet

Starlet and Vegas were on their way back to the squat when she grabbed his sleeve, tugging him down to the grass. "Let's sit," she said.

She chose a spot next to the overrun herb garden and under flowing branches of yellow hibiscus. Its branches arched nearly to the ground, forming a cocoon of flowing leaves and flowers and high grass. Its flowers had closed for the night. Brushing back a branch that was poking into her cheek, Starlet twisted a blossom, and pulled off its petals, one by one. She absently licked them, pasted them on her thighs, their silky petals like cool girlie skin against hers. The air was filled with scents from adjacent oleanders and eucalyptus, along with that of the mottled growth of oregano and parsley.

"Pick me some parsley?" Starlet asked, curling a bit of her hair around her finger.

"Sure," Vegas said, scooping up a handful for her.

Starlet blew away the tiny dirt clods hanging from the roots and chose a long-stemmed piece to place between her lips. She said, "Remember Onge chewing these like toothpicks? When I think of *him*, I really want to go home. I don't know what's safe anymore."

"Me neither."

"Like now, is it better to be in the squat or out here protected by the bushes? It's hard, but hey, I'm strong. I can handle it."

"He was good, that guy. You could call him a hero."

The dim light from the loose back porch bulb flickered as it shined on the off-kilter cement steps and slightly past them, creating an arc of light in the yard of the bungalow.

"This is way private, a hiding place," Starlet said as a siren whined in the distance. No noise could be heard from the squat.

She pushed closer to Vegas, their hips now touching. He jerked a little as she touched him, as though still surprised that she liked him so much. *He's getting skinnier*, she thought.

"How much money you got left?" she asked Vegas.

"Five bucks and some change. You?"

"Twenty-two upstairs and two in my shoe. So, how much for us to get bus tickets back? We'll be safe back with my mom."

"A lot?"

Starlet rolled the petals off her legs, discarding them. She smoothed out her skirt. "My mom despised this skirt – said it was a cheapo-teaser. Whenever I wore it she said I was out for attention, but hey, I like attention, I guess. In class I used to squeeze my thighs together preventing peak shows, but here, everyone hangs out, a lot. Beach girls *and* street girls." She threw a message out there for Vegas without actually telling him what she was thinking, seriously thinking. Pulling at the skimpy skirt fabric, she said, "I did like it, but it's filthy. Gross."

"Starlet, you sure about home? Me going?"

"Yeah. You can crash on the couch. I bet my sister clued Mom in about Ralph because I told her to lock her bedroom door, but I didn't tell all. She kind of guessed he was all over me. I mean, she could see it. He threatened to hurt them if I told all."

"You're worried about her, huh?"

"I told her to damn stay away from him. Go over her friend's house. Call the cops if she had to, but leave Mom out of it."

"Want to call her?"

"I'll call her, but not yet."

"Any jobs near your home?"

"They always hire at the Dome. Concessions and stuff. Photo shops, too. I think Mom was getting suspicious about Ralph, how he hung around us kids, bought us those cheap satin robes. She didn't say anything, but I heard her swearing in the bathroom about the way he hung those nauseating polyester shirts that stunk like him, Old Spice shit, in the tub. Always dripping. You couldn't take a freaking shower without them dripping on you."

"My father smelled like crap. One day I found some of his rubbers in a Band-aid box in our medicine cabinet behind his million colognes. First, I pin-holed them, then I said, "Fuck you," and flushed them down the toilet, purple cellophane wrappers and all."

"Okay, Vegas!" Starlet said, high-fiving him. "Hey, I'm cold."

"Here." He took off his outer black T-shirt, wrapping it around her legs. It smelled bad, but she acted like it didn't.

Around midnight they trudged up the stairs to the squat. After an hour, Starlet was still awake. She bounded out of the sleeping bag, still tired, but her mind was kicking. A zillion times she had forced her eyes closed only to have them burst open again, feeling grainier than ever, as though she'd popped an upper, but she didn't do pills. She had tried taking deep breaths, but couldn't calm down. It was weird because it was only her and Vegas there; the others were out, but still, she was amped up. She had decided: later that day, she and Vegas would take off.


Just the night before she had shimmied up next to Vegas and tried to get some sleep. She finally passed out for an hour or two. She eased her body from Vegas's. His eyes were still closed, his mouth slightly open with the faint tic of a smile. Her hair was a disaster, but she fluffed it up, swished some mouthwash around in her mouth, spit it out the window, and intentionally left her silver jacket so Vegas would know she'd be right back, then she slipped away towards the door.

Starlet turned back, and tiptoeing back to Vegas, she bent down, then kneeled and dropped a kiss on Vegas' forehead, leaving an imprint of apricot gloss in the shape of her lips on his skin, each crease and puff implanted like a fingerprint. Whispering, she said, "I'll be back, my blue boy. We'll dance." She flicked her curls back, brushed aside a stubborn hair that stuck in her lipgloss, squirted perfume behind her ears and down the front of her crotch, and, touching each shoulder to complete the sign of the cross, she headed out.

The air was chilly on her bare legs, causing the soft down on her thighs to stand out from her skin. It was a bitch walking with blisters on her feet, but she had no time to stop. She'd get *it* over with. The plan was to say that she found the money. He might not believe her, but it was the only way she could stay clean in his eyes. She thought, *God, I'm screwed here.*

The corner bench was slicked with heavy dew that glistened in the sunlight. Starlet dried the seat with a discarded *Times* that featured a giant picture of a hottie-star, no older than Starlet, punching out a paparazzi. She laughed at the thought of a size-four chick decking the guy. She sat down, looking at the sunrise, its clouds floating like a pink chiffon dress on the horizon. The office buildings threw long shadows over palm trees along the street. Soaking in the lovely warm sunlight, Starlet swallowed her discomfort. It wasn't so much a physical thing but a screeching loneliness that shook her insides. She tried to overcome it by chanting in a whisper, "I'll be home soon. I'll see Mom soon."

Sure, she was missing her badly. There had been the usual teen flip-outs when she and her sister threw hissy fits for ridiculous reasons, like who took the last tampon. Starlet remembered waking up cranky, fresh for no reason. Acting spoiled. Her mother told her to quit her high-horse princess act and actually told her to shut up. Her mom was in a bitch-mood. Starlet thought it was because she had just received a hang-up call and said it was a telemarketer, but Starlet thought it might have been from her missing dad. Her mom was pretty good most of the time. Starlet recalled neat things about her: the buttered linguini smelling of crushed garlic, the laughter in the kitchen. Pure laughter: that was something she didn't hear a lot of in the squat. She did hear mocking tones and nervous giggles when the tension was hot, but it wasn't a comforting sound.

And now, in LA., it was summertime. The gentle morning breezes were blowing off the ocean. As Starlet wrapped her arms around herself, tucking her hands under her armpits, she realized that Californians didn't know true cold and the fun of snowflakes, especially LA. people but, then, there were always birds singing in the morning and scads of flowers everywhere, in pots hanging off the city street lights with big museum signs, in the tiniest bit of dirt next to sidewalks, in postage-size lots in front and in back of bungalows—behind fences, growing through holes, hanging over.

A lot of folks were loaded; they drove amazing cars, but this early she only saw a few gardeners' trucks rumble by along with delivery trucks heading to coffee shops and markets.

Two small-bodied gray sparrows slept on a wire across the street, so close their wings were touching like linked arms, their heads tucked. A fat crow came from nowhere, swooped down in front of Starlet and started poking madly at a burger wrapper that crackled with each peck. He'd glance up every third or fourth peck to see if she was watching. The sun caught his glistening feathers, shining jolts of turquoise and green on black, as he moved. His eyes darted from his meal back to her. Back home she had seen crows in run-over fields. They gathered in bunches at certain times of the year and plunged onto roofs, squawking. A country bird, he didn't belong in Los Angeles. Some kids didn't either. She didn't expect to see a crow on this day here in a city where sea gulls flew overhead at the beach and quite far into the city. Two gulls flew down, landing six inches from the black bird. From far away they had been stunning laser flashes of white in flight on the sky, but close-up she could see the dirt encrusted on their belly feathers. She recalled the ornery gang of them fighting like young street boys when they swarmed the sidewalk at the beach, yet nothing could mar her memory of that thrilling day. The sun had been warm and she and Vegas decided to take in the crowd at the beach. The two of them could have passed for local kids playing hooky. Now she was alone with her thoughts and her intention of getting cash for the trip home. Even if she was uncomfortable and scared, she knew what she had to do. Maybe it would be easy. She remembered Victoria's warnings, but she had made it through years on the street. Starlet was asking only for this one time and then she'd go home and take Vegas along.

A boy with scarlet hair and spreading toes clamped on his skateboard rattled past Starlet, his music blaring from his headphones. The beat went straight to her body, her head moving, as well as her hips, before her mind registered the sounds of the words. He was ten or twelve years old, she guessed, as the boy glanced at her with a crooked grin and popped a wheelie for her benefit. He bore down, braked and took the curb with a three-quarter turn. She yelled, "You go, boy. Sick!" as he flew down the hill, his body swaying, as though glued to the board, a part of it. A natural-born surfer, she thought, imagining his spiked hair all slicked back, his rubber suit dripping. Although the suit was unzipped down to his crotch and was hanging half off, nearly trailing behind him, she pictured him, deftly swimming in the waves like a shiny black seal, shifting his board out of the sea foam, high on the taste and smell of sea salt, his tingling legs, and his own bitching ride in.

*There was magic in that ocean that washed in treasure every day,* she thought, like the shells she and Vegas found in the sand, the pearly pink one he strung on kite string to make a necklace for her. *My sister would dig the Pacific. From the way she runs track, her long legs reaching out ahead of her, her arms spare and in balance, she'd make it as a surfer girl.* Had she finally got the hang of using mascara without clumping it all over her eyelids and hands? *I could call her. No, not yet.*

Starlet had removed her shoes to examine her blisters when a crazy-long limousine with darkened windows drove a few feet past her, stopped, backed up. She checked it out front to rear. It was probably full of drunken chicks pulling an all-nighter or rock stars heading home from a twenty-four hour taping session, she thought, but still, the windows spooked her. If her mom were there now, she'd say, "Blackened windows are illegal as all get out. You have to watch out. Especially downtown." She'd grab her hand and cross the street, just the same as if she were in Detroit City. She was cautious with her daughters around traffic, in boats, stuff like that, but Starlet had heard that her mom had been a daring kid, having swum the whole width of the lake when she was thirteen.

Mom, young for her age, had hair still thick and shiny.

The limo had parked; its engine was quiet, its headlights off. Leaning forward, Starlet cautiously peered from her place on the bench into the windows. It was impossible to see who sat inside. She was about to split when the driver jumped out, ran around the front of the vehicle, and stood within three feet of her. He was near enough for her to see his bulging eyes and his gut, a steel drum the size of a barrel. He wore a flack jacket too small to be zipped. He stood, his hands on his hips, glaring directly at her—as though she was a doe and he was beading on game. For a quirky second she focused on his ears that flopped out ridiculously beneath the rim of his chauffer cap.

Barely moving her torso, she reached down to grab her shoes. She inched up, one vertebrae at a time, and then took off, running and then she heard, "Hold up, you're coming with me."

"No," she said. *Danger. Snake-Bastard.*

Even as this was happening, Starlet thought she could escape, out-run him. Then wham, he tackled her. The man's arms were locked around her, his muscles hard against her body. She flung her mouth at his ear lobe. Catching the slightest bit of soft flesh in her mouth, she bit down.

"Bitch," he roared, loosening one arm to brush her away from him. Her body lurched forward. Her knees banged hard on the cement, the skin shredding open. She thought she heard one of them crack, like a bone was breaking.

"Help," she screamed. "Help me, somebody."

The back door of the limo swung open. Starlet punched at the driver's belly, as he carried her towards the door. *Fucker.* She scratched at his rough bumpy neck. She could feel his fingers digging into her sides. Her bare feet were bicycling in the air, her hips scrambling, as her skirt hiked up to her waist. She knew she was fighting hard, but he was too tough. *Too strong. Too strong. Too damn strong.* Heaving her body inside the back of the limo, he then snatched each foot she was kicking, and nearly caught them in the door as he slammed it shut.

## Chapter 13
## Search: Vegas and Green

That night Starlet and Vegas lay together, their skinny legs entwined like roots of a willow, on top of the sleeping bag where a few grains of sand had worked their way loose and imbedded in his elbow. He brushed them off, leaving tiny pockmarks. A light breeze drifted in from the open ceiling window. The night was clear with a huge, low-hanging moon. It reminded him of the quiet desert sky at home.

Sometime in the early morning hours, Vegas awakened from his dream. His body was hot and sweaty; he anxiously tried to recall the details of his dream. There had been a woman wearing a dress in a lush blue color similar to that of his blue dress. Her rich-lady thick pageboy appeared freshly washed; it swished as she moved, a wisp of it sticking to her cheek. The fragrance of gardenias surrounded her shoulders.

It might have been the same woman he met at the chapel who caught him bold-facedly robbing the place. He'd been hunched over to hide, but when he stood up to bolt, she looked directly at him yet never spoke. Was she frozen with fear? He hadn't known she would be in the suite – tourists rarely were: he hadn't known after he had taken the photos of her wedding that later he would bump into her again. And, strangest of all, he hadn't planned to steal her blue dress that was to become his symbol of freedom.

As truth mixed with imagination, Vegas sorted out memory and dream. Here he was in California, flinty memories caught up where the woman was faceless, eyes floating above her head. They had followed him. His stomach lurched, a rope of guilt around his gut tightened.

She sat across from him in a rowboat slicked with yellow paint. He said, "Don't mother me." The scissors in her hand were enormous. They made a loud chopping sound, as they feathered the hem of the dress, pieces flying in the offshore breeze. She stood, and slithered out of the dress. He slammed his eyes shut. *Naked.* He couldn't look but imagined the small rise of her soft belly that had molded the shape of the garment and the hollows of her armpits in the sleeveless dress. He gathered up the pieces that lay across the insteps of her feet, but the blue color was still undulating around her legs.

Vegas now dug his sharp knuckles into his eye sockets. He sat up, focusing on the rough-hewn ceiling of the cramped room where he had slept. The foggy dream had passed. "Starlet," he whispered, reaching for her. He flipped his thin hips over, expecting to feel Starlet's body warmth against him. "Starlet?" His hands moved in a furious search of the sleeping bag. "Starlet. Hey, Starlet," he croaked. His mouth dry, he tasted panic. *She's gone.*

The last thing he wanted to do was to wake up Green. He braced himself for her onslaught. *Wait.* Rising quietly, he stepped carefully, easing around Green's and Pepper's bodies. He stood on his toes, trying to peer out the window. Starlet might be using the garden hose to wash up. He saw nothing — he heard nothing, no swish of water. There was only the thick breathing from Green's mouth and Pepper's sputtering snore and a motorcycle racing down the alleyway.

Vegas' lower back ached, especially his tailbone; he inched his fingers along the bumps on his spine. *Yes, he was getting skinnier, just as Starlet had said. There was barely an inch of flesh padding his bones.* He approached Green and tapped her lightly on her left foot.

"Get up. Hurry," he whispered.

"Huh?" she answered, without opening her eyes.

"It's Starlet," he said, leaning within inches of Green's face. "She's gone."

Green threw her arm up, catching her forearm under his chin and against his Adam's apple, shoving him back. "Quit breathing on me. What?"

"Starlet's gone!"

"What? Gone? Maybe she went to get a donut or something."

"You don't get it. We had plans."

"I thought you were watching her. Freaking loser!"

"I know, but…

"But, shit."

"Come on, Green," Vegas pleaded, his face tweaking up.

"You know a freak was following her."

"Alright. Alright. Hold up," she said, scowling and buttoning her shirt. She was moving fast now, tying her boots and sloshing water from a bottle on her face. "You know, Lily left me. Just because a girl acts cool doesn't mean she won't split."

"Let's go, Green. Hurry up!" Vegas said, his stomach in a ball, his heart beating. He rolled the sleeping bag, unrolled it, shook it out, rolled it again, folded and refolded Starlet's jacket, mumbling, "Got to find her. Got to find her."

Once down the stairs and out in the yard Vegas ran around ducking under bushes, circling the house and garage with Green following him. Dawn had broken, the smog lifting, yet it layered above the tallest buildings and trees. Satisfied Starlet wasn't nearby, they hunched under the fence. As though Vegas knew where to look, he took off, glancing back to make sure he had hadn't lost Green in his haste. He nearly tripped on a homeless man, whose legs spread out on the sidewalk. Curled against a picket fence overgrown with nasturtiums, his face appeared filthy-brown against the bright yellow and orange flowers. His swollen feet were the color of ashes, as though he'd tread through them.

"Watch it," the man uttered.

"Pitiful, man. In the toilet," Vegas said.

Ten minutes later they reached the diner where they heard cracking and clunking sounds seeming to come from the alley. They stopped and proceeded with caution. A bare-footed boy, about eleven, was heaving rocks against the metal roof and watching them bang their way down.

"Get out of here," Green screeched at him. "Get lost!"

The boy crouched, picked up a loose hunk of black asphalt and shot a teasing expression at Green. He wound up and let go, popping one of the letters in the blinking, neon sign. "Jeronimo," he called and hopped over the back fence.

"Dummy!" Green bellowed after him, as she scouted around, lifting the lid to the dumpster.

"She ain't here, Green. Come on, screw it, she ain't here! She wouldn't eat trash," Vegas said, kicking a green container against the wall. He picked up a tin can
and heaved it up on the roof. Vegas and Green watched as it clanged its way down and clunked on the asphalt sidewalk.

Green stepped up in front of Vegas, her hands on her hips, "Face it, she split—without you."

"No, she didn't!" Vegas said, hating Green right then. "She left her jacket – she wouldn't have done that if she was taking off!"

"She don't need you hanging on her."

"No, no, no, you're wrong," he insisted.

"I doubt it, but what about cash? Did she have any?"

"Not much. But check this," Vegas said, lifting his shirt to reveal a gold chain tied with rope around his waist. His indented skin had taken on the serpentine shape of the chain. "I never showed Starlet. Hockshop on Third will see me beaucoup bucks with this, I bet."

"Big frigging deal, Vegas. Your timing is off," Green said.

Ignoring her, Vegas moved to the steps where he dug into one of the cardboard cartons from early morning delivery. He scored a giant package of muffins, tore open the saran wrap and stuffed one in his mouth. He tossed one to Green.

"Got it," she said, with her mouth already bulging.

Just then, Gonzales, the cook, leaned his head out the screened back door. "Hey you!" he shouted, holding the door with his hip and wiping tomato sauce on his apron.

He and Vegas stood eye to eye, and Vegas thought he spied a quick grin flash across Gonzales's face, as he shook his head, his black hair shifting over his ears. The Mexican was known to have a soft heart when it came to runaways, handing them hot beef tacos and coffee. *He knows hunger—first hand.*

"Sorry, we're leaving," Green said, gesturing with her thumb up. "We chased a trouble-maker out of here. You heard him, right?" Green asked, "And the rocks on the roof?"

"I heard it. Okay. No problem," Gonzales said. He turned and went back inside, the door banging behind him.

They scurried back to the front of the diner while swiping crumbs from their mouths. Above, the neon sign blinked in semi-broken letters; it cast a greenish glow onto the metal. The loose railing wobbled when Vegas grabbed it as he rushed up the freshly swept steps. Fissures in the cement had trapped sand, a skinny pen, and a green wad of gum.

## Chapter 14
## Party Day: The Whole Gang

Joe-Mack, located about ten hours out from Los Angeles, came up on puffs of blue-white fog, whimsical in its flight across his dash in the early light of day. It quickly turned to a heavy layer, a gray ghost too stubborn to move — the kind that taunts a driver to cut through it. Joe-Mack's truck sliced through wafts of air split aside by the yellow fog lamps. He glanced down at the Jersey barrier and the road under him, using instinct to perceive distance. When he considered pulling over, the fog lifted, and, within a mile, socked in again. *Same old game. Fading fast here. Coffee break coming up...*

Exiting and rerouted due to construction to nowhere, Joe-Mack rumbled along a two-laner, an old road that existed before the freeway he assumed. The ping-ping and twanging noise in the engine could be the result of his imagination working overtime or the ruts in the road causing havoc. Once he maneuvered quickly into a dry-dirt parking area of a one-horse stop, raising billows of dust from his rear tires; he hopped out, rubbed his sweaty palms against the side of his jeans and peered under the cab to see if anything was hanging. As he straightened up, stretching his stiff spine, the sun burst through the sky.

Heading into the building, he noticed two small, barefooted children playing with industrial-sized coffee cans in a sand pile. The girl, petite enough to fit in a baby swing had brown eyes that took over her whole face; she shifted sand from one can to the other. The grainy trail, sparkling like copper, mesmerized her. A light layer of dust shimmered across her loosely parted hair that hung to her teeny waist. As he watched them, the boy spoke, "Hey mister."

"Hi buddy," Joe-Mack said, grinning at the kids.

"You, a trucker?" the boy asked, pointing to Joe-Mack's long-haul. "That big one."

"Yup."

"You a cowboy trucker?" he asked, as the little sister glanced up.

"You could say that, son."

"Papi say cowboy, no horse."

"You got that, buddy. I'm riding that hunk of steel over there," Joe-Mack said. "Hey, have fun, you two."

Once inside, he swung up on one of the six dilapidated counter seats. A thirtyish-looking woman adjusted the coffee maker, spilling grounds on the counter. She scooped them along the edge of the counter into her hand and back into the filter. Turning to him, she asked, "You want help?"

"Yes, coffee and a burrito please."

"You want cheese and beans or only beans."

"Don't matter. Whatever you got."

"Sure," she said, smiling and swiping the area in front of him with a rag. Her breasts swayed with her movements under a flowered blouse tucked into a long man's apron. Joe-Mack conjured up deep rose nipples under that blouse. She caught his stare and turned her face away.

"Excuse me," he said, "Those your kids outside? Cute little buttons."

"Good ones, my Raimundo and Rachel. Twins."

"Wow, I didn't know that."

"Raimundo come first. Big brother."

Joe-Mack hustled down the food and coffee, used the john and paid for two Snickers on his way out. He tossed the candy at the children; they tore the paper off and had their mouths full in a quick second.

"Bye, cowboy," Raimundo said.

Joe-Mack yelled back, "Be good to your sister, little guy." He waved from inside the truck and pumped a rat-a-tat-tat on his horn. Not hungry, yet an empty feeling filled his gut.

Word had it that certain drawbacks to over-the-road gigs in California stumped newly minted truckers. The laws were quirky; the fines were out of sight, the courts were full on a daily basis, and the lights were set to bust them. A trucker's ass-end could hardly make it through a yellow when bang, the red flashed. Still, Joe-Mack liked the mix of terrains, the hick towns in the desert and the cities, crammed with a tremendous mix of outsiders drawn to the La La Land mystique. They added to the excitement and struggles, the synergy, all within spitting distance of each other.

Five hours out now, Joe-Mack floored the pedal, bounding in and out of the passing lane, rushing for no good reason. Guilty thoughts filled his head. He again questioned his desertion, his ditching Lucille, his purposeless life. Frenchy gone, he'd lost his best friend. Miffed, and trying to escape his inner voice, its condemnations, he allowed a billboard to beckon him. Swerving ahead to catch the exit, he took the cutoff and wheeled into the parking lot. *A few pops won't hurt.* Inching in between a shiny BMW and a Honda with gray Bondo patches in the shapes of clouds plastered over it, he turned off the engine, combed his hair with his fingers and placed his cap back on. Approaching the scarred wooden door, he recognized the White Fence gang tags surrounded by bold strokes of graffiti. Stale booze and musty perfume smells met him inside the tunnel-like passageway as he angled through a tangled, beaded curtain. *Man, a lot of hurt passed through this place.*

A young thing with piled-on make-up and spike heels jockeyed up to him, ready to escort him. "This way?" she asked, pointing to a rear booth.

"Naw, I'll hit the bar, thanks," Joe-Mack said, noticing the intentional sway of her slight hips as she moved while balancing a tray of drinks over her shoulder. *Fresh on the job.* The cherries he yanked from the bartender's stash and popped in his mouth were red yet sour-tasting.

"Becca," the barkeep yelled to another chick bending over a nearby table; her lace undies flashing beneath a skimpy skirt that floated on her pelvic bones. "She'll serve you," he said, fiddling with the cufflinks on his overly starched white shirt.

"Whiskey neat," Joe-Mack ordered, twirling on the seat, his eyes at the level of Becca's breasts that pumped out of her satin weskit.

"Double?" Becca asked. "Thirty-two fifty."

"Holy, I didn't want the whole damn bottle, but here," Joe-Mack said, handing her a hundred dollar bill. "Hang on to this. I ain't done yet, Sister."

Two young men with fresh buzz-cuts sat around the curve of the bar slamming shooters, sucking limes. *Amateurs.* An old guy with hangdog earlobes hunched over four beers, slurping from each one intermittently. A couple of senior ding-dongs sat in the booth nearest the restrooms. The woman read from a New Yorker magazine under the dim lighting, gumming her personal size bag of pretzels and sipping pink martinis. The old gent used opera binoculars to eyeball the waitresses as they passed by.

Two fireman poles stood opposite each other on the stage that ran parallel to the bar seats. A heavy beat of Credence Clearwater's *Proud Mary* pulsed through giant speakers, nearly shaking the establishment off its hinges. Joe-Mack signaled Becca for a refill. The jerks down the way pounded the lacquered bar, missing the beat by a mile. The taller fellow ripped off his tie and swung it in circles above his head, hooting, "T and A, T and A, T and A."

"Jesus H. Christ," Joe-Mack said.

The lights lowered; a spotlight shone on the curtain. As the Orphan Annie dancer pranced out, the shorter guy yelled, "Over here, Baby!" and lapped the air like a dog. The young girl shimmed in white knees socks that reached up to her shiny kneecaps. She wandered around the stage three times, flipped over into a handstand with her legs split in the air and held herself there. After landing back on her feet, she continued slithering and shaking as she stripped off her skirt and schoolgirl blouse. She ended up on her hands and knees with her fanny wagging, revealing two tattoos on her cheeks as big as apples. Joe-Mack whistled. "Those babies must have smarted."

"Another round?" Becca asked.

"What's the deal? The bartender keeping his shirt clean for a big date or what?" Joe-Mack asked, emptying his glass.

"No. We make more tips. Split with him. You know."

"Sure, I know, Cutie."

The next three acts blurred by. Joe-Mack downed more booze. He rolled a hundred around a toothpick, stabbed a cherry with it and handed it to Becca. She ate the cherry off the end and giggled as she pocketed the cash. "I'm toast," he said, laughing at his own humor. "I'm out of here."

Out in the alley in the afternoon sun Joe-Mack caught sight of Orphan Annie, still with red painted circles on her face and freckles dotted across her nose, shuffling around with a big dobie of a guy against the cinderblock wall. His hands cupped the girl's head, pushing it down towards his open fly.

Joe-Mack's stomach turned. *The kid probably needs the money for food, her mom in a wheelchair, for drugs, for her kids who sleep in a shitcan car.*

"Crap," he said, reeling against his cab, "she doesn't know how bad her life is. She's stepping in it." *Me, my hero days are over.*


The night after Katha met Vegas and Starlet, she hardly slept. Although she didn't care to admit it, she'd been battling loneliness and damn confusion for some time, left with weakening memories that flitted in and out like butterflies. It would not be an easy task preparing for party day at the diner, yet the challenge revved her up. She rose carefully, desperately babying her left knee that had been buckling on her of late. Her thoughts ran to her new student, Starlet, who, with a bit of craft training and special attention to lips and brows, could become something special. Although Meg Ryan and other young gals had started their path on the soaps, Katha wanted her ingénue to work directly in film.

Starlet's dream of starring in film touched Katha. It had been her dream decades before; however, society had changed and frightful business deals twisted the hearts of artists. Gone were the days when the gut of the audience was drawn in by story and sheer beauty and romance. Katha had been around a long time, collecting tidbits regarding sordid affairs, smutty photographs, and family messes. *It would be quite possible to write a book,* she thought, *yet some matters should remain untold.* As her mother would emphatically state, "Some things should go to the grave."

Now Simon tickled his mistress' leg. "Shush, shush," she said, yet he continued to wind around her and meow. She reached down to scratch the top of his head, musing, "How romantic. Those vagabond children have found me and that old car." Then, as he shoved against her with force, she remembered the cat dish. After filling it, she paused on the loveseat. *If that car could talk. Oh my.*

The road trips back in the day had been frightfully exciting. Katha accompanied Blake up Pacific Coast Highway along the spectacular coastline with its splitting precipices, crashing waves, all with the Cabriolet's top down, and the wind swirling. A newspaper triangle dangled over her nose held on by her sunglasses as well as a lovely straw bonnet that flew back in the breezes, refusing to protect her skin from the sun' rays. *Blake drank from a Tiffany flask. The show-off. He handed it to me; I caressed the delicate etchings, and, as I did so, I teased Blake about sleeping arrangements at the castle. It was all before his tryst.*

It would be impossible for Katha to forget her first overnight party. The lady guests had been provided with billowy chiffon togas and the men were given nude-colored suede loincloths. The pool's cobalt blue tiles entwined with eighteen-karat gold designs provided a perfect backdrop for glamour girls and leading men.

*Today, however, the gathering would call for pearls and diamonds,* Katha thought. It wouldn't be a grand venue, but she would put her best foot forward. She dressed and packed four stemware glasses in a plastic bag, and then adjusted her hat at a flirtatious angle. Once down the hill and inside the diner, she noticed that she was the first to arrive.

She passed her usual stool and stopped to gather her breath, placing her hand on the bronze cash register, and there she bid the cook good day. Slyly, she glanced at the painting that hung high on the wall to the left of the fry stove. It occurred to her the image of herself might elicit conversation with Starlet regarding her glory days. She continued on to the last booth and placed her things down on the table. When, at last, she eased onto the leather seat, she reached for the hem of her skirt with both hands and fanned her hot legs with the material.

The cook, Gonzales, brought her water, and said, "Good Morning, Missus. Tea? Eggs?"

"Not quite yet, Mr. Gonzales. Thank you kindly. I must wait for my guests," she answered, beaming.


Seemingly, only a few minutes later, Vegas blasted in the door of the diner. "You see Starlet?" he asked Gonzales. "You know, the blond I come in here with."

Gonzales continued slicing onions; the air filled with a spicy stench, and he shook his head no. Vegas cased the place. In the last booth Katha sat alone, wearing a goofball hat, that Starlet might have liked. He rushed up to her. "Hey, did you see Starlet?" he questioned.

She appeared not to hear him. Looking up with a startled, squirrelly expression, she cupped her ear. "Oh, Vegas, it's you. Beg your pardon," she said.

"Starlet," he yelled, bending down closer to her. "Starlet! She here?"

"Why no."

Vegas slid in across from her. "She's gone. Missing."

Reaching for a napkin from the dispenser, Katha folded it, and refolded it. "Naughty Starlet," she said, looking befuddled. "She's tardy. Naughty girl!" Looking up, she noticed Green who was standing next to Vegas. "Who is this?"

"That's Green," Vegas said.

She fixed on Green's hair, blinking. "So I see," she said, and then suddenly she glanced down at her ring finger. "Oh dear me, it is gone. My opal. Have you seen it, Simon? Oh no, my goodness, you're Vegas. I'm so confused these days. Names, names, names: so baffling."

"I'll find it," Vegas said, glancing around the booth and looking in the bag she had brought. Green got down on her hands and knees and peered under the table and came up with it. She placed it in on Katha's wobbling finger.

"Oh, oh Lord." Katha said, sighing. "Thank you. I must keep track of my jewels. Losing things is a bad sign. I'm afraid I'm having a dizzy spell," she said, her voice tremulous. "May I have a glass of juice, please?"

"Sure, I'll get it," Green said, and headed over to the counter. Katha perked up and made a clucking sound while eyeing Green's dingy men's trousers.


Joe-Mack had been driving in a fuzzy state after he parked his truck and rented a big-ass Lincoln. He tooled around the Santa Monica beach area, stopping finally at the Venice Beach parking lot to sleep off his liquor buzz in the car. He wasn't going back to work for a week no matter what, even though his phone had vibrated all morning. The company and Lucille, who'd been leaving messages for him for two weeks steady, could both take a hike. The sun beamed through the front window of the vehicle, waking him up; he rubbed his crusty eyes, and then curiosity got the best of him and he listened to the backed-up messages. He was surprised and not surprised when he heard Freddie's voice. The kid had garbled on about his plan to leave California, hitching a ride, maybe from Joe-Mack. But things were screwed up. He needed help now!

His mid-day headache from the bender pissed him off. The Alka sat in his glove in the rig doing him no damn good at all. He didn't feel like stopping as he headed up Lincoln to Olympic to Fairfax. Once in Hollywood, he stopped at a convenience store and bought a breakfast burrito and a can of beer and Excedrin. The air outside, steaming from the asphalt, quivered in the sunshine. *Another hot one.* Joe-Mack popped the beer, and considered where Freddie might be: the shelters, the streets, jail. There was no way to reach him by phone, but he listened to the message again. He was definitely asking for help. The shelter on La Cienega he swung by was closed up tight for the daylight hours. He drove a big loop around the streets where kids congregated on corners and in alleyways. *No dice.* Okay, last place he saw him was the diner. *That's it, last chance Charlie here.* The same parking lot he had used when he dropped off the kid had space for his big-boat vehicle.

"May be a while," he told the attendant, who wore a USC sweatshirt, but his matted hair and mud-tinged shoes hinted that he might have crossed the border recently. "Here's fifty. That ought to do it. Keep an eye on this turkey," he said, gesturing towards the car. Then, he rolled off a twenty. "For your trouble," he said.

The guy smiled, rather reluctantly.

What the Christ am I doing? Joe-Mack thought. *Wild goose chase here.* After he entered the diner, it only took a minute for him to scope out the motley bunch in the last booth. *There he is.* Freddie sat across from an old woman, all gussied up in a hat, and next to a space-y looking chick with a mass of green hair.

Joe-Mack moved quietly up to Freddie where he could smell the kid's body odor. When Freddie turned his head and saw Joe-Mack standing next to the table, the skin on his face flushed red with blotchy white spots. He leapt up, scrambled out of the booth, shouting, "Holy shit! Wow, it's you! Jesus, I can't believe it!" He reached out for the trucker, kind of stumbling into him.

"Yeah, it's me, Kid, one to a box, huh?" Joe-Mack said, with a wry smile on his face. He reached out to shake the boy's jerking hand. "I got your message. What's happening?"

"I'm all jammed up," Vegas said.

"I get that," Joe-Mack said, his eyes shifting to the people at the table.

Vegas said, "That's Green there, and the lady is Mrs. Willis."

Joe-Mack offered a quick hello to the group and suggested that Freddie step outside where they could talk privately. He turned, expecting the boy to follow, and he did.

As they stood in front of the diner, Vegas, in the midst of the noise from the traffic, bungled through his story: how he'd lived in a squat, how he made a friend, and how she disappeared.

Joe-Mack looked him up and down. "You okay, Freddie?" he inquired, shifting his cap on and off with one hand and holding his coffee mug with the other.

"I'm Vegas," he blurted out. "I go by Vegas." As Joe-Mack searched his face and eyed his miserably beat-up clothing, loose on his bony frame, the kid yanked his sleeve down to cover his tattoo.

"Tattoo? Waste of money if you ask me, but look, it's no big deal, Vegas. Tell me about your friend."

"Me and her were close, you know. It's like this — we were leaving, see. I even thought we could borrow some cash from you, I mean… or a hitch home, but boom, just like that, she's gone," he said, snapping his fingers. His words spun out with barely a breath between. "Like, she disappeared. I'm freaking."

"Simmer down," Joe-Mack said, easing onto the top step and patting the space beside him. "How did all this come about?"

Vegas sat down. "After you dropped me, I hung out. I got mugged. Then, I slept under this crumby bridge with birds screaming all night, then I met Green. She took me to the squat. Starlet was there. Me and her were tight."

"How do you know she's in danger? Maybe she ran away?"

"No, no, she wouldn't." Vegas said, explaining that someone stalked her before.

"Specifics, Vegas. You're shook up, but give me something to go on."

"We were splitting Hollywood today."

"We're beyond that now. Have you searched?"

"Yup."

"You starved?" Joe-Mack asked, pinching Vegas' pitifully thin arm. You're emaciated, kid. Let's get you some food."

"No. I had a muffin this morning."

"Okay, but listen buddy, we're wasting time here. Let's get down to brass tacks."

"What?"

"We go back to where you met her. Shadow her days. Post haste."

"Huh?"

"Fast! Like yesterday!"

"Got it," Vegas said, after hearing Joe-Mack's harsh retort. He knew he'd better hustle, and, although this guy had been good to him, he was reminded Joe-Mack was the adult here, the one who had the smarts. The situation with Starlet missing was his fault. *Dumb fuck.* He was to blame. Letting her go off on her own. He had an idea what she was up to but couldn't bring himself to believe that she'd actually hustle guys for money. He'd find her. He had to.

He jolted off, half-cocked, when Joe-Mack grabbed him by the elbow. "Wait buster, get a grip. Go tell your people in there to stay put in case the girl shows up and then, you take me to the last place you saw her."

"The squat?"

"Yes, pronto."

## Chapter 15
## Common Ground: Joe-Mack and Vegas

After the ten-minute hike up the hill, Vegas stopped short in front of Katha's house, glanced up and down the street, and gestured for Joe-Mack to follow him to the side fence area. His eyes darted as he snapped his head left to right, as though he was on alert back in his hometown, Las Vegas. He lifted the twisted section of the wire fence, motioning his companion to step through.

"Wait," Joe-Mack, cautioned. "You sure about this?"

"No worries."

"Who owns this place?"

"The old lady – Mrs. Willis. She can't see worth shit."

"Look Vegas, don't be a pain in the ass. Learn some respect!"

"Uh, sorry, didn't mean it."

The houses they had passed on the street had been built in the same era as the bungalow they were now facing. Potted herbs and yellow daisies, tricycles and Tonka trucks crowded wooden-slat porches. Miniscule yards with lawn chairs tucked next to bougainvillea bushes and occasional swing sets surrounded the buildings. A few more recently built, box-shaped homes with second and third floors used up nearly every inch of their lots with barely room for a sidewalk in front. They were sprinkled with glass blocks and turrets and the lines of their roofs were much taller than the thirties bungalows.

The neighborhood had a daytime-quiet about it: blurred sounds of rapid-speaking voices on Spanish TV, the rapping-tapping of hammers on construction sights of remodels, and a baby crying. This particular area was unfamiliar to Joe-Mack. He'd read about old-time Hollywood, Bette Davis and Nancy Davis, who had married Ronnie Regan, and the Black Dahlia myth, but this was a side of the city he'd never personally perused. Now, he inhaled the scent of flowering bushes near a bungalow set back with privacy attained by a fence and overgrowth. It appeared a gardener left the tall greenery alone while tending to a patch of grass and symmetrical plantings near the porch.

Joe-Mack followed Vegas under the break in the fence, through the yard, and in the window into the interior of the garage. Right away he spotted the vehicle. "What's the deal with the antique car?"

"Not much, except Onge was mad for her."

"Her?"

"Yeah," Vegas said, slapping the side of the hood. "He named her Leontine. We all had street names"

"Yes, but, a car? That's ridiculous!"

"Not to him. Onge was cool with it. Look here," Vegas said. "Some rat-bastard scooped the hood ornament. Never would have happened if Onge was alive."

"Tell me about him?"

"He bossed us."

"A gang leader?"

"Nah. He took charge. Kept a lid on. Before he took the pipe," Vegas said, his chin dropping, looking aside to avoid Joe-Mack's eyes.

Before Joe-Mack could inquire about Onge's death, Vegas cut up the stairs. Joe-Mack had heard about places where homeless youngsters hung out, but he had never seen one. Long ago he volunteered with youngsters; they were down and out, but they all had homes, of sorts, even if their houses and apartments were wrecked-out and crowded with losers.

He tailed Vegas, thinking twice about his decision to look up this nut-ball. It was preposterous to think that the boy was only slightly older than his first daughter would be. What was it about Vegas that compelled Joe-Mack to find him? Was it the uncertainty behind his damp lonely eyes, the false bravado in his loser black clothing and safety-pin necklace? Was it his own need to salvage a thread of dignity in his soul that had gone sour?

"What about the owner?" Joe-Mack asked, grabbing Vegas's elbow as they stood on the second floor landing that squeaked under their movements.

"The woman at the diner. Remember her?" Vegas answered. "No worries."

"What's her story?" Joe-Mack asked, still holding his grip on Vegas. "Is she aware you people are squatting?"

"Like I said, no worries. She's ga-ga over Starlet," Vegas said, and then he told how he and Starlet were invited into her house. The old lady wants to teach Starlet acting. Starlet digs the idea."

"That's a little hard to fathom, Vegas. Wouldn't she be wary of strangers, especially a bunch of ragtaggers?"

"Nope. She wasn't scared of us," Vegas said, circling his finger round and round the air near his ear. "Space-cadet, but she and Starlet got on big time." he said, shoving the door open, then he shrank back. "Yuck, it's fucking putrid in here."

Joe-Mack stepped past him into the tight space. "You're not kidding. Whew," he said, but watch it with the f-bomb. Where's everybody?"

"Beats me," Vegas answered, shimmying by Joe-Mack and thrusting trash aside with his foot.

The scent of candle wax, the tug of perspiration and grime, and the stench of leftover fast food and pot smoke permeated the air. Vestiges of belongings sat in different areas — not much individual stuff, as though the kids had set up camp and could break it down in a flash. A stepladder sat in the open space in the middle. Some of the books piled high under it had library white numbers squiggled along their spines. Joe-Mack opened a copy of *Roman Architecture* that was stamped "Hollywood Public Library, State of Florida." Another new paperback with its slick cover still shiny, *Chinatown, Revisited*, had Oren B. Brown scrawled on the title page, as if he wanted the author to know he was reading it. As Joe-Mack fanned through the pages, an orange peel with a hint of citrus scent spilled out.

The squat was unbearably small, the size of a guest bedroom in a tract home, but he could sense how the kids could feel safe there. It had a peculiar likeness to a dormitory without rich-kid electronic trappings. There was one scummy tufted armchair, the sort left out on porches, and a filmy gauze bedspread draped over a box with nail polishes in silver, black, and red lined along the top. Joe-Mack questioned how the kids found this place. He was told that Onge made the original discovery and got the word out he'd take on kids.

"Are these kids druggies?" Joe-Mack asked.

"No. Onge was down heavy on use."

Joe-Mack learned there were rules in the squat. No drugs were allowed inside the squat. Starlet was clean, but Vegas wasn't sure about Green and Pepper, the chick from Chicago who got dumped by her boyfriend, and John-John, whose family had money up ass. It was clear that Onge had a sweet spot for Starlet — the way he'd wink when he spoke to her.

"Pepper was drugged up good or coming down when I met her; she was wasted. I heard John-John was hooked on white stuff up his nose. You might be thinking that Onge was all good. Not really. He used to nip whiskey every morning when he went down to clean up under the hose, but with us, he lay down laws. 'No pills, no booze, no sex. Go outside to get your needs on, come back clean.'"

Joe-Mack held his open palm up in front of his mouth, breathed on it, and sniffed in the stale liquor odor. *Christ. I should give it up. The juice is killing me.* It occurred to him that all the men in Vegas's life were on the sauce: his drunk-ass father, this Onge fellow, and, if he would come clean and admit it, he hit it heavy himself. He'd always told Frenchy he could put it down, but he never had. He prided himself in the fact that he wasn't a mean drunk except when he kicked Lucille's cat and, Jesus, the damn cat wasn't to blame for her whining.

Vegas opened the cooler. "Rank!" he said, coughing and slamming it shut. He grabbed a chewed up broom and started sweeping. "Starlet used to sweep. She'd hate this."

*The old story of an innocent attempting to sweep some order into a place, but she could have been a mess, and Vegas couldn't see it,* Joe-Mack thought.

Vegas scooped up trash with his hands, and then he scored a section of cardboard from a pizza box. Using it as a dustpan, he shoved wrappers, soda cans, and old tee shirts that stunk of sweat and booze, and emptied it into a pile of junk to the left of the door. He rolled up a shag rug littered with the remnants of a take-out meal and glanced over his shoulder at Joe-Mack for approval.

.    "Did the girl have money? Enough to leave town?" Joe-Mack asked.

"Yeah, she had a little, but not enough to split. She wanted a job, that's how it was"

"How about run-ins with the cops?"

"Me and Starlet, no, but there's always shit going on: John-John was busted for rolling guys, Pepper dinged for shop-lifting. I mean, come on? The Gap? They tag kids at Bev Center. Anybody knows that."

"So you know it all, a regular wise-acre?"

"Nah," Vegas answered, scratching at the blush crawling up the side of his neck. "But, I keep my eyes open. The *authority* ignored us. If they paid attention, they might have to dig down and help out, you know. Hollywood is flush with invisible kids."

"She's not here, Vegas. I need clues," Joe-Mack said. "Where did you kids spend your time?"

"Around here, and Venice one day. You know Venice, don't you?"

"Venice, oh sure, full of whackos."

"I know, how cool is that!"

"If you say so."

"I mean, insane," Vegas said, his face lighting up. "Starlet and I bussed it there, then we walked past the Erwin Hotel, wishing we could crawl into a clean bed. Standing on the Pier, the ocean smells like salt. There's artsy freaks, run-down apartments, luxury hotels — all jammed in together. Starlet bought a pair of movie star sunglasses. Two bucks. The humongous white frames hid half her face, and then we got churros from this old Mexican lady. She tells us twenty-five cents and hands us the two biggest ones. A bitching day, man. Super hot, not sweat-hot like home. We ditched our shoes.

Waded along the water's edge. All of a sudden, Starlet sees this pack of dolphins and goes wild. 'I'm swimming with them. I always wanted to,' she says."

Vegas is over-handing his arms here in great swoops like he's swimming. "I say, 'No, don't,' but she unbuttons her shirt, drops it in the sand. Off comes her shirk, her panties flashing white, she wades through the shallow incoming waves. The water's past her knees, her thighs, and she's pushing hard, heavy water against her, and it's level with her waist when I see a spectacular wave, like tidal, sweeping towards her. Quick, she dives under the cap of it just before it crashes and I'm looking killer-hard. I feel like my eyes are failing me, and maybe it's only one minute, and finally, I see her head pop up like a seal, her hair all matted down. She bobs up and down with the flow of the water around her, getting closer to the surfers on long boards. I mean what's the deal with them passing up that huge one, but three dudes are still out there with her. Their timing must have been off, missing a monster ride like that. She's getting closer to them when one points out the dolphins to the others. Looks like they're having a conversation, but Starlet, she's heading out further — nearer the fish. Their bodies, like mirrors, sun glinting off them. The surfers must think *big fucking deal*. They're straddling their boards, vegging until the next set. Starlet's swimming, looking pretty first-rate, still shooting for her dream of swimming with the dolphins."

"Was she alright?"

Joe-Mack watched as the memory roils up in Vegas's head, his face comes alive, he gestures madly, and demonstrating the giant movement of the waves, even wraps his arms together in front of him as though holding Starlet. He's found his purpose.

"Yeah. I'm yelling her in, the lifeguard's down where the waves are foaming. He's hopping over easy ones, moving out, blowing his whistle, but he's in slow motion. He starts paddling. I'm freaking worried. She ignores us. I'm thinking, mother, she's going to drown. The lifeguard heaves his rope and buoy. It takes him a freaking long time to get to her, but he does, and hauls her in like she's a rag doll, before she can reach the dolphins. *She was so close.*

"He gets to the shallow part. I wade in up to my knees, but the kid shoves me a backhand, killing my collarbone. Starlet's dragged in, her knees buckling under her. He plops her on the beach on her back. Her ribs stick out and I think she's hungry, but then I feel stupid to think that cause she could die. Her lips are purple, blue on top of pink. Her eyes are closed but she's moving her lips. I imagine her saying, 'Let me. Let me go. I want to touch the big one and the baby, the baby dolphin.' She opens her eyes. After puking up a ton of salt water, she sees me. 'I'm okay,' she says, brushing away the lifeguard with her hand, after he pumped her chest, before this gigantic gush of water jumps from her mouth.

"The lifeguard points to the black flags along the beach. 'Undertow, fucking undertow, man,' he says, rippling his arm muscles. I see him beaming in on her, getting that she's a babe. I know he's ready to flirt her up. You know, the hero shit. She says thanks to him. He says, 'No sweat,' and I heard him say *hottie* under his breath.

"Then I'm mad. I think he wants to jump her, but next thing I know, she reaches up, and, because I'm bending over her, her lips touch my face. The kiss lands on my chin. Her lips are salty. The lifeguard dude shoots me a look and says, 'Fucking unbelievable.'"

"Sounds amazing, Vegas. I knew a girl like her. Swimming was her thing. You'd think her legs would have been all muscled up, but they weren't. They were fine-boned as could be, especially delicate in little pumps." *That's Gloria all over,* Joe-Mack thought.

"Starlet, she didn't swim all that great, but she took the risk.

He told more about how Starlet loved the ocean — that went on forever until it reached the sky. She chased the twiggy-legged sandpipers and reached out her hands to touch them, and then the birds would do this helicopter-hop, hover and take off, and land only a few feet away, and she would laugh hysterically."

"Excuse me, Vegas, but we should get moving," Joe-Mack said.

Holding his arm up to silence Joe-Mack, Vegas said, "Wait, wait, listen. The lifeguard gave Starlet a towel to wipe off with. It was wet, but we sat on it for the rest of the afternoon. The sun was flaming. Starlet twirled curls into her salty hair by twisting it around her fingers. The salt dried on her skin that was pink and hot to the touch. Every time she went in the shallow water, I thought she might head out again for the fish. They were still out there, only further. She hopped over the waves crashing on shore and tried to pull me in. The horizon, a supernatural blue, Man, mirrored in her eyes. No josh. Silver, like mercury. The beach was magic, Man. I thought it might pull her away from me."

"That's neat, Vegas, but we've got to move on," Joe-Mack interrupted.

Vegas nodded, yet he kept on with his story. "So then, these seagulls were flocking us, flapping, hovering. Beady-eyed. Intelligent. Hey, they had guts. Two of them had a wildcat war in mid-air, bitching feathers flying. I pulled out my camera. I take pictures of Starlet and all them birds. The sandpipers scooted to miss the waves. Their timing was beautiful — skittering on those tiny-clawed feet.

"There were these little squirts, two boys and a girl, a toddler. They'd been working on a sand castle with a moat and everything. Windows. Flags. A stonewall. When they waved to their mom to come and look, she blew them off. She sat on her butt puffing a bone, all out in the open with two dudes, not beach people. They were fully dressed, only their shoes and socks off, pants rolled up."

Joe-Mack was impressed that this kid had taken in so much. He seemed able to judge the difference between a kiss-off mother and a good one. Perhaps his girl had brains, insight.

"Starlet's stuff is over here," Vegas said, pointing to a spot near the wall. A shell strung through a purple ribbon hung on a nail under a silver jacket. "Listen, Starlet was smart. She nailed her dollars up here, under her jacket."

As though the shell were a precious stone that might turn to dust, Vegas picked it up cautiously. Placing the ribbon over his wrist and letting the shell dangle: he reached up and ripped the safety pin necklace from his neck. With great dignity he lifted the ribbon over his head, and the delicate pink-tinged ivory shell that had been shaped by ocean water dangled on his chest, its smooth crust touching his skin the way it had graced Starlet's bony chest.

Joe-Mack had been shifting through the belongings, fingering a tiny blue sweater, running the fringed bottom against his hand. He lifted the fabric to his nose, sniffing it. *Now,* he thought, *I am getting weird, but the scent has some familiarity to it. Sometimes girls and women act all the same, flirty, but in the dark a man can make out a woman's scent.*

"Hey, what's that?" he asked, noticing the necklace.

"Nothing. Private," Vegas answered, wrapping his fingers around the shell.

"Give me a look-see?"

"No! Don't touch it." Vegas said. He bit his lips, hunkering away, hunching his body over.

"Okay, calm down," Joe-Mack said, patting Vegas' shoulder. "Trust me. Let me take a peek."

The boy opened his fingers one by one revealing a shell that shimmered with a tinge of pink in the stream of sunlight that flowed through the attic window. Joe-Mack gently took the shell in his hand, his rough palm against the silken exterior, soft as a newborn's heel.

"Okay, careful. Give it back now! I keep it until I can return it back to *her.* I mean, we got nothing, me and her."

"Okay, okay, don't come unglued," Joe-Mack said, handing it over.

Vegas lifted the shell up, looking as though he wanted to kiss it, but instead, he blew on it and polished it with his tee shirt. "This is all I got, and my film here." He pointed to his pocket. "That's all."

They had been examining the shell together, kneeling close to each other on the hard floor. Vegas put the necklace on again, and said, "Be right back. Going outside to pee."

"Make it fast."

Alone in the squat, Joe-Mack again shuffled through the girl's things: two bottles of water, a folded towel, cleansing wipes, jeans, and the blue sweater. *Not enough to keep her bones warm on a rainy day.* He felt odd, intrusive, examining a young girl's personal belongings. His own daughters must have their secrets, diaries and such, and they wouldn't want a stranger nosing around.

When Vegas returned, Joe-Mack asked, "This all she had?"

"Pretty much.

"Let's look local."

"Okay, like Lucky, The Quick Mart?"

"Let's hit it, then. We'll grab a snack, too."

"I've been trying to avoid the police routine, but maybe we should give it a go," Joe-Mack said.

After checking the stores and wolfing down chili-dogs, Joe-Mack and Vegas went to the police station. The stairs at the police station were crammed with suited-up lawyers hiking leaden briefcases and a few hangdog clients spruced up for the big day. The lawyers glanced over their shoulders at their assistants whose pumps clicked-clacked on the cement steps. As if to show these girls off, the men waved at each other, slapped one another's back and winked. One particularly rotund fellow pressed his hand against the small of his young woman's back, and held it there — longer than a polite gesture. His assistant, decked in serious black-rimmed glasses, wore a mini-skirted tweed blue suit with white fishnets that barely covered an ankle tattoo. *A Campari and soda type*, Joe-Mack thought. *Easy chick. Nothing says hooker like tattoo.*

The trucker and the boy waited in line and then moved up to the desk. After Joe-Mack ran through the missing girl scenario, the Duty Officer said, "Can't help," as he itched a scar on hairy hands. "Too early in the game."

"What's the deal?" Joe-Mack asked.

"She ain't gone forty-eight. We don't know she's missing."

"Give me a break here. I mean, this is L A," Joe-Mack said, grinding his baseball hat in his hands.

"Take is easy, buddy."

"And, Sir," Joe-Mack said, "if it was your daughter, would you be dicking around with the clock?"

"Look, pal, this ain't no city of angels. The girl could be stoned out, sobering up somewhere. Run off with her boyfriend. Whatever."

"The boyfriend's right here," Joe-Mack said, waving his hat towards Vegas. "Anybody else I can talk to, Sir."

"Hold up," the officer answered. Turning away from Joe-Mack; he picked up a phone, pressed an extension on the receiver against his shoulder, and said, "Plumstead, you busy? Yeah, yeah, I get it, the one armed-paper hanger routine. A gentleman here needs assistance. Give him the skinny, will you?" Without even glancing at Joe-Mack, he pointed back, and said, "Through the doubles, second office on right. Watch it, she's a ball-buster."

"Thanks, mighty grateful, Sir."

"Righto."

The office door, held back with a metal bunny doorstop, opened to a dull room with tan walls and an oak desk. The desktop, hardly visible under mile-high stacks of paper, practically hid the woman behind them. A giant paper clip, hand-painted with "Fit and Forty," a dying spider plant, its babies brown and wilted, and three paper cups with bits of left-over coffee sat on a small table at the far end of the room.

The woman behind the desk swished her curly, mud-brown hair over her collar. She angled back in her chair and quit stamping forms, casually glancing up at Joe-Mack. Her suit jacket, with buttons pulling against her chest, was the same color as the walls. A lone calendar hung high up on the wall, an afterthought, crooked. Three pictures in clear plastic frames sat on the shelf behind her, a black-and-white photo of a pre-teen boy, a toddler on a tricycle and, the last, a poodle with a pink bow tied on the top of his head. The pink was the only color in the room.

"Excuse me," Joe-Mack said.

"Sit down," she said.

Joe-Mack sat on the edge of the chair, leaning in on the desk.

She went back to stamping forms. "Due yesterday," she said. "Not even close."

"I get that."

"Plumstead, here, Ms. Plumstead to you," she stated, while thumbing through the top half of the files she had stamped.

"How do you do. Joe Johnson, here." Joe-Mack thrust his hand over to her all the while thinking his full name sounded weird to him. He never used it except to sign his paycheck.

"What's shaking, Joe?"

"Missing girl. This boy," he said, pointing to Vegas, "lost his friend."

"How long?"

"Since this morning, early, like five, maybe even last night," Vegas said.

Plumstead beaded in on Vegas, her expression hardening in a millisecond. "What business is it of yours?"

"We live together."

"So, a love feud?"

Joe-Mack jumped in. "Not really. They were squatting together. Not bad eggs as far as I can see. The girl was clean, he tells me."

"What's your deal with this?"

Joe-Mack told her how he happened to be driving his rig past Las Vegas when he picked up the boy hitching and dropped him in Hollywood. Now today the heads-up call on his cell led him back to this area. "The kid was in high panic when I found him."

"You playing hero here?" she said, softening her gaze at him with a wink. Although he didn't much feel like it, Joe-Mack knew he could get more with sugar than salt, so he'd sent off a quick wink to kiss up to her. "That your boy in the picture? Good looking kid."

"Yeah, that's Sam."

"Sam ever been in trouble?"

"We live in L A, Mr. Johnson. What do you think?"

Nodding in agreement, he said, "But, the thing is, is he okay now? Thanks to you?"

The woman threw him a look that said she knew what he was pulling, but she'd go for it anyway. "I don't usually talk about my son, Joe, but, seeing you asked, he's on the right side of the fence. Tough road, but he made it to eighteen."

"You've been there, huh? You got to have compassion, being in this job."

" I had it, but it's worn down to nothing."

"I get that. Hey, this missing girl belongs to somebody. It's tough out there for kids."

Plumstead took a deep breath, peeled off her jacket, exposing bra straps that hung down on her upper arms outside her sleeveless blouse. "You divorced, Joe?" she said, her eyes sliding over his left hand.

"Estranged."

"Me, too. Jeez," she said, rushing her fingers through her hair. "I'm a mess." She adjusted each black lace strap, took a deep breath and massaged her back in circles against the swivel chair. "Whew, toasty in here. Son of bitch air hasn't worked for ten years. City don't care if we sweat. And that's how it is. Give me your number, Joe. I'll buzz you if I get wind of something?"

## Chapter 16
## Missing: Joe-Mack and Gloria

Joe-Mack, now seriously enmeshed in Vegas's problems and in the odd happenstances of the squat kids, still flashed back on his wife and daughters. He longed to hear their voices, tuck them in at night, and sit at the old picnic table in the yard at his in-laws' lake place. Something in his head clicked. He whipped out his cell - dead.

A frown lining his forehead, he spoke rapidly to Vegas. "Follow me. Got to find a phone." He remembered the booth outside the QuickMart. Heaving in a deep breath, he mentally made the sign of the cross and made the call. Punching in the numbers was automatic; he had done it in his daydreams a million times. The words to Gloria might stick in his throat. They were tough to speak, almost impossible. He chewed the skin on his right hand, while he wondered if he would blow it. Would she know that he was never quite right after he left his family? Was she also off base? *How many men had touched her velvet tummy in the last eleven years?*

As the dial tone rang in his ear, Joe-Mack scratched the toe of his boot along the edge of the floor, shuffling scraps of paper and dirt; the green distant Hollywood hills in his sight, he leaned on his elbow, but he hardly saw them. When Gloria answered, he said, "It's Joe. I want to speak to the children, please."

"What? Joe? Why now?"

"I met a loner, a boy, and well, he made me want to. I mean, if it's okay."

"I don't get it."

"I'm worried."

"Now you're worried?" Gloria asked. Her voice rose in pitch, and then, backing down, she sucked in a deep breath and measured out her words, "You don't know. I'm sorry. I can't..."

"What, Gloria?"

"Joe, Oh God. Jen's missing," she burst out, then spoke, through her hiccupping sobs, "I can't believe it."

He jammed the phone tight against his ear. "What? Where is she?" An ambulance passed, speeding around the corner. The siren's pulsing sounds drifting off in the distance.

"I don't know. Oh God. I don't know. We've had cops out, put up fliers. I'm so scared."

"Jesus Glo, why didn't you call me? Damn it all. I'm her father, you know!" Joe-Mack yelled into the phone, his hand gripping his throat.

"But, but, you've been gone."

"I know, but Jesus. I'm sorry."

"She ran away, Joe. I'm afraid to think anything."

"Have you asked everybody, inquired everywhere? How about her sister?

"Yes, damn it. Don't give me the third degree."

"Oh Jesus, Glo, I'm sorry. Shock, I guess, but what about Amy?" Joe-Mack said, glancing down at the scruffed-up boots he wore and the faded shirt, wondering what she would say if she saw him right now.

"She said that her sister had been acting secretive, locking her bedroom doors. I thought it was teen stuff."

"Any girlfriends or guy-friends missing?"

"No, Oh God, this isn't helping, Joe."

In the background, he heard, "Mom, the receipt. Tell him about the receipt."

"Oh, right. Amy found an airline receipt in a water bottle this morning. God, I almost forgot."

"To where?"

"Los Angeles. I'm scared, Joey."

*Joey.* He could almost imagine her lips mouthing his name. "Listen, I know you're scared. This isn't about *you.*"

Briefly, Joe-Mack ran through the fact that he was in California searching for a runaway, a young girl, a friend of a friend of his. He had connections.

"So what now?"

He told her that she and Amy should come directly out. Let authorities back there continue their work. "You, me. and Amy need to hang tight on this. Leave no stone unturned." He forced his voice to sound confident even though he was shooting blind.

"I can't leave," Gloria sobbed. "What if she comes home?"

At this point Vegas leaned into the booth, wrinkling his nose at the stale urine smell inside the booth, and asking, "What's up?"

"Get out," Joe-Mack said, nudging him back. "I'll tell you later."

"Who's that?" Gloria asked.

"The kid. Don't worry about him. Station your mother at the house in case Jen comes home."

"Alright, but, you really think she's out there?"

"Jesus, Hollywood is a damn magnet. The ticket and all, I'd say it's possible. Hey, is Amy alright?"

"She's devastated, blaming herself."

"Tell her I love her," he said, softly.

"Yes, but are you okay?"

"Not about me. Pack. You forget something, I'll buy it," he answered while watching a ladybug fly through the doorway, land on the hanging phone book, sprout its wings again and land on his hand. He shook it out the door to freedom in the open air.

Gloria's breaths sounded fast and heavy. "I'm shaking. I can't control myself."

"You can! Go straight to Northwest. I'll get tickets. Pick you up at LAX."

"I have to go to the bank before I leave," Gloria said.

Don't worry. No sweat with money. I got it. See you at the airport."


Tail lights lined up for what seemed like miles in front of him. Headlights went back as far as Joe-Mack could view in the mirror – a couple of lane jockeys squeezed in and out. His eyes stung and the glare from the mirror gave him a headache that reached from his eyelids up over the top of his head. He flipped the mirror up. Looking ahead at the stream of cars, as was his habit, along with scanning to the right and left of him, he tapped his brakes during endless slowdowns. *Spaghetti bowl.* "No way to blast through this mess. Okay, Lincoln it is," he said, taking the exit at Olympic.

Vegas clasped his spiny arms around himself, as though he was cold. "Been trucking long?" he asked.

"Yep. No time for small talk, kid." Sweat collected under the rim of Joe-Mack's baseball cap. He had pictured taking this cutoff, skimming down Lincoln past Sid's Baby Goods, the biker bar on the corner, and the good view of the tower at LAX, and curving the wide ramp that feeds into the airport so many times in his mind, but always, he was the one going home. It hadn't happened that way; he'd never had the guts. He had to tamp down the squirrelly feeling in the pit of his stomach while the tangle of excitement over Gloria zinged up his throat, but then he asked himself why did the girl run. Did Glo screw up? He should have been the first one called; his address and phone number was on all his checks. He'd ask her again. They'd be together soon if the holy damn plane didn't crash.

"Airport ahead?" Vegas asked.

"No kidding, genius. I'm trying to drive here," he said, although he could drive half-blind. Bright lights illuminated fat-bodied planes rolling in, each one on the other's behind, low in the sky and roaring.

"I'm sorry, but are we going to keep looking for Starlet?" Vegas asked.

"Of course! Her and Jen. Listen, don't mind me, I'm fried. Stick close after I park, okay?"

"Sure."

"Hello reality," Joe said, as he glanced over at Freddie. *Whatever mess of a family he left in Vegas, I don't see them out searching for him.*

There was no way Joe-Mack could settle in a chair. He jerked up and down on the balls of his feet, paced in front of security check. Freddie hung back by the row of seats next to the window while Joe-Mack read and reread the arrival screen. Finally, the flight lit up. It had touched down. He thought he couldn't wait one more minute. A young woman with two toddler girls sat next to Vegas. Joe-Mack remembered Gloria brushing through the tiny snarls in his daughters' hair, braiding it, and letting them choose colored ribbons for their pigtails — how Jen loved red and Amy yellow, how the three of them stirred up pancakes, initialed them with wiggly letters made from frosting. *Gloria was a good mom back then.*

Joe-Mack signaled Vegas to wait. He half-smiled at the poor boy whose future was in question. Clusters of passengers moved along the corridor after exiting the plane; squinting and blinking, Joe-Mack thought he spied Gloria, recognizing first her walk and then the ponytail swinging over her shoulder. *The lovely tall girl holding her hand — it's Amy. Sweet Jesus, so grown up.*

He waved. Gloria ran, hand and hand with Amy, but when they got closer, Amy stopped. The look on her beautiful teary face tore Joe-Mack up. He rushed to her, one foot nearly stumbling over the other and reached out, pulling her against him. He grabbed Gloria with the other arm. She nuzzled up, her hair letting loose, her crisp scent familiar. He dropped his cheek, rubbing it against her hair, hugging it against his shoulder for just a moment. A sob broke loose from his throat. "Oh God, you're here," he managed to say.

Both Gloria's face and Amy's face were awash with tears. Amy pulled back, swiping her wet cheek with her sleeve. Her mom said, "It's okay. He's your dad." Amy hung by her mother's side. "Come on," Gloria said, "It's okay." She took her by the hand as Amy looked down at the floor, her mouth clamped tightly over her teeth.

Joe-Mack reached out and lightly touched her under her chin. "Buck up, honey. I'll find her – somehow."

Amy asked, "Can you, really?"

"Yes, Honey, I can, if anybody can." Joe-Mack stared into Amy's eyes, the same eyes he remembered. *Soft believing eyes.* He had always thought she could depend on him, her daddy.

"Mom said you left and all this time…"

"Not now, Honey."

"I'm sorry," Amy cried out, "I'm so lame. I didn't know she'd take off."

"We'll find her. We have to," Joe-Mack said, gesturing to Vegas. "Vegas, this is Gloria and Amy, my daughter."

Vegas glanced down, acting bashful and full of shame, muttering, "Hello."

Joe-Mack figured the kid was seeing himself in their eyes: faded out hair, flaking black nail polish, the dumb frog tattoo on his arm. "You're alright," he said, slapping Vegas' shoulder. "You're part of the team here." He led the little group to the parking garage.

Gloria paused by the car, seizing Freddie's forearm, sinking her nails in. "You live here. Do you know Jen? Where is she?"

In the dim yellowish light and acrid oily air of the parking garage, Vegas froze, challenged by the girl's mother, and weakly answered, "I don't know."

"Ease up, Glo. This kid's straight-up. Heart's in the right place," Joe-Mack said, gently helping her into the car. "He's got an in with homeless kids. We'll scope it out soon as we get the hell out of this airport."

Once inside of the vehicle, he reached over for Gloria's hand. "It'll be alright. Have faith," he said. Her cold fingers shook under the warmth of his. As soon they took off, Gloria undid her seatbelt and twisted around, kneeling on the seat, facing Vegas.

"My Jen, have you seen her?" Gloria asked, her eyes wild. "Was she safe?"

Vegas leaned up a little, straining, his wet eyes looking sideways. "Maybe. A lot of girls out here survive. Some whacked out. Me and my girl were okay until she left, but really, I don't know nothing about your daughter." And as he said this, embarrassment reddened his ears. "Sorry."

Joe-Mack slammed his fist on the steering wheel as he pushed ahead, trying to break out of the swirling traffic.

That night Joe-Mack's sleeves were twisted, binding his skin, the plaid fabric, wrinkled and sweaty, and his shirt bunched up in the back leaving a rib of flesh exposed to the cold morning air. The last thing he remembered was lying awake, his mind roiling in images of the past and the future: expectations, fears, a jumble. It could have been any place, any motel, but this one was on the edge of Hollywood, a testament to earlier days. It was quiet except for an occasional car alarm or siren or the slam of a car door close by that seemed to shake the loose plate glass picture window. Or it could have been shook up by the gusts that ran under the portico like a wind tunnel. Joe-Mack had glanced through this window when they first arrived, as if there was anything to see besides the concrete wall separating the building from a storage unit facility and the Petco beyond that. The glass was streaked where a maid must have made a few lackadaisical swipes at it the day before — probably with a weakened solution purchased from the Job Lot or a bargain store of its ilk. The dust and dirt pocketed itself in the inside corners of the window. The outside surface was spattered with brown spots, a result of hard rain that arrived in Los Angeles the previous week, pounding the dry dirt surrounding the widely-girthed palms and overgrown Birds of Paradise.

The drapes in faded maroon hopsacking material adorned with voluptuous chartreuse ferns didn't quite stretch across the total length of the window so that a band of light went into the alley where strangers might see if the room were occupied or might even glimpse a narrow band suggesting a lady undressing or the removing of a man's undershirt or might even imagine sweat trickling down his sternum. The palm fronds waved shadows across the window at night, up and down like giant fans, as if to cool an arduous moment.

The hours after the time at the airport had blurred by. Finally, when Joe-Mack saw the bleak exhaustion on Gloria's and Amy's faces, he decided they should all get some downtime. They had checked into the last room available slightly before two in the morning. The manager, who was missing a tooth up front, the matching one gaping prominently over his lower lip, rolled off the messy-looking, slip-covered couch, spilling Playboy magazines with man-handled covers and curled edges from his lap, and signed them in. He pocketed the sixty bucks. "Don't sign the register," he said. "Hardly half a night any-hoo."

"Might be a couple," Joe-Mack said.

"No bothers," he answered, taking a good look at the women. "Done deal," he said, flipping off the blinking fluorescent motel sign, leaving only the yellow uncovered light bulbs that ran along the outside corridor.

Joe-Mack led the way along the shadowy sidewalk, scrutinizing the numbers on the doors under the skimpy lighting. Insects flitted round and round the hot lights, spitting sounds so weightless they were nearly lost in the night.

Mellow jazz rifts emanated from room two through the air spaces around the door; sounds from number 6 blasted an old *I Love Lucy* show on, her laugh blending in with Ricky's screaming. The next two rooms were dark and silent. *Harmless. Hapless occupants. Maybe not.* It was the silent and darkened windows that bothered Joe-Mack. Perhaps an adolescent female lay overdosed. Dead, to be found in the morning by a stunning long-legged Lupita or a squat glowering Rosa, who may have just arrived from Guatemala to work with her cousins. Perhaps a victim, a young girl, sat quivering with fright, slowly dying the death of a pounding heart, roped to a chair by her captor, praying for the cops to come, come and release her arms and wrists and rip the green tape from her mouth. Her kidnapper could have been clipping his toenails that clicked softly as they hit the floor.

The sky, tinged brown, as though lit up by a string of failing streetlights stuttering with an electric brownout, shadowed the city. A taxi horn sounded. The swish of the sprinklers misted the air. A bird in a tree shrieked.

When Joe-Mack first drove up to the hotel, he had apologized. "Not so hot, halfway clean. It's open, though. I'll find a better place tomorrow. At least they have a coffee machine." The day had been rough for all of them. Gloria's tired face appeared thinner, her cheekbones prominent. Amy had been resting against the rental car window that left a crease along her flushed, soft-skinned cheek. Gloria hesitated in front of the row of vending machines. She began digging in her purse for change.

Birds of Paradise

"I got it," Joe-Mack said, shoving his hand in his pocket. "Let me," he said, peeling off three one-dollar bills from a roll. "Here," he said, handing her those first and then two fifties for her purse.

"Gosh, Joey, so much money?" She smiled weakly, inserted the bills and let both Cokes slam to the bottom before she retrieved them. "Peanut butter crackers?" she asked Amy.

"Whatever," Amy answered.

The first package of crackers was a mess of crumbs the color of dry desert earth. She opened the second. The peanut butter had faded to butter color. "Oh well," she said.

"Want me to get burgers at Ihop?" Joe-Mack asked

"No, thanks," Gloria said, "We're all too exhausted to eat much."

Amy paused by a growth of flowers nearly as tall as she was. She crunched off the stem of a brilliant orange flower with a small tuft of violet sprouting from a pair of flat leaves. It was shaped like a bird, ready to fly.

"What is it?" she asked her father.

"Bird of Paradise. Like it?"

"Yeah, things are different here. These flowers are tall as me. It's not like California on TV."

"Yeah, Honey," Joe-Mack answered, placing his hand on the her shoulder and gently pushing her along. "Now, let's get some rest."

"God, I haven't even seen the beach or anything. No T-shirts, nothing."

"After we find Jen."

"Of course, like yes. So now I'm selfish, I guess."

"No, you're just fine, Honey," Joe-Mack said, noticing the curl of Amy's lip, a possible spark of envy. *A first sibling gets all the goods first thing.*

After dropping the girls' overnight cases, Joe-Mack sat on the bed with a large dip in the center. He imagined guys and their hundred-buck hookers, the prostitutes who serviced them with their expressions dull, eyes on the ceiling. Gloria dug facial cleansing tissues from her purse and led Amy into the bathroom to clean up. Emerging from the bathroom Amy and Gloria then headed for the two scratched, maple-finished chairs plunked in front of the window. Gloria coaxed Amy to eat an apple she had carried all the way from Michigan.

"I can't, Mom. I feel like I'm gonna heave."

Gloria lifted the Coke can to Amy's mouth. "Drink a little, Honey. The sugar will give you strength. You'll feel better."

Joe-Mack yanked back the stained bedspreads. "The sheets are cleaner than the spreads in these places. Maids wash them every day. Gives them something to do." He recalled maids, working in pairs, running their mouths while folding towels and making beds. "They work cheap."

As Gloria dragged herself to one of the twin beds, Joe-Mack watched her; she appeared even shorter than he remembered, or maybe it was her tragic slump and her dimmed spirit. The desire to scoop her up in his arms, hold her so there was nothing between them, not even old thoughts, rose up, yet he didn't dare

"You two take the beds, " he said, "I can sleep in the car if you want."

"No Joey," Gloria answered, "Amy and I will sleep together. I feel safer with you in the room."

She shuffled Amy into the bed, got in fully clothed next to her and pulled the sheet up under their chins while he kicked off his shoes and flipped the light switch. After a minute or two, he murmured, "Hey Glo, you still awake? I got a handle on a detective. She's keeping an ear out for Starlet and maybe she'll get word on Jen." When Gloria failed to answer, he listened for her breathing. He walked quietly to the bathroom, and, leaving the door ajar, he showered and put the same clothes back on. Once back in bed, in the dusky light, he prayed, *God, I promise. I'll straighten up. Do better.*

As his eyes adjusted to the dim light, he focused on a huge gash in the geometric wallpaper on the opposite wall. After all his suffering, bitching about Gloria, there she slept, mere feet from him. It was a reunion of sorts, but *Christ,* here they were in a derelict motel in twin beds.

He awoke, realizing that he had finally crashed even though he had no idea what time. A strip of sunlight beamed in through the crack in the heavy drapes. The solitary flower rested against the side of a plastic glass on the night table between the beds. Gloria must have placed it there some time during the night. She and Amy had sobbed under their sheet and into their pillows, but finally, they too, had slept. They lay very close together; two heads of long curls, the mother's auburned and the daughter's streaky blondish brown mixed together and billowed out over the pillow.

It was another lifetime when Amy used to dash to their bed afraid of scary, two-headed monsters. The three of them would finish off the night in the same bed while Jen braved it alone in her room. Joe-Mack rubbed his hand across the stubble on his chin and whispered, "I love you" in their direction.

One of Gloria's legs was thrown out of the covers - *she still does that* - her sneaker, still on, swallowed up her tiny foot, out-sizing her delicate ankle. Joe-Mack had adored those silly little ankles of hers, how they wobbled slightly when she walked, how she'd stop and pose for him, in her trim heels just before leaving for work. Where were those patent pumps, the ones she shined with worn-soft diapers and Vaseline? Where is the hippy dress, all cotton lace, she wore when they were married? Would she recall her sprained ankle when he scooped her up like a doll, set her on the bed, and poured the anniversary champagne? If only he could return to that day.

## Chapter 17
## Return to the Squat: Vegas

Time had flown since the meeting at the airport. Vegas rode along with Joe-Mack and his family as they searched the streets and the brightly lit local areas and the shadowed alleys, realizing that he was merely an extra, a weak thread in the connection to their loss and his own loss. Before the others headed for a motel, Joe-Mack dropped him off within walking distance of the squat. "On your toes, kid!" he said. "Call me later."

Heading up Sunset, Vegas ached all over; he dragged his heavy legs along and rubbed his neck, stiff from gawking at would be Starlets. He began to feel desperately alone just as he had when he discovered Starlet missing. His gut twisted, his eyes blinked from sheer emotion.

It couldn't be easy for Joe-Mack and Gloria and Amy, getting acquainted again - in crisis. Their missing kid gave them a purpose, yet Vegas understood there were questions. Trillions of them. Did Joe-Mack really want to know about Gloria's years without him? Did she want to know about his *road* life? Were they hesitant to talk about their pasts the same as he held back about Rose and Frederick? He imagined unspoken anger and confusion. Amy wasn't going to be a pushover; he had watched her dark-circled eyes, sometimes glaring, and other times welling up with tears. He could see the sister was irate at times and hysterical, yet trying to stay in control.

When he reached the bungalow, Vegas didn't expect to see Katha's house ablaze with light, yet it appeared every light bulb in the house was lit. Had she forgotten to shut them off? Was her pitiful old body plopped on her ancient couch, as she lay there trying to stay awake for word of Starlet?

Vegas dipped under the fence and, quickly entering the yard, he approached the bush where he and Starlet had sat together and peered under it. *No Starlet.* He climbed in the window, recalling the last time the two of them were there. The sight of Leontine drew him in, the way it had called to Onge and Starlet. Now he badly wanted to believe that Onge had never died; he wanted to pretend that Starlet was upstairs combing her fingers through the golden threads of her hair like she had at the beach.

Reggae music blasted from the squat interrupting his thoughts. Onge would have busted a gut if he'd heard it. "Can it," he would have insisted. "Immediately!"

A foul stink met him at the open door. The room, loaded with tequila bottles, lime skins floating in half-filled paper cups, and open refried beans cans, had gone south. Cigarette stubs and roach clips sat in garbage filled foil dishes. Vegas held his breath and walked to the window, stood on his toes, and lifted it, shoving a stick in to hold it open. Powder and paint chips flaked down on him, one settling in his eye. He went to Stripe's mirror, stretched his bottom lid out and dug in to retrieve it. Finally, although his eye was itching and red, it was gone.

A dude Vegas had never seen before, stoned out of his mind, lay on top of Vegas' sleeping bag. His gelled crew cut had been bleached white - his clothes, expensive, but ruined, and the curve of his butt cheeks revealed bare skin above his belt-less pants. *John-John.* He hauled in the booze and weed, Vegas thought. It looked as though he was chasing his high and wanted more. The jerk had returned to the squat with a bag of tricks and thrown temptation in the kids' faces. Pepper lay stretched out on the floor, her face down, legs and arms in an X. Green flopped next to her, her knees turned out, her mouth stained with thick drool. *Escape. Was it worth it?* "Drugs don't swallow no pain," Onge had claimed. "Just eat you up, day by day."

In a fit of confusion, Vegas turned to Starlet's pile of candles and lit the largest white one. It sent vanilla fragrance into the air and a quivering light against Green's hair. When he moved past her, she stirred.

"Hey, who's that? Vegas?" Green asked, swiping her chin with her sleeve.

"Green, you screw-up. What happened here?" he asked, in a low voice.

"Shut up, shut up, my head's screaming."

"You're pissing me off, Green," he answered, his temper boiling up to clenched fists.

"Get up," Vegas said, handing Green a bottle of water. "Here, drink. You seen Starlet?"

"No."

Green sat up, slugged down the water and rolled up her loose sleeves. Vegas leaned close to her face, his eyes drilling her. "You son of a bitch: you promised to wait at the diner. You screwed up. What if she went there? Jesus! I can't take this shit."

"Where's the trucker?" Green asked, shoving aside a dish full of food and butts.

"Never mind him, what about Starlet?"

John-John woke up; he eased his body over as though he was in pain. His pants slipped down, revealing a fleshy tan stomach and a jeweled belly-button ring. He reached for a smashed pack of cigarettes on the floor. Vegas scooted past him, nearly stepping on him. "What the fuck?" the kid mumbled. "What's with the fucking noise?"

"Nothing, Lush," Vegas said.

"Who you calling what? You, the crosser." He sat up, strumming his fingers along his shirt, singing, "Devil with the blue dress on."

Vegas' mouth set straight in anger, he screeched at Green, "You told, you son of a bitch told," and, out of the blue, he leapt on John-John, punching the brown stubble on his square jaw. Green yanked him off by his shirt. Vegas took a step back, and while Green still held him, he screamed, "Prick! Fuck-face!" at John-John. And then he grabbed a book and hurled it at John-John's head. It whacked him on the ear with a loud thud.

"Ouch! Jesus, my head. You ripped my ear off," John-John moaned, crashing against the wall and down to the floor with a bang. Vegas tore away from Green and shoved his knee in the boy's chest.

Pepper stood up and helped Green rip Vegas off John-John.

Vegas shook the girls off, breaking away from their grip. He seized his pack, and, plowing through junk on the floor, he ran out and took the stairs by twos. At the bottom of the stairs, he gasped in breaths and quickly listened for anyone following him. When he heard nothing, he made his way to the fence. It was then he felt the stinging in his hand that turned red and swollen. He blew on it and his hot breath made it hurt more, yet he was oddly proud and charged up. After all, he'd stood up to John-John. He stood up for himself and the blue dress. *Joe-Mack should have seen me.*

The sun wasn't up yet and Vegas didn't expect to hear from Joe-Mack until later so he decided to head down the hill and find a place to rest - finally entering the doorway of The Blowfish Tattoo. The whipping flag that slapped itself when the stiff Santa Ana breeze scurried through swiped across the top of his head. Exhausted, he sunk to the cement, and, clutching his backpack in his arms, he closed his eyes. Memories of the chapel came to him. He remembered back not too long ago; it had been a quiet wedding week – hardly any money rolled in. Frederick, all over Rose, ranted, "All that living together, cohabitating crap is ruining my business." She told him that it would get better. He told her that he would head out and drum things up. She expected he would come home drunk.

Vegas knew the drill. Frederick would hang flyers around the casinos before management tore them down. The Lily of the Valley Chapel Bonanza featured a ninety-nine dollar wedding ceremony with a free bottle of champagne. Foil-wrapped, the bottle's label would be obscured. Frederick had gone all out with the flyers; he copied a photo of the stunning woman in the blue dress and her big deal husband with the chiseled jaw and the suit that shouted money. Would-be clients could almost smell the fruity, romantic odor of the massive bouquets of gardenias surrounding the couple.

"Stick around, Slackers, I got my savvy on today," Frederick blared, stomping his butt on the stone step. "And hey, sweep these God-damn steps."

At the time Vegas lay on his bed, snacking on great handfuls of chips that left his lips salty. As he passed his mother's room on the way to the john, he heard the usual drivel from the shopping channel.

Several hours later, Frederick bombed in, shouting, "All hands on deck, double wedding on the way. Told you, didn't I?" Vegas readied his camera; Rose chose her purple sequined muumuu, and Frederick's purple and gold silk tie, and prepped the living room: plumping out the crepe paper flowers stuck in a pail of sand and straightening the white plastic doilies on top of the piano. Frederick stepped out to smoke.

"The ladies are shopping for their dresses at Caesars as I speak. Gucci, Pucci, who gives a rat's ass. Pile on the extras, the fools are high, coked-up, I think, and drunk as skunks," Frederick said, through an open window, as he took a last toke under the Joshua tree.

Now, deep in dreamscape, Vegas awoke to the sound of someone talking to him.

"Well, lookee here. Look who's back for another tat," Rocco said, nudging the boy in the doorway with his sandal. "You like my work."

Startled, Vegas shrank away from the door. In his groggy state, it took him a second to recognize Rocco.

"Don't sweat, Kid. It's me. It's early. You want a cup of coff?"

Yawning, Vegas answered, "Ahh, yeah sure. I'm dead on my ass. Hey, you still got the birds?"

"I not only got them. I got time. Big marathon over to Brentwood. Quiet day," Rocco said, pouring two coffees from his thermos and flipping on his radio. He seized Vegas' wrist, asking, "How's the frog?"

"He's good."

"Excellent, my man."

Vegas moved closer to the rear wall. He traced his fingertips lightly over the stencil of the birds of paradise. *Fantastic.* Cooler even than he remembered. He imagined how they'd sound if they were alive, zooming across the tops of trees in the jungle, squawking like hell, their flashes of color brighter than any rainbow.

"Save these for me, will you?"

"How long?"

"'til tomorrow."

"Love at first sight, huh?" Rocco said, amused.

"I'll be back."

"Got it," Rocco said, adjusting to a new music station with his broad thumb. "Remember," Rocco called out, his voice over the opera music on his tape, "second-time-around discount." He shoved a bag of day-old donuts in Vegas' hand. "Eat kid. You're wasting away."

"Okay, be back later."

Vegas's spirits lifted. He wolfed down the doughnuts and tossed the bag in a dumpster – all the while thinking that it would be high time to hock the chain. *Starlet will dig the birds. I know it.* On his way to the pawnbroker, Vegas passed the drug store. Then and there he decided to develop his last roll of film. He recalled the pictures of Starlet they took on the beach would be on that roll, and, as thrilled as he was about that, he remembered she was dead on stealing. He'd sneak the flipping knife back into Pepper's things.

He entered the twenty-four hour drug store and quickly dropped the roll of film at the counter. His shoulders were stiff, and his knuckles were raw. Outside again, he absent-mindedly counted parked cars, peering inside the windows for signs of Starlet. He caught sight of a blond-haired girl in the back seat of a beater-pick-up. The chick shot him a nasty look when he brought his face so close to the glass that his breathe fogged the window. It sure as hell wasn't Starlet. He swiftly stepped back, nearly losing his balance and falling into the street. Bummed and glaring at the oncoming traffic, he yelled, " Hit me. I dare you, sons a bitches."

Settling back against the wall of a Starbucks, the fresh coffee smell surrounding the building, he realized he was still hungry. His stomach gurgled and popped; he now regretted tossing the last donut crumbs in the bag Rocco had given him in the trash. Reversing his path, he headed back to the drugstore and lifted a bottle of orange juice in deference to Onge and a candy bar. He glared up at the round reflectors on the ceiling, but he made it outside without a flicker from the employees. It didn't seem right to be eating without Starlet, but he wolfed down the candy as the beeps of car horns, conversations of passers-by, and the whirring din of two police copters above surrounded him. He wandered aimlessly up the street and found himself at a familiar bench. With thoughts buzzing in his head, he slumped down, allowing the sun to beat on his hair, down to his scalp, and on his forearms. Sweat collected under his arms and across his sternum. The sky was now a cloudless quiet blue. *Free, but alone? I go home now, who's to say, I even existed here.*

The memory of wearing the dress, the fabric so slick on his hips, surfaced. *Starlet was cool with it, but who cares now?* No longer a screaming desire, it had seemed almost more important thinking about wearing the dress than the act itself.

Vegas shifted his weight from foot to foot. The soles of his feet stung; people rushed by with hurried looks on their faces. When he couldn't wait any longer, he darted though the folding doors that were plastered with ads and missing kid posters that he quickly scanned: *no Starlet,* and then, he went to the line of customers, vaguely noticing them. Across the counter, a teenager with mucky green scum on her teeth waited on him. Her stringy hair that he guessed would feel slimy to the touch, separated into clumps. *Homeless.* He pictured clear plastic bags filled with her belongings, all kinds of crap, but no toothbrush, sitting in a grocery cart in the alley behind the row of stores. *At least she's got a job.* He'd never again ignore down-and-outers.

Counting his money and lacking the last thirty-seven cents, Vegas said, "I'm short."

The chick said, "Forget it. Go on." He clutched the envelope close to his chest, and said, "Thanks," and, out under the awning, he wondered if the girl behind the counter had taken a sneak peek at the pictures. *Not like they're dirty.*

Vegas nervously thumbed through them: the first photo's image was of the birds' stencil from Rocco's place, the next, Green, who hid her face while peering through a fence of spread fingers, and then, Starlet at the beach. Captured in mid-air, her gorgeous legs spread in a V and high off the ground, she leaped after the skittering sandpipers along the foamy edge of the waves. *Oh Starlet. Your eyes, the liquid color of the ocean.* Touching the photo gently, he squeezed his eyes shut to memorize her, every possible detail. There were two more photos. Starlet had taken a picture of the horizon, the big orange sun seeming to touch the deep dark-blue sea at its farthest point. Next, she aimed the camera up the coast capturing the curving coastline and the Ferris wheel on the pier. *Why didn't I take her for a ride? I might have kissed her at the top.*

With the pictures safely stowed in his pack, he headed back to the squat. Tiptoeing up the stairs, he heard no sounds. Empty, the place was in tough shape, and so was he - lonely, but his body was beat down, he'd collapse there. *At least I don't have to deal with the messed up kids right now.* He shoveled the trash to one side and tidied the area where he and Starlet had last slept. He assumed Green and Pepper had gone out for food or for drugs. John-John might have led them on a wild goose chase for drugs, maybe to his boyfriend's house where they'd screw that place up.

While smoothing out his sleeping bag, he dumped a small pile of crystal sand that must have dragged in on his body and Starlet's body after the beach day in Venice. He scooped up a few grains and put them in his pocket — for luck. It was then he found a note that had been tucked into the sleeping bag with a crinkled twenty-dollar bill folded inside the paper. He knelt down and read it.

> *Vegas -I split.*
> *I got to find Lily.*
> *I hocked Katha's silver spoons. Sorry.*
> *Hey Vegas. Don't fold. Green*

Vegas crumbled on the floor, the note in his hand. He could hardly believe how sad he was. *Wow, I miss her. I didn't even like her that much.*

Vegas wouldn't see Joe-Mack until later that day. He lay down, stretched his arms over his head and tried to sleep. In the quiet the birds twittered on the roof; one flew in and hopped around the sleeping bag, pecking at donut crumbs. A sparrow, not one of the beauty birds, but Vegas liked it. The pecking felt like raindrops on his head. Was he a messenger? Although he and Starlet had heard the birds before, one had never before angled his way through the holes in the screen over the window.

## Chapter 18
## End of Squat

The day nearly spent, Joe-Mack suffered a myriad of feelings. The joy of being around his wife and daughter was dulled by nagging guilt over his own screw-ups and by naked fear for Jen. The sun's light diminished, melding pinks and purples with an overlay of golden shimmer, its last hurrah.

The reservations about him and Gloria making it after all these years stacked like a wall of bricks against his chest. He could read mixed emotions in her eyes, too, eyes that were mostly full of fear for her daughter, but she rested them against his intermittently and even reached for his rough hand. This was not a time for them to be intimate, yet when close, he smelled her citrus perfume – the one she wore when they were together - on her skin, and he held on to the idea that she, too, had desires.

*Keep it real.* Just live each moment and try to be smart about what is severely important - finding their daughter, and then, carving some kind of future for the family. Helping Vegas. *A redemption of sorts.* A miracle was needed here, perhaps the road angel. Joe-Mack looked to the sky, trying to read the shapes of the clouds. *Nothing.*

Over the last decade a lot of women had sidled up to Joe-Mack. Each took her turn flirting him up. If it wasn't his "adorable eyes," it was the "sexy crinkles" around them, they cooed. The flattery was a bunch of bull - that he knew. The gals often gave up the ship and turned to Frenchy, spilling their secrets to him. All types of women dropped their panties pronto in his friend's cab, without so much as a drop of alcohol or a joint involved. Joe-Mack's thoughts were spinning. This was not the time to worry, to reminisce, or to lament years gone by. *The past is what it is.*

Quiet, Amy dug deeper into her shell, shutting out her mother's attempts to comfort her. Although she looked like a teenager in a slump, jet-lagged and cranky, her reasons surely ran deeper. Joe-Mack tiptoed around her angst, similar to straddling the white line in the black hours on a deserted highway. His daughter needed a firm hand, but what right did he have? He had ignored a bitch of a headache for hours, but now, he thought, *Bourbon. A glassful. Trying like crazy to cut back, but ...* Gloria hadn't mentioned his liquored-up breath. It had been some time since he managed to throw back a quickie beer and shot. Eleven years ago the girls' night out thing started their troubles, and, in an odd moment, now Joe-Mack considered that Gloria might have been drunk when she took to bed with that bastard, and then the big blow-up took place. At this point he could hardly discriminate between foggy truth and his imagination. The slim chance to start over with his woman loomed ahead; he and Gloria seemed to be in sync, understanding without talking, yet they hadn't ironed any wrinkles of the past. Truth told, Joe-Mack had been unprepared for this reunion, even though he dreamed of it happening.

After searching the area, including the street corner, the shops, the Quickmart, Joe-Mack and Gloria finally collapsed on a city bench. Amy moved around listlessly, circling them. She plopped down, her lanky legs sprawled out.

Leaning in, Joe-Mack spoke softly, politely, as though he and Amy were sitting in the back of a church pew, "Amy, are you okay?"

Her head remained lowered when she answered, "Dad, me and sis were tight. How come I didn't know?"

"Two little bugs in a rug when you were little. I remember that."

Gloria gazed at the ground, pretending not to listen, but then spoke up, "Not much to remember, is there?"

He faked it, ignoring her comment. The three sat in silence. After a bit, Joe-Mack took Amy's hand in his, "I'll be right back," he said. "How 'bout I take the kid here for a snack? She's weak."

"Good. Be careful, Joey," Gloria answered.

"We'll be across the street," he said. "Give a wave if you need me."

Joe-Mack led Amy to the Schaeffer's deli where he chose a table next to the plate-glass window. A group of teens clutching around the rear of the shop twittered like a gathering of sparrows circling a pile of deserted fries on the blacktop. The air around the kids was tart with young perspiration and apple gum. They adjusted their mini skirts and rolled-over sweats, and zipped and unzipped their hooded jackets and pockets. Another group of boys and girls, all with dragging laces on their running shoes, were smoking just outside the door. White puffs of smoke curled up the window. The ash barrel overflowed with crunched up cellophane, pop cans and butts, some of which were still blazing red at the tips. A girl with long stringy black hair tipped with pink, ceremoniously stomped out her cigarette on the asphalt and immediately lit another one.

A homeless man, who appeared normal except for the toothbrush in his pocket protector and his loafers that were slashed down the front to make room for his toes, hovered by the inside trash can. He stood caressing a large paper cup of coffee, warming his fingers. A woman with a baldish head in an over-sized UCLA sweatshirt, licked the chocolate frosting on her fingers and offered the man the last half of her donut; he turned his nose up at her. She shrugged and smiled at Amy as though she might have a granddaughter her age.

Amy toyed with the split ends of her hair, holding a straggly clump of her long hair in front of her eyes. She twisted several strands through her fingers, and, as though preparing to thread a needle, she brushed the ends along her teeth absently. The man with the slack jaw and long artistic fingers wrapped around the cup, looked her way; she winced, shaking her fingers like a needle had pierced her skin.

Joe-Mack, who'd been eyeing her closely, said, "No Amy. You got the wrong idea. That guy might be homeless, but Jen's only been gone a little while. Maybe she's staying with friends or at a hotel. Somewhere."

"Yeah, but you don't know where. Do you? You don't know anything!"

"Look Amy, if she's anything like her mother was at sixteen, she's a pistol. A survivor."

"I hope she didn't cut her hair," Amy answered, her voice child-like, as she tilted her own hair over one shoulder, stroking it nervously. "It's lighter than mine. I love it."

Joe-Mack moved his chair closer, placing his arm over the back of Amy's. Leaning in, he said, "Remember the flower that thrived in the holy mess in front of the motel?

"The bird of paradise? Yes, I do."

"Listen, Amy: It's ironic how beauty survives the poundings nature sends out. Your sister will survive, too." He reached down, wrapped his arm around her thin waist, and gave it a good strong squeeze. "I believe it, God help me!"

Amy looked as though she didn't get what he was saying. She shook two packets of sugar into her green tea, dropping half the crystals on the table.

"Here, I'll do that. Tea is big out here, huh? A bazillion choices?"

"So what," Amy stammered. Licking her finger, she dabbed at the sugar on the table and sucked it off.

"Hey, germs."

"So, like I care. My sister could be dead. Where were you all this time? No fun having no dad!"

"I know," he answered, disappointment covering his expression.

"Mom was working her head off listening to us snivel about crap and you, you? Where were you?" She spoke in a voice that said without articulating it, *I'm only pouting. Love, me anyway.*

"I know. I'm sorry. If you knew how sorry..." His face darkened, shadowed by anguish, his uselessness. "Here eat," he said, offering her a sandwich he had purchased. "You've got to keep your strength up."

"Whatever," she said, taking miniscule bites. She ate in silence for a bit before she spoke. "Jen drank tea, but she was big on water. I mean, obsessed. She made this humongous chart on pollutants. She went on about rust, chemical garbage, E Coli, all of it. I'd tease her, saying 'water is water,' and she'd knuckle-punch me hard. She fooled some people with a sweet face and fluffy hair, but she was tough. Her attitude could turn in a flash."

"Really?" Joe-Mack asked.

"Absolutely! I mean, her water bottles cluttered up the whole house, her bedroom, because, of course, she re-cycled, and came unglued when Mom and I didn't. She bitched about a lot of stuff." Amy averted her eyes, rubbing a crack in the corner of the slightly off-balanced tabletop and her mouth broke into a slight smile. "We fooled around a lot. I took her for granted. We used to race, and I always won." Tears nested along the rim of her eyes. Her face had that look of sad and happy – when in the midst of a memory, it rings true.

"You run track?"

"Yup. Trophy winner five times."

"No kidding. That's terrific."

She set her chin down on her chest and crossed her arms, hiding her pleasure at being praised.

"Me, too," he said, " Your mom was my number one fan." It was thin, but he was creating a line of family history here.

"I know. Me and Jen found pictures in the attic. How about those really weird shorts? Skinny legs."

"Still rail-thin I'm afraid, but I could run some back then." He laughed and she echoed it. The laughs trailed on a little longer, like they both were working on it.

Then, right after the laughter, she scooped in a big breath and burst into tears. "Damn. Damn Ralph. I could kill him."

"Why, Amy?" Joe-Mack asked.

"It's like Mom changed around him. She hung on him, but he made her crabby. Me and Jen knew he was a sleaze, but Mom - she - I don't know? Clueless, you know?"

"What are you not saying? Tell me more."

"No. Mom booted him out after Jen left anyhow, but I have my suspicions.

"Like what?" Amy stood up to leave. "I can't talk right now," she said, cringing. "Let's go."

"Just a minute," he said, pulling out the photograph Gloria had given him this morning. He rushed over to the counter and asked the boy behind it who was filling the coffee urns with water, "Excuse me, have you seen this young lady?"

The pimply-faced kid glanced at the photo. He brushed it aside with his plastic-gloved hand. "Hell if I know. You expect me to remember any blond chicklette come by?"

Joe-Mack tried to connect Jen with this place, any place he had seen so far. Had she come in here? Was she alone? Held against her will? Was she hooked on meth? Some say it only takes one hit, one shot.

Amy and her father returned to the bench that was in close proximity to the squat. Large succulent leaves that had tumbled from a magnolia lay on the bench and bunched around its legs; they were part of the gigantic beauty that flossed over the scary parts of Los Angeles. Gloria sat quietly scrunching a satiny jade-colored leaf in her hand and opening her fingers, she let it flatten out again. Staring at the tree of veins, as though they were roads to follow, she was mesmerized with this simple task of closing and popping open her hand. Her back rounded over, her hair parted at her shoulders, drooping over her cheeks and jaw. When she heard them approaching, she pushed her hair back behind her delicate ears, and glanced up. The skin around her eyes was red and thin. Joe-Mack's face told her there was no news; she glared dumbly at the ground. Her arms were crossed, her hands clutching her elbows, appearing as though she didn't want Joe-Mack to see her deep disappointment.

He shook his head, hesitating, not wanting to say aloud words that would injure by their very presence, not wanting to hear himself declare failure again. He whispered, "Nothing yet, Honey, but we will find her. I promise." He longed to hold her in his arms, yet he felt not quite right about it, stung by a shyness that goes with a separation that held secrets.

Amy plopped on the grass next to them. She began ripping clumps of it and throwing them on the sidewalk. Joe-Mack and Gloria let her alone. He thought she must be frustrated and inwardly hysterical. She might be in her head focusing on teen fights she'd had with her sister over dumb things: clothes, boys, blond hair envy. She might be suppressing clues about Jen's disappearance and the man in their lives. He'd ask Glo in a private moment.

Quiet now, the three of them were stumped as to their next maneuver. A city bus rumbled by. Its wake of black exhaust swirled behind it. Each of them stared into the windows as it passed. Joe-Mack's cell rang.

"Vegas?" he said, as he flung it to his ear, "Oh it's you, Plumstead. What? Holy Mackerel, are you kidding? Be right there."

Gloria seized Joe-Mack's shirt sleeve, pinching the fabric, yanking it, "What, what is it?"

"Info on a young girl in an accident. The detective was thinking, maybe Vegas's girl, but I'm thinking it could be Jen."

"Oh Lord. It could be," Gloria answered, rushing her hands through her curls.

The trip to the hospital was surreal; the wild rhythm of the city streets and the gypsy sky overhead, with its illusive colors, fell away. A life hinged on possibility. The three ran, their hearts beating, each with his own thoughts. Joe-Mack wondered if hope would float away on the soft Santa Ana breezes. *Lost.* If ever he considered that he'd be depending on a skinny-ass detective, who seemed more worried about her toned butt than anything, he would have kissed the ground, but he had confidence in Plumstead. She'd been around the beat-up offices of the department for a couple of decades and would know a real tip from a phony one. She had sashayed around her desk for his benefit when they met, but, at that time, he sensed something in her eyes when she glanced back at the picture of a toddler in an out-dated sailor suit. The fleeting softening of her look told him she knew something about lost children. He imagined a piece of her crushed inside her chest every time she ran identity checks and came up with nothing but an image of a splayed out body, a bruised face with dead eyes.

The change in Joe-Mack's pocket jingled as they ran. *Possibility.* It could be Jen; it could be Freddy's Starlet. Sprinting now, gulping air, he pulled the girls along. Amy bounded with her long legs, her sandals whacking the pavement. Gloria skittered along in her loafers, sliding in the sand that dotted the sidewalk. It took six minutes flat – time enough to hope.

"You praying, Glo?" Joe-Mack asked.

"I am, Joey."

*I place my trust in thee* - his mother's prayer popping into his head, but hell, now *he* needed to make a valid plea here. His mind blanked; he had forgotten how. But he could make promises. A deal with God. *Anything.*

As the cold stone façade of the hospital complex came into view, Amy skidded to a stop in front of a vendor. She grabbed a bouquet of Shasta daisies with gigantic velvety white petals. "For luck, Mom," she said to Gloria.

Before dashing up the stairs, Joe-Mack, his baseball hat flying off, threw a ten at the man. Amy turned to chase after his hat. He yelled, "Leave it. Damn it. Leave it."

A flock of Cherry-head parrots flew over, their startlingly green bodies, a mass of new mown grass, their red heads bright enough to be tulips dotting the landscape. Their flash of color—a play of bright kites across the sky. They landed on the palm tress that lined the boulevard, clustering on branches, shaking and bouncing. They cooed and squabbled, pecked each other's feathers. This swarm of birds, squawking in unison, squatted there for just a second or two and then took off in tandem. *A Greek chorus.* They flew north in a loose bunch. In a flash of thought, Joe-Mack wondered if they had they seen the *road angel* in their travels.

Locating the room, and tiptoeing in, Joe-Mack saw a nurse in faded, rainbow-colored scrubs punching a digital box with green blinking lights next to the hospital bed. She shifted a bulky cast that ran from the young woman's clavicle to her wrist and the patient yelped. Her fingers, blue and swollen, contrasted her tan-washed willowy neck. The blond-headed girl turned toward the outside window ledge where a covey of pigeons nestled in a corner, cackling and necking each other. She was sheathed in white, in the same sort of gauze a child might wrap around an injured robin. It was an airy and light coverlet, gentle on an injured wing. Sun-gilded memories of daisy crowns and mock weddings misted through the room, a harp of twigs and string, a strumming.

For some odd reason the young woman in the bed slid down, pulling the covers over her head. Amy, long of leg, with the spontaneity of a head cheerleader, was the first to reach her. The hair. It certainly was her sister's hair. She had seen before the girl dove into oblivion. She had the blondest hair in her whole class at Pontiac High, but here in Hollywood everyone was yellow-haired: the chicks, Rod Stewart, the poodles.

Lifting the starched, yet worn thin hospital linen, she peeked. Then, she flung the daisies madly across the white blanket, the white railing, the translucent tubes, as the warm sunlight shafted across her dull brown hair, lending a sheen that would almost be acceptable in Los Angeles.

"Jen, Jen, gosh sis. It's you," Amy wailed. There was a great clash of hugging and crying between the sisters.

"Ow, watch it, my arm," Jen cried out. "It's really sore."

Gloria lunged forward and cupped Jen's face in her trembling hands. "Baby, my Jen. I love you," she said. Looking over her shoulder, she glanced at Joe-Mack, standing mere feet away. She motioned for him to come closer. "Your father," she said, her voice unsure, to Jen.

Amy chimed in, "It's him."

He cautiously stepped up, wiping tears from his face with his wrists.

"Oh Glo, she's beautiful," he gasped, reaching to touch Jen gently on the arm, as if she were breakable. "Are you okay? Are you alright?"

Shocked, Jen spread her fingers across her mouth, pressing against her soft lips. "My father? My real father?" Jen asked, in a weak voice, her eyes mining for familiarity.

"It's him, really," Amy answered, slinging her arm through her sister's good arm, and squeezing Jen's hand.

Joe-Mack leaned in to kiss her cheek and halted when she spoke.

"I don't get it," Jen said. "You've been gone – so long. You hardly look like your pictures."

He moved back a few inches and said, "Right, I'm old now, but I'm here," and then he lightly brushed his lips across the top of her head.

"Where did you come from? Were you looking for me? I dreamed I'd see you. Isn't that weird? Like mystical."

"Meant to be," he answered, and "Mighty glad, so glad it happened."

Sobs filled the room.

"I'm sorry," Jen whispered. "I screwed up."

"No, no, no! You're safe, that's all. We don't care about anything, except that you're safe." Gloria said. "My fault. It's my fault." She reached down twisting and pulling at the front of her blouse, as if to hide her body. "This whole thing is my fault. You all can blame me."

"No, Glo. No blaming here," Joe-Mack, his face still full of emotion, said, reaching over to lightly stroke his daughter's shoulder, "I can't believe this – my girls, all three of you - don't you see – we're together. It's crazy, but somebody up there likes us – we're together."

Amy and Gloria perched on the bed; Gloria ran her fingers along the bright-white rough cast. Joe-Mack pulled up a metal chair, placing himself where he could reach out and touch both of his daughters.

"Do you want some water, Sis?" Amy asked. "I can go get your fav, if you want?"

"No, I'm okay, but my mouth is totally dry," Jen answered, running her tongue over her teeth, "but give me some out of that pitcher over there. She pointed to the pink hospital container.

As Amy poured, Gloria reached over for Joe-Mack's hand, and spoke to her daughter. "Do you feel alright, Jen? Like enough to tell us what happened?" She proceeded to gather up the flowers Amy had thrown into a bouquet. "These were for luck. You got that right, Amy," she said, as she handed them to Jen.

The room seemed quite silent as the family waited for Jen to speak: Amy, biting the side of her mouth, Gloria, tugging her hair with one hand, Joe-Mack, his eyes on fire, waiting, fearful. Sunlight poured in beaming a wide strip of light on the bedcovers. The florescent glow from above the hospital bed turned Jen's bruises an odd purplish and greenish color. Outside, the middle-of-the day blue sky mottled with clouds blanketed the area as tons of flowers flourished in their terribly wonderful fuchsia and yellow and orange colors along the sidewalks surrounding the hospital. Small birds collected in the coral trees and seagulls far from oceanfront swells, swooped down on a scattered pile of popcorn on the sidewalk.

Jen sniffed the largest daisy in the bunch, dusting a tiny bit of golden pollen against her nose and pulled a few petals from it, meticulously placing them on her bedside table in a line. Then she handed the whole cluster to her mother. "Get a vase, Mom – ah, please?"

Gloria fussed around looking for a vase and found an extra plastic pitcher; she filled it with water from the sink and arranged the flowers.

Jen took a long sip of water and a deep breath. She gazed out the window as she spoke. "I'll try to tell you guys. It's complicated," Jen said, wrapping her good arm under the cast, hugging herself then with both arms. "I can tell a little anyway. I left – I had to. But I wanted to be a star," she said, lifting her chin, allowing her long hair to flow down her back. "You know that, Mom. I thought I could, you know, make big money, get my tooth fixed, and yeah, get you and Amy out here, but..." Jen hesitated, coughing.

"Here, have some more to drink. Are you hungry?' Gloria asked.

Amy laughed. "That's Mom, huh?"

"I could use a cheeseburger."

"I'll get it, and Polar Spring, too," Joe-Mack said, jumping up, grateful to be useful. "Anybody else want anything?"

"Fries," Amy said, "I'm starving! Big-time."

"I'll go. Maybe you girls will want some time together – fill me in later, okay? I'll ring your house and let your mother know we've found her, right Glo? But listen, don't leave Jen alone!"

Gloria nodded. After the door closed behind Joe-Mack, Jen said, "I couldn't talk in front of him – like I don't know him."

"I understand, Jen. He's been so lovely to Amy and me, isn't that so, Amy?" her mother answered.

And Amy shook her head yes, and said, "This is better. It's just us."

Gloria took a small bottle of lotion off of the table. She saturated her hands and rubbed Jen's fingers gently with the medicinal smelling lotion. Amy stuck her hand out and Gloria squeezed some into it. Amy worked it into her palms and swiped her hands on her jeans to dry them and then she bit at her thumbnail and pushed the wisps of hair off her forehead. The room was quiet. Outside the noises from the hallway could be heard: the announcements, bells, clanging of equipment, and someone screaming.

"Someone's in pain out there. I hate this place," Jen said, fingering the edge of her blanket. "I'm sorry."

"It's me who is sorry," Gloria said, "I guess I was caught up in Ralph's promises. How dumb of me."

"Looking back, the whole thing was nuts, Mom. I thought you and Amy would be safe for a while. I told Amy to stay away from Ralph. You know he didn't like her anyway," Jen said.

"Did he hurt you?" her mother blurted out. "Hit you? I didn't think he was mean."

"Listen, Mom," Amy said, turning to her mother, "he ignored me and that was fine by me."

"It's over, mother. Don't ask," Jen said, signaling stop with her hand.

"Tell me."

"Not now."

"Well, he's gone and better late than never your grandpa would say," Gloria mumbled, kneading her fingers together. "But honey, how, how in God's name, did you end up here in the hospital?" Gloria asked.

"I snuck out of the house and flew to the L.A. airport. It was my first flight ever. I bused it to Hollywood, hung around and finally stayed in a motel for two days. A wacky girl from Mississippi directed me to a place to stay for free. A stunner, but dumb as dirt. This guy, Onge, took me under his wing, and gave me a place to crash with homeless kids."

"Wait, what are you saying?" Gloria asked.

"Don't get all on this, Mom. Onge watched out for us. He was kind of a leader who knew things, like a father would. It was so awful when he died."

"What happened?" Amy burst out.

"I don't know for sure. He got shot, Amy, and I was right there. His eyes, blank. Dead. His shirt all bloody - I couldn't believe it," Jen said, her chin trembling, as she spoke. "I never saw somebody dead. It was the worst thing that ever happened to me in my whole life."

"What about you?" Gloria asked. "I want to hear about you!"

"I'm getting there. I left the squat really early. I was minding my own business," Jen said, "when this limo pulls up and this bull-guy, huge, grabs me up and heaves me into the back of the limo. In the backseat – Vicky's pimp.

"I fought. See," she said, practically breathless, holding her forefinger up, "I ripped a nail – he twisted my arm, broke it, I think, but he didn't cut me. I can't tell how much he hurt me cause of the accident. I think he got injured too," Jen sobbed, bringing her swollen fingers up in front of her eyes. Her whole body shivered, as though a fierce wind passed through. "I was terrified - scared to death!"

"I know, Honey. I know," Gloria said, in a soothing voice, wrapping the covers up over her daughter. She reached to caress her daughter's hair, smoothing out the flyaway curls around her face. "This is too much." Her eyes blinking back tears, she rubbed Jen's leg like she used to – to comfort her when she tossed and turned in her little flannel pajamas and couldn't sleep – after her father left.

"Onge died. I don't know why. He didn't gang-bang or anything. It could have been an initiation, some ghetto girl flying colors. That's what a witness said."

"Are you sure he wasn't involved with those Cripps or Bloods?" Gloria asked.

"Positive, Mom. Things are different out here. Like I met this woman, Vicky. You wouldn't get her. She was a street walker but cool."

Gloria kept her mouth shut yet her face darkened when she heard this.

Jen told how she had met Vicky before this on the street and had breakfast at the diner. It had been Vicky who warned her to keep off the street and told her to go home.

"At least I'm glad of that," Gloria stated, crossing her arms across her chest and clucking.

"Mom, just wait, you get all bent," Jen said, her voice rising. "Give me a break."

"Alright, alright, I will," her mom answered, letting her pent up breath out. "Take your time."

Jen shifted her bottom, straightening up, as if to see more as she gazed out the window, as though she were looking for someone in the distance. "I'm wicked scared for Vicky now."

Gloria and Amy learned that Vicky had been around the city for a long time. The Mexican cook at the diner knew her. They were told by Jen that people out in L.A. get it. The craziness and the chances.

"Hollywood is nothing I expected, more like a neighborhood. You see the same shopkeepers and kids hanging and no movie stars at all – except on billboards.

Vicky had a tough life, lost a baby, I think, but she loved her grandma; Vickie wanted to be a singer. I want to be a star – too late for her but not me. She called my hair Cinderella hair. Silly, I know, but that's so me, isn't it?" Giggling, she said, "She made me laugh.

"Then, in a flash, she's out of there. Taking off in a cab. A weirdo stranger came into the diner searching for her. He didn't notice me - I thought."

"These horrible people. Dangerous people!" Gloria said.

"You can't tell by how someone looks, Mother! They're not all dangerous, just messed up."

"But, Honey, why did you leave? You could have come to me," Gloria said.

"I tried, but forget it. You look thinner, Mom? Your cheekbones, they're sticking out."

"Never mind me, tell me, why did you leave?" Gloria pleaded.

"I don't know. It's all blurry."

The girls' conversation ended when Joe-Mack entered the room. "Did I interrupt something?" he asked. Gloria took the food from him and gave it to her daughters. She pulled him aside to a corner of the room and whispered what she knew - Jen had been kidnapped by a man who wanted to pimp her out, and would have, except for the car crash. Thrown from the vehicle, he quite possibly lay somewhere in the same hospital or in the morgue. Joe-Mack's face turned boiling red; he balled his hands into fists. When Gloria noticed, she said, "Don't do anything. Don't do anything right now." She leaned into his body, holding him back. He embraced her. "We'll be alright," she said. He nodded his head and squeezed her tighter.

"Wow," Jen said, smirking at Amy, "look at them."

Joe-Mack vowed to guard Jen every minute of the days to come, forever, if necessary. The massive feeling of guilt he felt for not being there for her for so many years crushed him.

In the midst of all this, Joe-Mack had nearly forgotten about Vegas until his phone rang. He told Vegas to come to room 333 at the hospital right away. He imagined how the kid would feel. Jen had family. Vegas had squat. Joe-Mack hoped to take the family to their home, but what would Vegas do – go on searching for his girl?

When he heard the tapping on the door, Joe-Mack rushed to open it, and he enveloped Vegas in a huge hug, slamming the boy hard to his chest. His voice cracking, he said, "I am indebted to you," and with that said, Joe-Mack broke into sobs, guttural and hoarse that sprang from his gut, his head crushing against Vegas's scrawny shoulder.

Jen screeched, "Vegas, Vegas, is that you? Come here. Come here quick," she waved her arm frantically towards him.

"Starlet?" Vegas asked. "You're here?" He dropped his pack and ran to her bedside and stopped stiff, hesitating a second while Gloria stepped aside. Starlet lurched, pulling the bedclothes with her, nearly sliding off the side of the bed. She grasped his wrist and held it across her collarbone up to her cheek. The tears from her eyes dropped on the hairs on his arm and on the frog tattoo.

Joe-Mack tried to tell Vegas the girl in the bed was Jen, his daughter. It was then he realized Jen and his Starlet were one and the same. "She's Jennifer, Vegas - Oh Lord, she's your Starlet?" He remembered the sweet scent of the blue sweater in the squat. It had been so like Gloria's lemony lotion, and now he realized it had belonged to his daughter. She had lived in the squat.

His breath caught, as he gently said, "It's Jen, Vegas. You actually know my own daughter."

"Dad, you don't understand. I am Starlet. It's my Hollywood name."

"Joe-Mack, why didn't you tell me Starlet's here?" Vegas asked. His eyes fired up, searching his friend's face.

"Christ, I didn't know," Joe-Mack countered.

"It's okay, Vegas. Come closer," Starlet said, rubbing Vegas' hand against her cheek.

"Damn it, Vegas, you could have told us, told us more!" Gloria yelled, frowning at the boy. "I mean, all these hours – we waited – we hoped – we prayed."

"Stop, Gloria, cool it," Joe-Mack said. "Not his fault. We're all confused here," he said, raising his hands to her shoulders. "Take it easy. She's safe and sound, that's all."

"Starlet? Starlet, I thought I lost you," Vegas wailed, his hands slamming his temples. "First, me and Green searched. I called Joe-Mack. Me and him went to the squat. We searched all over." Vegas said.

Jen told her family they could straighten out all the details later. She directed them outside so that she might talk to Vegas alone.

Vegas turned to follow the group, as though he hadn't heard Starlet. She pleaded, "Don't leave. Please, please don't leave me, Vegas."

Alone now, Vegas held Starlet's hand, very tightly even though he felt he could break the bones in her tiny fingers, even thinner than before, if he wasn't careful. He fought the urge to cry. "What happened? What's with the cast? Where did you go? Why?"

Vegas's tattered black clothing stood out in the all-white room. Starlet could hardly stand that he looked so shabby and forlorn. She wondered what her family thought about him being her friend, but Joe-Mack had hugged him and seemed protective of him.

"I didn't really leave you. I would have come back. I can't tell you everything, I'm just too beat, exhausted, freaked – some guy kidnapped me. It was awful, awful. We got in this accident. I'm okay, I'm okay, I'm okay," she repeated, quivering, breaking into tears. "I tried to be brave, but I can't anymore." She hunched in a ball. The hospital gown parted between the two sets of ties, revealing her smooth back.

Vegas pushed her over softly and got into the bed with her. "Starlet, let's lock the door. Keep the others out. So things don't change."

"I know," she whispered. "I know, we could, but... I need to know. Do you think I can be a movie star? Do you think I can? Truth?"

"I don't know. I guess, yes."

"Does Katha despise me? I screwed up so bad?"

"No. You're okay," he answered. "Hey, I'm going to get the birds. The tattoo. We can go back to the squat and ..."

"Hold it, Vegas. I'm weak. I'm hungry," she said. "Give me a bite of that cheeseburger. Take some yourself."

Weakly, Vegas agreed to eat with her.

"I'm not even well yet, Vegas," Starlet said, wiping her mouth with the edge of the sheet. I don't know what's next. My family's out there. Ralph is gone. The puke!"

"He's gone? So, that's good. I got an idea," Vegas said, easing off the bed. Opening his backpack, he retrieved the blue dress. After shaking out the wrinkles, Vegas delicately placed it on Starlet so that the luscious blue fabric took on the slight curves of her body. "You keep this," he said.

Saddened at his sacrifice, Starlet said, "I couldn't. It's yours."

"Don't matter. Take it."

"Help me," she answered, twisting to allow him to untie and remove her hospital gown. He grazed his fingers along the round of her shoulder before he unzipped the wrinkled garment that smelled of his perspiration and pulled it over her head. She scooped up her mass of curly hair out of his way. A thread of the dress tangled on her cast. He freed it and then, removed a scissors that sat atop the side table and cut a small slit in the sleeve so that it would fit. His face flushed with love.

"I want to stand, Vegas." Starlet said. Removing the covers that nested her legs, she swung her legs over the side, and let her feet touch the floor. Fragile, she fell against his bony shoulder. "Hold me. Dance. You can, you know how." As if they were covered by an angel's veil, they held each other. The cooing pigeons on the ledge strained their necks upward to view the couple.

"I'm not going to give up my dream, Vegas – no matter what."

The lavender sky deepened, a gush of wind shook the hydrangeas along the beach strand. Yet another ambulance's wail rose above the clicking of the oxygen pump. The wind brought relief to the sunset; changing beauty that threw powerful purples, oranges, sliced, angel-white and bloody reds every damn night to where the eyes dull, the speech slurred, but when the wind stirred, it shook the heart, the shifting sands, and the pelting rains. The earth split – helpless against the tide of nature.

## A note from the author:

The writing of *Birds of Paradise* has been a labor of love. I spent many snowy days in my office looking out at the snow cones set in the pine trees and listening to the winter birds while longing to be back in Manhattan Beach. The characters in this story lead me back to the settings, and people, so fiercely beautiful and complex, in California. When I called my daughter, Carolyn, to talk about my book and told her that a character had died, she was shocked - this young man and the others lived with me and my family, writing group friends and teachers, for a long time. They are real to us. It is my hope that readers will get them and care about them. Although quirky and discouraged, and confused, these children and one family maintain a thread of dignity while longing to achieve their dreams - it's meant to be a tribute of sorts to those children who run from home and their families.

Special thanks goes to my teachers and friends who read this book, usually in pieces, and kept me going- Woody Willow, Bruce Machart, Steve Almond, Jamie Cat Callan, Tara Masih, Kevin Donahue, Virginia Young, Deb Kurliecz, Louisa Clierci, Nancy Antonietti, Lenora Levine, Kimberly Davis, Sherrie Ryan, Eileen Malone, Mary Eastham and Fran Riley. I'm especially grateful for Meg, my brilliant granddaughter and Stephanie Blackman, the whiz-kid of Riverhaven Books and, of course, all of the Grub Street folks.

Special love to my husband, Edward Handley, my mother, Mary McNamara Hope, and father, Duncan Hope, who taught me to be curious, my twin aunties, who were curious and individualistic themselves, my daughters, Elizabeth Nightingale and Carolyn Clark, who inspire and surprise me, and my grandchildren, who delight me with their wit and wisdom and love.

To my friend, Donna, who is a greater storyteller than I'll ever be and my gal pals no longer with us - Gretchen, Margie, and Sue: I honor you.

And to my readers, thank you!
Kathy Handley